It was bullyboy tactics of the worst kind. And right out in plain sight.

There were three of them, armed with six-guns and clubs, standing out on the deck at the top of the stairs under the POLLING PLACE sign. They stopped and questioned everyone who came up. If they didn't like the answers, they beat the would-be voters and shoved them down the stairs.

Martin looked up the stairs at the leader. He was a husky man in a derby hat, a stub of a cigar in his mouth, a billy club in his hand. When he realized that Martin was watching him, he stood, legs apart, hands on hips, daring him to come up. All three of them watched, weapons ready.

For a few seconds, Martin tried to think of a way to coax them down to fight one at a time. Finally, he said, "Hey, you! You with the billy club! You man enough to come down here and fight fair for the first time in your life?"

Around the stub of the cigar, the pug sneered, "Why don't you come up here, shitface?" The other two toughs stood beside the cigar-chomper, hands on gun butts.

A growing sick fear was beginning to settle in Martin's stomach. He couldn't outshoot the three of them, he'd be killed on the spot. His back stiffened; he'd be damned if he'd back down. Damned if he would.

"You want me to come up there, huh? Well, maybe, just by God maybe I will."

DOYLE TRENT
FEAR TOWN

ZEBRA BOOKS
KENSINGTON PUBLISHING CORP.

ZEBRA BOOKS are published by

Kensington Publishing Corp.
850 Third Avenue
New York, NY 10022

First Printing: June, 1994

Printed in the United States of America

Chapter One

It could have been Martin's face, the way it was deformed on the left side, or maybe the red-bearded young man in a floppy gray hat was mad at the world as he came out of the Silver Tip Gaming Palace. Whatever the reason, Martin got his first hint of trouble when he stood on the plank sidewalk on the main street of Vega in the new state of Colorado and asked directions to the Mossman Ranch.

The red-bearded one frowned at the scarred face, then growled, "Mossman Ranch. Why'd you wanta go there?"

"Ray Mossman is my brother."

"The hell, you say." Unfriendly bloodshot eyes looked Martin up and down. A pistol which Martin recognized as a Navy Colt, .36 caliber was seated in a holster just above the man's fingertips. Martin had stuffed his Remington single-action six-gun, holster, and cartridge belt in one of his saddlebags before riding into town. He didn't want to look like a hard case. "Yeah, I know where Ray Mossman lives. Ever'body knows where he lives."

Keeping his voice amiable, Martin said, "I believe his ranch house is only two miles north of town, but I've never been there."

"Mister, I wouldn't tell a Mossman the way to a shithouse. Get outta my way."

Puzzled, Martin stepped aside. He'd been in his share of brawls, more than his share, and he didn't believe in taking insults from anyone. But a brawl was the last thing he wanted now. He watched Redbeard walk down the plankwalk to the next saloon and go inside.

It was early evening, but a sign on the door of the Mossman Mercantile said the store was closed for the day. The saloon across the street and down the street a half-block was doing a good business, with laboring men and a few well-dressed gentlemen going in and coming out. Tinny music from a ricky-tick piano reached the street.

Martin had left his tired horse at a hitchrail in front of the mercantile and headed for the saloon to ask directions. Now he stood on the plankwalk wondering why the red-bearded one had been so unfriendly. Oh well, some men were like that. Martin went inside the saloon and worked his way through some twenty-five men to the bar.

The music was louder here, and so was the hubbub of voices. He didn't order a drink because he didn't want whiskey on his breath. "Pardon me," he said to the gent on his right, "I'm looking for the Mossman Ranch. I wonder if you'd mind telling me how to get there."

The gent hadn't shaved lately, and he wore a bill cap pulled down to his eyebrows. He too frowned at Martin's face a moment, but Martin was used to that. "You a friend of Ray Mossman?"

"I'm his brother."

"Shit." The word came out with a sneer, and he turned his back to Martin.

This was getting nowhere. Maybe if he found someone who wasn't a saloon patron he could get an answer. Outside on the plankwalk, he mulled it over. It was obvious some of the men in Vega didn't like Ray Mossman. But why? Ray was no troublemaker. He didn't start fights. Ray didn't like to fight. Martin was the one who was always getting into brawls.

When two cowboys dismounted in front of the saloon, Martin stepped up. Maybe they would be more sociable. A cowboy could recognize another at a glance. "Pardon me, gentlemen, I'm looking for the Mossman Ranch. Would you know where I can find the ranch house?"

Their eyes drifted over Martin, paused only a second on the scarred face, then the tall one asked, "You a friend of Ray Mossman's."

"That I am."

They gave him a second looking over. Both carried six-guns in holsters on their right hips. Then the tall one pointed down the street and drawled, "Wal, you go that way till you come to a fork in the road—it's only 'bout a quarter of a mile—then you take the north fork and go another mile and you come to another fork, then you take the one that goes northeast and you'll come to the house. It sets back up against Bear Creek."

"Much obliged," Martin said. He felt the two men's eyes on his back as he walked across the street to his horse.

It was nearly dark when he rode up to the house—a two-story wood frame building, whitewashed, with a white picket fence around the front yard. Flowers grew in the yard and a flower box full of red tulips sat under a window on a wide porch. Lacy curtains filled the windows. Before he dismounted, Martin took in a long barn built of rough lumber, four plank corrals, a low building that looked like a bunkhouse, and an open-sided shed with a freight wagon, a buckboard, and a buggy parked under the roof. Two horses were standing in one of the corrals.

Ray Mossman was doing right well. The successful brother.

Without getting off his horse, Martin hollered, "Hallo-o-o. Hallo-o-o the house." He hollered it twice before the door to the bunkhouse opened. The man standing in the lamplight held a rifle. Martin watched him, wary. Then the front door to the house opened and Mary stood there.

"Who is it?"

Though she'd put on a little weight, she was still a pretty woman. He said, "It's Martin. If I can get down, Mary, you'll recognize me."

"Martin? Martin, is that you?" Two young boys were peering around the woman's long skirt.

"It's me, Mary. That must be Joshua and Benjamin with you. Is Ray at home?"

"Not at the moment, Martin, but please get down and come in. Where did you come from, anyway?"

The man from the bunkhouse was walking toward him, still holding the rifle. Mary spoke to him, "Everything is fine, Luke. This is Martin Mossman, Raymond's brother."

"Oh. All right, Mrs. Mossman." He lowered the rifle and turned back to the bunkhouse. Martin dismounted, wrapped the reins once around a hitchrail in front of the picket fence. He opened a narrow gate in the fence and stepped up onto the porch. A quick frown crossed the woman's face when she saw the old bullet wound, but just as quickly she smiled. "We weren't expecting you, Martin. Raymond will be happy to see you. He's attending a meeting of the county board of commissioners at a neighbor's, but he'll be home soon. Come in, won't you?"

He stepped inside a parlor and looked around. This was no homesteader's cabin, not like the one Ray had described in a letter as the first home for the family in

Colorado's South Park country. A moss rock fireplace dominated the room, and a sofa with soft pillows sat a safe distance in front of it. Four chairs, upholstered with plump seats, were arranged on either side of the sofa. A hemp carpet covered two-thirds of the floor, and a staircase went up the far wall. Family photographs hung on the walls.

"Boys, this is your uncle Martin. You've heard your father tell of him. Martin, you've never seen our sons, have you."

"No. This has to be Joshua." Martin nodded toward the tallest of the two, a sandy-haired boy in a faded plaid shirt and baggy cotton pants. "He's seven now, isn't he?"

"Seven and a half. And this is Benjamin, the baby of the family. He's five. Boys, shake hands with your father's brother."

The older stepped forward and offered his right hand. The younger one took his turn, and asked, "What happened to your face?"

"Benjamin," the woman scolded, "we don't ask questions like that."

Looking down at him, Martin smiled a crooked smile. "You've heard of the war? They're calling it the Civil War nowadays."

"No sir."

"Well, you'll learn about it soon enough."

The woman explained, "Your uncle Martin was in the war, and he was wounded."

"Was you shot?"

"Yeah, Joshua. I was shot."

"Martin, have you had supper? We had to eat early because of the board meeting, but I'll find something for you."

"Yes, I've had supper." He hadn't, but he didn't want

to put her to any inconvenience. "I've been pushing that horse out there pretty hard to get here before dark. Is there a place for him in one of the corrals?"

"Of course. Joshua, take a lantern and show your uncle where to put up his horse. And feed it."

It was dark outside now, and Martin untied the horse and followed the boy and his lantern to the barn. "I know about the war," the boy said. "Mama told us about it. Bennie's too little to know about things like that."

"It was a bad war. All wars are bad."

"I know about gettin' shot too. I seen people that was shot. I seen a dead man once."

"Well . . ." Martin didn't know what to say to that.

The boy opened a corral gate, and Martin led the horse through. "There's water in that tub and I'll get some hay from the barn. Papa told me never to go in the barn loft with a lantern, but there's some hay that hasn't been ate yet in one of the mangers."

"You hold the light and I'll get the hay. That way there won't be any accidents."

"It's good timothy hay. We grow it ourselves. We grow some oats too."

"This old pony will be happy to have it."

"We irrigate the vega with water from Bear Creek. It comes out of the mountains north of Wilkerson Pass."

"That must be the pass I rode over a few hours ago."

"You can see Pikes Peak from up there. Mama says you can almost see clear to civilization."

"You mother doesn't think this part of the country is civilized, then?"

"It ain't yet, but it's gonna be. Papa is gonna see to that."

The boy talked on, but Martin was thinking about his brother's wife. Mary had always been polite and accommodating to him because she was brought up that way. And because he was her husband's brother. But he knew she wasn't fond of him. She didn't approve of him and his carousing ways. Well, he wouldn't stay long, just long enough to get reacquainted with the only other member of his family who was still alive, and his two nephews. Then he'd drift on. He'd always drifted on.

It was getting late. Martin reckoned it was after ten o'clock. Mary was worried, though she tried not to show it. She'd been making polite conversation, and Martin did his best to be polite and make small talk without mentioning his adventures. He sat in one of the cushioned chairs and wished for a smoke, but Mary didn't approve of smoking. His headache was coming back too. He volunteered to sleep in the bunkhouse, but she insisted that they'd find a place for him in the house. Then she said, "Joshua, did you hang a lantern on the porch so your father can find his way?"

"Yeah, Mama, I done it."

"You did it, Joshua, not done it. It's time for you both to go to bed. No need to wait up for your father. He'll be angry if you're still up when he gets home."

After the boys had gone upstairs, she sat quietly, hands in her lap, fingers twitching nervously. Then she said, "He should be back by now. The board meetings usually don't last this long. He should be back."

Martin asked calmly, "Is there trouble, Mary?"

A weak smile flickered, and a worry frown reappeared. "No. Yes. Yes, there is trouble. Raymond and some of the others want to . . . there are men who disagree. Some very dangerous men."

Chapter Two

His sister-in-law's lips clamped shut, and Martin knew she didn't want to discuss it. He wished his headache would go away. Why did that have to flare up now? Unconsciously, he rubbed the side of his head, the scar. They sat quietly. Then they heard him.

Mary had been listening intently and was the first to note his coming. "Oh, I hope that's Raymond." Her husband hollered, "I'm back, Mary. I'll take the lantern and put this horse up before I come in."

Martin stood, started to go outside to greet his brother, then realized Ray wouldn't recognize him in the dark and might think a stranger had taken over his home. He stood and waited. It had been ten years. The last time the two brothers had met was three years after the war. It was in Denver. Ray and Mary had come west after the war started and Ray had opened a grocery store on Market Street. They were afraid they would never have a child, then finally Mary discovered she was pregnant. Mr. and Mrs. Raymond Mossman were a happy couple. Martin had left Denver, drifted on, before the child was born. The two brothers had exchanged an occasional letter, but hadn't met again until now. When Martin heard boots on the porch, his heart beat faster. Ten years was a long time.

Raymond Mossman came through the door with a question: "Is that a strange horse in the . . . ?" Then he saw Martin. He stopped short, his mouth still open. Martin smiled his lopsided smile. Ray gaped, and then a wide smile split his face.

"My gosh. It can't be. It is. Mart, where in the wide world did you come from? My gosh, I can't believe it."

The two met near the door, shook hands vigorously, patted each other on the back, and grinned from ear to ear.

"Where in the world did you come from, Mart? How are you? Are you all right?"

"I'm fine, Ray. Older, but no worse off." He grinned again. "No better off, either. Looks like you're doing good."

Mary said, "I'll stoke up the stove and put the coffee on." She left the room.

"Sit down, Mart. My gosh." Still grinning, shaking his head, Ray went on. "I hadn't heard from you for so long. Mary and I talked about you often. The mail is so slow. We never knew whether you were dead or alive. The last letter we got from you, you were in southern New Mexico working on a big cattle ranch."

"I've been a lot of places, Ray, done a lot of things." He grinned again. "None of which I can brag about, but I've stayed out of trouble. I helped drive three thousand cattle to some grasslands north of Denver, then drew my pay and came over here to see you and Mary and the boys. They're fine-looking boys, Ray. Mary's as pretty as ever, and you're looking good. A little more beef on your frame, but looking fit enough to take on a mountain cat."

"How are you feeling, Mart? Do you still get those headaches?"

"Now and then. I'm used to it."

Mary was back. "The coffee's perking. I'll leave you two alone. You've got a lot to talk about." She kissed her husband swiftly on the lips, said, "It's grand to see you again, Martin. Feel welcome in our home." She went up the stairs.

"Come on in the kitchen." Ray led the way into a big kitchen with a four-hole Windsor range. The stove had a nickel trim, a high shelf, and a hot-water reservoir. There were cabinets on the walls, linoleum on the floor, and a long table lined with eight chairs. "I've only got one hired man here now, but I've had as many as five. A woman from town comes out and helps with the cooking and housekeeping when we have a full crew to feed. Still like your coffee black?"

They talked for two hours about a lot of things, their dead folks, the sister who'd died at age seven, the old hometown of Indianapolis. One subject they stayed away from was the war. Ray wasn't proud of the way he'd avoided going to war, and Martin knew he didn't want to talk about it. He didn't blame Ray. He'd probably have done the same if he'd been in Ray's shoes. Now that Mary had gone to bed, Martin pulled his sack of tobacco out of a shirt pocket and offered the makings to his brother. Ray shook his head, but said, "Go ahead and smoke. Mary doesn't like for anyone to smoke in the house, but the smoke will clear out before she gets up in the morning."

No one would have known by looking that the two were brothers. Martin was the older, in his middle thirties, and the tallest at an even six feet. He'd always been a little underweight. Ray was two years younger, two inches shorter, and huskier. Martin was the handsome one—until he was disfigured in the war. He still had thick dark hair, while Ray's hair was getting thin. Both were clean-shaved, but Ray shaved carefully around his muttonchop sideburns.

Puffing his cigarette, blowing smoke over his brother's head, Martin recalled how the younger brother had taken over the family store when their dad died, how he'd run the store with experience and a talent for business. But Martin, he was something else. He liked the girls and the girls liked him. He'd stayed out of serious trouble, but he liked to drink, carouse, and get into fistfights. He hadn't been much help at the store, and, thinking back, he wished he had been. Then Ray had gotten married, and then the war started.

Martin had had no opinion at all as to which side was right, but he'd been caught up in the war meetings held on a street corner in Indianapolis. When the bands played "Red, White and Blue," and "Rallied 'Round the Flag," and speakers appealed to patriotism, the young men felt guilty if they didn't enlist. When the first had stepped up and signed, everyone cheered and made him a hero. Others, including Martin, had followed. Ray wanted nothing to do with the war. Mary wanted nothing to do with the war. As the war dragged on, there was talk in Washington about conscripting young men to fight for the union side, and Mary had persuaded her husband to sell the store and move to the Territory of Colorado. The brothers had never been close after that.

"Got any plans, Mart?"

"None. I won't stay long. I only wanted to say hello and get acquainted with my nephews."

"You ought to settle down, Mart. You're not getting younger, you know. Pretty soon you'll be old and have nothing."

"You're right. I know it. I keep telling myself that, but I get to wondering what's over the horizon."

"There's still some land available for homesteading in this territory. You can do what I did. I homesteaded a hundred and sixty acres, claimed another quarter section under the Timber Act, preempted another quarter section, and bought out two other homesteaders. I was lucky enough to get some irrigable land along Bear Creek and Granite Creek. I learned the hard way you can't grow groceries here. The growing season is too short. But I can grow good prairie hay and I've got four acres in oats. There's a demand for hay, and a good profit in growing it. You, after serving four years in the war, can pick a quarter section that the government hasn't offered for sale yet, live on it a year, and own it."

With his lopsided grin, Martin said, "I'm no farmer, and the good land is probably already claimed."

"I know two homesteaders who won't even consider growing anything but potatoes, corn, carrots, and other food crops, and they're about to give up. You can buy their claims cheap. And what with the new horse-drawn mowing machines and hay rakes, harvesting hay isn't as much work as it used to be."

"Well, you know me, Ray. When the snow flies I'm like the wandering goose and start looking for a warmer climate. This looks like deep-snow country to me."

"That's why hay is a profitable crop. These cowmen around here can't grow enough, and during a hard winter they'll pay anything for it. I bought a few percheron mares and bred them to a big horse over on the other side of the pass, and I'll raise a few horses. Draft horses are in big demand here. Saddle horses are too, but if you've got some good harness horses for sale you can name your price."

Grinning again, Martin said, "That's why you're gonna get rich, Ray. You think about things like that and you look ahead. You're like Papa, always thinking about business. Wish I was that way."

"You're plenty smart. You went as far in school as I did, as Mary did. The only difference is we read a lot, and yes, we try to look ahead and find ways to make a profit."

Martin had been sitting with his chair tilted back on its hind legs. Now he let it down on all four, crossed his legs, and allowed, "It's folks like you and Mary who will bring civilization to this territory. Folks like me, we just pass through. I'm not proud of it."

"The General Assembly has divided Colorado into counties, and we've had county elections. I'm chairman of the county board, and we've got a sheriff and a clerk and recorder. We have authority to levy taxes. What we don't have yet is a permanent county seat, but we will have soon, and it will be the town of Vega. Not only that, the Midland Railroad is building west to Leadville, and it will come right smack through here. Our little town is going to be an important trade center. This is a good spot to settle down on, Mart."

"That's what I ought to do. I know it, but a man who settles down wants a wife, and with my face I doubt there's a woman who'd have me."

Shaking his head, Ray said, "I don't believe that. It's like Mary said once, after you've been around a while nobody notices. Sure, you don't look quite normal, but you're not ugly. It's those headaches you get that worry me more than your face. You—"

Hoofbeats, running hoofbeats, stopped Raymond in midsentence. Moving fast, he blew out the lamp and said, "Get down on the floor, Mart. Get down."

Gunfire popped like cannons outside. A window in the parlor was shattered. Bullets thudded into the walls.

Then, as quickly as it had started, the shooting ceased. Running hoofbeats faded away.

Martin sputtered, "What the humped-up hell's going on? What . . . ?"

Ray was running up the stairs, finding his way easily in the dark, yelling, "Mary. Mary, are you hurt? Boys?"

From the first floor, Martin heard their voices, Mary's and the boys', excited. He stood in the dark, afraid to light the lamp and make a target of himself. It was the gold fields of California over again. It was the mining town of Silver City in southern New Mexico Territory. It was Dodge City, El Paso, Cimarron. He wished he'd brought his saddlebags in and had his Remington. He was helpless without a gun.

Then the voices calmed, and they came down the stairs, the four of them, Ray leading the way with a lamp.

When they gathered in the kitchen, Ray said, "I don't think they intended to hit anybody. It was their way of showing me they don't agree with some of our goals."

"They might have shot us, Raymond." Mary's voice was trembling. "We could have been killed in our beds."

Joshua was excited. "Boy, did you see the window. They shot right through it. I wished I had my rifle loaded, I'd of burned their hind ends for sure."

"Joshua," his mother scolded, "that's enough of that kind of talk. And don't you ever point that rifle at anyone. If you ever do I'll take it away from you."

"Well," Ray said, "it's over now. They've gone and they won't be back. We can all go to bed." To Martin, he said, "Law and order isn't fully established here yet, but it will be. If we don't let the hooligans scare us away and if we stick to our goals, we'll have a justice system and a police force."

Shrugging, Martin said only, "It happens."

As he went to bed in a small room off the kitchen used occasionally by a hired cook, he muttered to himself: "It happens, all right. Too damned often."

Chapter Three

Martin was introduced to the hired man at breakfast. His name was Luke, middle-fifties, short, and broad-shouldered. Luke wore brogan shoes and the stiff new Levi's denim pants held up with leather suspenders. He took off his floppy black hat when he came in the back door to the kitchen. "I heard the shootin'," he said, "and I come over to see if anybody got shot, but I seen you-all through the winder and I didn't wanta bother you."

"You didn't see who did the shooting, did you?" his boss asked.

"Nossir, I was sleepin' like a dead man when the shootin' started, and by the time I got out'n my blankets they was gone."

"You said there's a sheriff," Martin put in, "will he do anything about it?"

"Breakfast is on the table," Mary said. She wore a long white apron tied at the back with a big bow. Her dark hair was done neatly in a bun at the back of her head. "Boys, did you wash your faces and necks?"

"Yeah, we already done that, didn't we, Bennie?" The younger boy nodded in agreement. "Yeah, we already done it."

"You did it, not done it. Joshua, you should set a better example for your brother."

"Yes'm."

"And it's 'Yes, Mother.' "

They all sat, all but Mary. She filled the men's coffee cups, then set a platter of hotcakes in the center of the table. The platter was soon emptied, along with a platter of bacon. Raymond Mossman was at the head of the table, and Joshua sat next to his uncle. Mary served more hotcakes. When the younger boy, Benjamin, stood and reached for a bottle of corn syrup, he was ordered, "Sit, Benjamin, and ask for the syrup. And say please."

The boy sat. "Please pass the surrup."

"Uncle Martin, have you got a gun?"

"Well, yes. It's out there with my saddle and blanket roll."

"If you'd a had it would you'd a shot back last night?"

"I doubt it. I wouldn't have had time."

"Papa don't carry a gun, and Luke don't neither."

"Doesn't either, not don't neither."

"Well, a man shouldn't need a gun nowadays."

"I got a rifle. It's a single-shot thirty-two. It'll kill a deer."

"Joshua, don't talk so much, and eat your breakfast."

"Yes'm. I mean, yes, Mother."

They ate silently a while, then Ray said, "In answer to your question, Mart, I doubt Sheriff Little will do anything. He was elected too, and we members of the county board have nothing to say about what he does or doesn't do."

Around a mouthful of hotcake, Joshua said, "I don't have to go to school again all summer. I wish I never hadda go to school."

With a sigh, Mary said, "I'm beginning to wish the

same. You pick up all your bad grammar at school. The older boys are a bad influence on the younger ones. Martin, would you have believed, when we were in the Indianapolis Middle School, that boys and girls from six to sixteen could be in the same class?"

Grinning, Martin said, "It must be kind of awkward. I pity the teacher."

"Mrs. Harrison does her best, but it's just too much. I hope that someday we will have a bigger schoolhouse and divided classes."

"That's another one of our goals," Raymond said.

"Please pass the surrup," the younger boy said.

"Benjamin, you're drowning your breakfast in syrup."

Meal over, the three men and Joshua went outside where Luke got his orders for the day. He was to get on a horse and ride around the hay lands, see that the wire fences were all up, then round up the Mossman horses and drive them back this way. After dinner he was to irrigate the Bear Creek meadow. Luke nodded his head and said, "Yup, yup," then walked away toward the corrals.

The sun had come up over Wilkerson Pass and was casting a long shadow on the west side of the house. The few young elm trees that Mary and her husband had planted were making thin shadows. Ray looked at the solid blue sky, and mused aloud, "If it would rain more we wouldn't have to irrigate so often. Would you believe, Mart, that this is a dry climate despite all the snow in the winter?"

"Everything is green. No, I wouldn't have guessed it."

"We've got two big hay meadows," Ray explained. "We're growing hay on sixty acres over east under the pass, and we've got another hundred acres under irrigation a mile north where Bear Creek comes down from the

South Platte. It's a floodplain, and it produces good hay."

Joshua said, "The Mexicans call 'em *vegas*. That's what they call all the flat land, and that's what the town was named after. Mrs. Harrison told us that."

"Mart, I've got to go open the store. You can loaf or do whatever you feel like doing. If you want to go to town, you can catch one of our horses and let yours rest."

"I'll walk around here a little. It won't hurt me to walk."

The first thing he did was go back into the kitchen and offer to help Mary with the dishes. "I've done a lot of batching, and I'm used to washing dishes."

"No, I can do it. When the work gets too heavy, Raymond hires a woman to help. But thank you anyway, Martin."

With the two boys at his side, Martin walked out onto the prairie, gazing long at the mountains on the east and north and the land lying flat to the south. It was a pleasant morning, and he was enjoying his walk and his nephews. When a cottontail rabbit jumped from under a clump of grass and ran off, Joshua held his hands up as if he were aiming a rifle. "Bang," he said. "I could of got him. Do you like to hunt, Uncle Martin?"

"When I need the meat. If I don't need the meat I'd rather see the wild animals running free and pretty than dead and bleeding. Wouldn't you?"

"Well, I don't know. I guess so."

"If we kill 'em for sport there soon won't be any left. They'll be gone like the buffalo."

"Mrs. Harrison told us about the buffalo."

"There's a lesson to be learned there."

The hay land was surrounded by a smooth-wire fence, sagging badly. Martin knew from experience that a change in the weather caused the wire to sag. The younger boy, Benjamin, pointed and said, "There's Luke." The hired man was using a nail puller to stretch the wire against a corner post. "That's a never-ending, job," Martin mused aloud.

Looking up at his uncle, Joshua said, "Papa's gonna get some bob wire. Cattle can't go through bob wire. The only cow we got is old Grandma, and she gets through the fence whenever she wants to. Luke milks her every morning and night, and we got milk and butter."

Lunch was leftovers from last night's supper—thin slices of boiled beef, mashed potatoes fried into patties, and canned peaches. For the boys, there was milk. "I wish we could get more fresh fruit," Mary said. "When the railroad gets here we'll have more produce to choose from."

"Poppa don't come home for dinner most of the time. He gets somethin' to eat at the Vega Cafe."

"He doesn't come home, Joshua, not don't come home. Raymond usually has too much work to do at the store to take the time to come home for lunch."

"Speaking of the store," Martin said, "I'd like to see it. I reckon I'll walk to town."

"We can ride to town, Uncle Martin. I got a horse I can catch with a handful of oats. He's a paint named Patches. I'll catch old Barney for you."

"Don't be a pest to your uncle, Joshua. Maybe he doesn't want you tagging along."

Scooting his chair back, grinning, Martin said, "One of the reasons I came here is to get acquainted with my nephews. I'll be tickled to have his company."

The store was another two-story frame building with a staircase outside leading to a balcony and door over a vacant lot. A sign painted on the side and also over the front door read MOSSMAN MERCANTILE and GENERAL MER-

CHANDISE. A plank door flanked by two windows faced the street. Martin and the boy tied their horses to a hitchrail on the street, climbed two steps, and went inside.

The merchandise was general, all right. On one side of the big room was a long wooden counter, and on the far end of the counter tobacco, bags of coffee, beans, and flour were stacked. A crank-operated cash register sat on the near end. More groceries of all kinds, including hermetically sealed cans of fruit and vegetables, filled shelves behind the counter. Clothing and bolts of cloth were stacked neatly on tables, and hand tools from axes to crosscut saws were on display against a wall. In a corner next to an inside door was a wooden case filled with guns, including lever-action rifles, long-barreled trapdoor single-shot rifles, and different calibers of revolvers.

In another corner was a short counter and pigeonholes on the wall behind it. A sign on the wall read U.S. MAIL. The inside door opened onto a storeroom in the back and a staircase that led to more storerooms upstairs.

Ray Mossman was putting groceries on the counter next to the cash register as a woman in a poke bonnet and a long calico dress read from a list she held. When he saw Martin and his son, he said, "Have a look around, Mart, I'll be with you in a minute." Wooden floorboards creaked as Martin sauntered across the room.

"It's a real nice store," Martin mused aloud. "Everything you need is in here? Is this the only general store in town?"

"Nope," Joshua answered. "Mr. Pritchard's store is down on the other end of the street. He sells groceries and stuff and he sells whiskey in bottles. Papa don't sell whiskey."

"Is your papa the postmaster too?"

"Uh-huh. When I get in the fifth grade I'm gonna help sort the mail."

"Well, what I need now is to find a laundry. Know where it is?"

"Sure. It's down on the next block."

Martin had carried his saddlebags into the small room he was using at the Mossman house and emptied them of everything but his one change of clothes. Now he untied the saddlebags from behind the cantleboard of his saddle, slung them over his shoulder, and looked down the street at a sign that said simply, LAUNDRY. The boy remained at his side.

Leaving their horses in front of the mercantile, they crossed the street, walked past the saloon where Martin had asked directions the night before, past a vacant lot and then a one-story rooming house. The plankwalk ended here, so they followed a dirt path in front of another weed-grown vacant lot to the small log building with the laundry sign.

Two freight wagons pulled by two-horse teams went by in the opposite direction, tug chains and singletrees rattling. A buggy pulled by a prancing bay horse passed, and two cowboys rode by on trotting horses. Martin and the boy stepped aside to make way for two women, one wearing a poke bonnet and the other with a shawl over her head. Vega was no boomtown, but it was busy.

As they passed the vacant lot again, on their way back to the mercantile, Joshua was challenged:

"Hey, shitface. Yeah, you, Mossman. I hear you eat shit."

Chapter Four

There were three of the boys, all older and bigger than Joshua. But young Mossman doubled his fists and stepped up to the foulmouthed one. "What did you say?"

"I said you Mossmans eat shit. You're all fulla shit."

Through gritted teeth, Joshua said, "Take that back."

"Your papa eats shit, your mama eats shit, and you eat shit." The boy was towheaded, in baggy overalls and badly worn shoes. "You're all fulla shit."

"That did it. Put up your dukes."

With a sneer, the bigger boy said, "Ha, ha. Go on home to your mama before you get hurt."

"Whoa, whoa, now, fellers." Stepping quickly, Martin got between the two boys. "Let's not have any fisticuffs. Josh, let's go back to the store." He took his nephew by the shoulder and turned him around."

"S'matter, Mossman, scairt? Who's this pissface you got with you, anyhow?"

Joshua tried to turn around and go back, but Martin had a good hold on his shoulder. "Pay 'em no mind, Josh. They're just trying to start a fight."

"But I gotta . . ." The boy was close to tears with frustration. "I can't let 'em say that."

"Come on. They're just troublemakers." He steered the boy toward the other side of the street.

"Let 'em fight, mister."

Looking back, Martin saw two men standing beside the three boys. "Come on," he repeated to Joshua.

" 'Fraid he'll get a lickin'? 'Fraid he can't take it?"

Martin tried to ignore the man.

"You Mossmans are yeller. You're scared to fight. You ain't even men. You're a bunch of old women."

Martin paused. Without turning back, he said to his nephew, "Go on over to the store, Josh. Go inside. I'll be along in a minute. Go on."

"But I—"

"Go on, Josh." Martin's voice was harsher than he wanted it to be. "Do what I told you to."

Reluctantly, the boy started on, head down. Then Martin turned back.

He knew the type. A brawler, a bully. You either fought him, left town, or listened to his insults every time you got within hollering distance of him. If he was bigger, you picked up the difference and broke it over his head. Or shot him. Martin's Remington was back at the Mossman house, while this gent was carrying a six-gun in a cross-draw holster. He was a broad-shouldered man, flat face, bill cap on his head. The gun was an old Army Dragoon, big and slow. The second gent was standing with his hands in his hip pockets, grinning. Martin stepped up to the big flat-faced one.

The man sneered, "What happened to your mug? You lookin' to get the other side busted?

No use talking. And it would be foolish to let him get in the first blow. Martin hit him.

It was a sudden, roundhouse punch that caught Flat-face on the left side, just under the heart. A left hook connected with the man's nose, and another roundhouse right to the left eye knocked him down.

It happened so fast, the big man couldn't believe it. He couldn't believe he'd been hit so hard. He sat in the weeds on the seat of his pants, blinking, shaking his head. Blood was dripping out of his nose, and his left eye was swelling fast.

Standing over him, fists ready, Martin said, "Care to repeat what you said?"

One of the kids goaded, "Git up, mister. Hit 'im back."

Martin glanced at the three boys and at the other man. No one had moved. To the gent still sitting on the ground, he said, "Well?"

Then the man moved. His right hand went to the six-gun on his left side. The gun didn't clear leather before a hard boot heel came down on the gun hand, forcing a pain-filled grunt out of the man. Martin reached down and took the gun from its holster. Stepping back, he picked the percussion caps off the nipples, gave the gun's cylinder a turn, then threw the caps and the gun into the weeds.

Martin repeated, "Well?"

Through clenched teeth, the big man asked, "Who are you, mister?"

"Name's Mossman. The fighting Mossman. Get up and I'll knock you down again."

"Next time we meet, you better be packin' iron."

Four pedestrians had stopped to see what was happening. A teamster riding on a freight wagon whoaed his team to watch. The big man stayed where he was. After glaring at him a few more seconds, Martin turned on his heels and headed across the street. Joshua was standing by the hitchrail, excited.

"Boy, you sure knocked the pee-waddin' outta him, Uncle Martin. Boy, you sure can fight."

"I told you to go back in the store."

"I started to, but I had to watch."

"You don't mind very good, do you?"

"Well, most of the time, but . . ."

"Your mother's gonna skin me alive. I shouldn't have let you come to town with me. I shouldn't have . . ."

The boy was near tears again. "I wish you wasn't mad at me. I didn't mean to make you mad."

"All right, all right." Looking back across the street, Martin saw the big man searching the weeds for his gun. The three boys and the other man were walking away. "Listen, Josh, fighting is something dogs do. I picked up the habit a long time ago, and I wish I hadn't. I'm not proud of it, understand? You don't have to fight to be a man, understand?"

"Yes sir."

"Your mother is gonna be powerful unhappy about this."

"I won't tell 'er, Uncle Martin."

"You don't lie. If your mother asks, you tell the truth. We'll both catch hell—heck—but we don't lie."

"Yes sir."

"Come on, let's go home and face the music."

It wasn't music Martin faced. Far from it. Mary Mossman was furious.

"You haven't been here one full day before you're fighting again. I had hoped, Martin, that you would have outgrown that by now. And with our son watching."

He stood in the kitchen, head down, feeling like a spanked puppy. Rather than wait for her to hear about it from other sources, he'd told her himself. Joshua tried to explain that it was because some older boys were picking on him that Uncle Martin got into a fight. "They called us bad names, Mama. We had to make 'em take it back."

"No, you didn't. Joshua, go to your room and don't come out until your father gets home. Martin, I don't know what to do about you. Please don't take our son with you the next time you go to town. You just can't stay out of fights. I'm only grateful that you were not armed. If you had been, it could have turned into a shooting fight and someone would have been killed. I don't want our sons exposed to that."

"I apologize, Mary. You're right. Trouble just follows me wherever I go. It's probably my fault. I . . . wish it hadn't happened."

Voice still trembling with anger, she said, "It is your fault, Martin. You're too quick to take offense. You'll never learn. You . . . you're a bad influence on our sons."

He couldn't argue with her, not with his brother's wife. All he could do was apologize. "I'll leave tomorrow, Mary. I didn't intend to stay more than a couple of days anyhow. I apologize." Wanting to get away from her before he did get into an argument, he turned and went outside.

At the corrals, he crossed his arms on the top rail, saw that his brown gelding was well-fed and not quite so gaunt. "Looks like we'll be traveling again, partner. Which way shall we go? Wherever we go, we won't be in a hurry. We've got all the time in the world." Then it came to him in a rush, everything Mary had said, and he felt that he was being blamed for something that wasn't his fault. "Goddammit, there are times when a man has to stand and fight. That's just the way the goddamn world is. Even Ray, her own husband, got into some scraps when we were kids. It's easy to say 'Turn the other cheek,' but I learned a long time ago if you turn the other cheek you'll get hit on the other cheek. Hell, if you don't hit back you'll have hooligans shooting holes in your house whenever they feel like it. Goddammit, she didn't have to blame everything on me."

To make matters worse, his headache was back. Ever since he'd awakened in a Union Army hospital wagon with his head full of sutures, he'd had the headaches. Laudanum had helped for a while, but soon he was taking nine or ten drops at a time, twice the normal dose, and it made him woozy and only half-alive. He'd tried morphia, but quit cold when he found himself getting hooked on it. Whiskey was the best medicine. If a man had to be dependent on something, whiskey was as good as anything else. He had a bottle of whiskey in his blanket roll, but he didn't dare take a drink. Mary could smell whiskey on a man's breath a mile away.

He stood that way, arms crossed on the corral pole, head down, headachy and heavyhearted. He didn't hear her come up behind him until she spoke his name.

"Martin," she said softly. Turning, he met her gaze. "Martin, I, uh, I was perhaps too harsh. Don't be in a hurry to leave. You and Raymond have a lot of visiting to do, a lot to talk about. You're always welcome in our home, Martin."

Her words lightened the load on his mind, but still he thought he ought to leave tomorrow, and he told her so.

"Don't leave because of anything I said." She turned back toward the house, paused. "Raymond will be home about sundown. Dinner will be ready then."

Raymond had already heard about it. All he did was shake his head sadly. "I guess it wasn't your fault, Mart. I only wish Josh hadn't been there."

They were washing for supper out of a tin pan on a bench outside the kitchen door. Martin wiped his face on a muslin towel and ran his fingers through his hair. "It's like I told Mary, trouble follows me. If you'd been there instead of me it wouldn't have happened."

"Yeah, it would. It was just luck that I wasn't there. I couldn't have whipped that big hulk. I don't know what I would have done."

"You've survived this long in a tough country. You don't need me."

"As a matter of fact." Ray had to bend his knees to see his reflection in a cracked mirror hanging from a peg. "I hate to ask you, but I need you to do a job for me." He half turned and faced his brother. "You don't have to do it, Mart. You don't owe me anything."

"Name it, I'll do it."

"Well, it's like this." The two men stood outside the kitchen door, out of earshot of anyone else. "What we merchants do is, we get our supplies from a warehouse at Florissant. You might have come through Florissant, east of Wilkerson Pass and west of Ute Pass."

"Yeah, I remember. A lumber town."

"A wholesaler in Florissant owns about twenty wagons and teams, and he hauls supplies from the railroad at Colorado Springs. We haul our supplies from his warehouse. It shortens what used to be a long trip."

"Uh-huh."

"Usually, we go in a bunch. We put together a train of eight or ten wagons, and make a four-day trip out of it. But a new vein of silver was discovered in the Buckskin mine about ten miles north of here and men have been pouring into town from all directions to work it. Well, the problem is, I'm running out of the main staples, like flour, sugar, cornmeal, and coffee. I'm going to have to send a wagon to Florissant."

"You want me to go?"

"Yeah, Mart, but you don't have to. I can maybe find somebody else. I'd send Luke, but he doesn't have the guts to do it."

"Takes guts, huh?"

"Yeah, but, aw hell, Mart, forget it. I've got no business asking you to risk your neck for me."

"I already said I'd do it."

"Listen, there are men who will kill for a few dollars, and even if they can't get cash, they'll kill for the horses. A man alone is . . . aw, forget it. Not only that, there are people in this county who'd like to put me out of business. No, I'll try to hire some men, enough to discourage any road agents." Ray looked down at his boots a moment, then back at his brother. "Trouble is, most good men are too busy running their own affairs, and that leaves only the, uh, unemployed. They're uh, not too trustworthy."

"I've run into road agents before, and I'm still alive. I'll go."

Chapter Five

They harnessed four big horses and hitched them to a wagon that had low sideboards but was wide and long. Two heavy tarps were folded in the back to cover the load on the return trip. Martin's blanket roll was under the high spring seat, and a pile of prairie hay had been forked into the rear end. Martin was wearing his Remington single-action revolver, .44–100 caliber, and a Winchester lever-action rifle lay across the seat.

Ray Mossman had wanted to wait until the next day to give him time to try to find someone with a shotgun to accompany Martin, but Martin said he didn't want any company. What he did want was to know why some of the citizens of Prairie County had a grudge against his brother.

Shrugging, Ray explained, "We want to make the town of Vega a good place to live and raise a family. To do that we want to get rid of some of the riffraff."

"How do you expect to do that?"

"We think if we can get rid of the cribs—Mart, have you seen much of Vega?—one street, Second Street, is lined with one-woman cribs, prostitutes. And if we can get rid of the tinhorn gamblers, the card sharps and the like, then we can sort of get a handle on things. It will take a county ordinance."

Martin was shaking his head. "That's hard to do. I've been in towns that tried it."

"We know we can't do it without citizen support. The citizens have to want it. So we're calling a special election."

"We being the county board?"

"Four of the five board members favor it, one isn't sure. Most of the merchants favor it."

"And," Martin said, "I can guess what's happening. Among them that don't favor it are the roughest and toughest and meanest of the citizens."

"That's it exactly. In your ramblings, you've been in towns like Vega and you know they're not fit places to raise a family. The fight you got into yesterday in broad daylight wouldn't have happened in Indianapolis."

Martin hooked a tug chain to a singletree, then straightened up and looked at his brother. "Is that why you left Denver?"

"Yep. Denver has become a big dirty city where the police and the politicians are crooked and the cutthroats and bullyboys have taken over the streets. Vega was a pleasant, peaceful little town until more float was discovered and all the toughs and whores moved south from the dying town of Buckskin."

"And," Martin said as he gathered the four driving lines, "as the town grows it gets worse."

"You're right again, unless we can get some ordinances passed that'll give us some tools to work with."

"Well"—Martin looked down from the high seat—"I don't know enough about your town to form an opinion, but I'm on your side no matter what."

* * *

He kept the team to a steady trot until they started up the road that led through the Puma Hills and over Wilkerson Pass. He wanted to get over the pass and on the downhill side before dark. By the time they started uphill the sun was at the one o'clock spot, and his stomach told him it was time to eat the sandwiches Mary had packed. His headache told him it was time for a slug of whiskey.

Damned headache. Damned war. Damned Army surgeons who'd had so many wounded to tend to they couldn't take time to do the job right. It was as if the Rebs had put a curse on him, a curse he'd have to live with the rest of his life. Whoever fired that shot didn't kill him, but he sure made him suffer. Damned war.

Reaching under the seat for his blanket roll, Martin fumbled it open and withdrew a quart whiskey bottle half-full. He uncapped it, took three quick swallows. As the whiskey burned its way throughout his body it dulled his brain for a few moments. That gave him some relief. Some, but not much.

There was just enough sun left, when he got to the top, to shine brightly on Pikes Peak, away off to the east. Between the pass and Florissant, the country was mostly rolling, with a few round-topped piney hills, wide draws, and deep arroyos. Pine trees, some tall and some short, and aspens dotted the country on the hillsides and along the streams. Florissant, Martin remembered, was just this side of a canyon that a wagon road had been built through from the settlement named Divide. Pretty country. Behind and below him, the wide, high, sagebrush prairie of South Park spread out as far as a man could see, and to the north were steep timbered hills. On the way to the top, he'd seen wagon tracks turn off the road and head north where they'd disappeared into the timber. One of the roads was well-traveled. Probably went to a ranch up there somewhere.

He traveled on a quarter of a mile, knowing it was a downhill pull from there on, then parked the wagon on a grassy spot barely out of sight of the road. There, he unhitched the horses, two bays, a black and a gray, stripped the harness off, and led them to a creek that came down from the higher hills to the north.

The best thing about traveling in a wagon was he could carry everything he needed, even horse feed. He tied the horses to the wagon, two on each side, so they could fill their stomachs with the hay he'd brought. They'd have to sleep standing up, but horses were able to lock their knees so they could do that.

It was good to have a fresh steak to fry in a skillet, red beans in a small pot to warm up, and coffee. After he ate, he took another long pull from the whiskey bottle to get some relief from the pounding headache. He smoked Duke's Mixture in hand-rolled cigarettes until after dark, then spread his blankets next to the dead supper fire. Looking at the sky, he saw nothing but stars, and decided he wouldn't need one of the wagon tarps to sleep under.

On second thought, he rolled up his blankets again and carried them and the rifle back into a stand of lodgepole pines fifty feet away. If anyone tried to sneak up on him in the dark, he intended to be hard to find. Pulling off his boots, he lay back, covered himself with a blanket, and tried to sleep. The headache was back. Another pull from the whiskey bottle turned the pounding ache into a light throb. Finally, he slept.

It was around midnight and a quarter moon had come up from the east when he was suddenly awakened.

He didn't know what woke him up—a horse's snort, a

footstep—but he was instantly alert, all senses straining. Only his eyes moved, slowly, taking in everything he could see in the dark. A black shape moved next to the wagon. Two black shapes. Man shapes. They were moving quietly, cautiously.

One climbed into the wagon and groped for whatever he could find. The other moved slowly around the long-dead campfire, and when he turned, Martin could make out something in his hand. A gun.

They were thieves, and they were ready to kill him.

Slowly, Martin reached for the Remington, got it in his right hand, thumb on the hammer. Then he realized he had a problem. If he cocked the hammer back, the sound would be loud and unmistakable in the quiet night. It would give away his position, and they could fire shot after shot in his direction until he was hit.

Thumb on the hammer, he watched them. Why hadn't they bushwhacked him before dark? There were plenty of trees and boulders to hide behind up here on the pass. Was it because they didn't catch up with him until now? Sure, that was it. The prairie country behind him was almost impossible to hide in. If they'd followed him he'd have seen them. They couldn't have gotten around and ahead of him, either. No, they'd had to wait until dark, then hope they could find him.

It hadn't been hard to do. Four horses did a lot of blowing through their nostrils, and a lot of foot stomping. And camping out in the open had been a mistake, making it easier for them. Too, if they hadn't found him in the dark they could have waited for daylight and shot him while he was cooking breakfast.

Did they plan to kill him just for the horses, or did they think he was carrying cash to pay for the groceries? And how did they know about this trip, anyway?

When he thought about it, Martin easily figured it out. Someone had seen him leaving the Mossman Ranch, and guessed where he was going. Vega was a small town. Word got around. These two had cooked up a scheme to bushwhack him and steal the money and the horses. Four big sound horses were worth more than four months' pay for a cowhand. They might even be bold enough to take the wagon too and sell it somewhere.

They wouldn't get everything they'd hoped for, however. Martin was carrying a signed note instead of cash. Ray Mossman's credit was as good as gold. But the two killers didn't know that. There were at least two. Maybe more.

Now they were walking in a half circle, looking for him. Eventually, they'd find him. Shooting was about to happen. Martin had to get in the first shot. He had to shoot fast and straight, with nothing more than a vague shape for a target.

Two of them were coming toward him, and then—oh boy—another dark shape joined them. There were three.

Carefully, Martin doubled a corner of the wool blanket he was under and used it to muffle the sound of the pistol hammer coming back to full cock. Still, a small clicking sound escaped. The three shapes stopped. They'd heard it. Any second now they'd start throwing lead in his direction.

Moving as fast as he could, Martin kicked the blanket off, aimed at the shape nearest him, and squeezed the trigger.

Chapter Six

The gunshot split the quiet night like a bolt of lightning. Without waiting to see whether he'd hit his target, Martin threw the blanket to his right and rolled to his left. Then the return fire began. Shot after shot sent lead slugs into the ground around him. He knew if he fired again the muzzle flash would give him away. He held his fire, looking for a better target, wanting to make his shot count. But the three were flat on the ground now, impossible to see in the near blackness.

Afraid to move again, Martin hugged the ground too, with only his head and his gun hand up, his eyes wide open. A slug slammed into the pine needles a foot from his right shoulder. He saw the muzzle flash, aimed, and fired at it. A man yelped, and hollered, "I'm hit, I'm hit."

The shooting stopped. Martin could hear them move now, and saw dim shadows gather where he'd fired his last shot. A man was groaning. Others were whispering. The dark forms were moving—moving away.

Lying on the floor of brown pine needles, Martin strained his senses to hear and see. Yes, they were backing off. The wounded man was still groaning. He was being dragged or carried.

For a full ten minutes Martin stayed where he was. All he could sense was the horses blowing through their nostrils, making fluttering sounds. The horses and the wagon were one big dark shape.

Slowly, carefully, Martin stood and went in his sock feet to the wagon. His first concern was the horses. If a horse had been hit, he'd have to buy another to get a wagon load of groceries to Vega. Talking quietly, he said, "Whoa, boys. Whoa now." Groping his way, he found all four horses standing. Any one of them could have been shot and crippled, but he wouldn't know it until daylight. Hell, they could all be hurt and still standing. All he could do now was wait for daylight.

Sitting on the ground, fifty feet from the wagon, he wanted a smoke, but didn't dare strike a match. The would-be killers could be somewhere near. The glow from a burning cigarette would be a perfect target too. And the headache was back.

Martin gave up trying to see in the dark, and sat with his knees up, arms crossed on top of his knees and face buried in his arms. He shut his eyes, hoping that by shutting off one of his senses he would strengthen his sense of hearing.

The horses were quiet, bellies full, sleeping on their feet. Or slowly dying.

That damned headache. Trying to find the whiskey bottle in the dark would be hopeless, so Martin didn't try. He'd suffered without whiskey or laudanum before, ever since the battle at Chickamauga a long, long time ago. Martin's battery, the Seventh Indiana from the 86th Indiana Volunteers, was in the middle of it.

At the time, Martin was on his knees with his head down, pulling a jammed paper cartridge out of that damned Mont Storm breech-loading rifle. Gunfire, cannon fire, was going on all around him. Men were yelling. Men were screaming. A rifle ball came from somewhere and smacked him on top of the head a little above the left ear. But instead of punching a hole in his skull, the ball had slid down the side of his face, just under the skin, and come out near his chin. The blow had knocked him unconscious.

At first the medical orderlies thought he was dead, and they attended to the moaning and screaming wounded. When they got around to him and found him still breathing they were astounded.

Martin had awakened on a narrow canvas cot in a hospital wagon, numb. He couldn't believe that what his fingertips touched was his face. It and the side of his head were nothing but sticking-plaster. He'd tried to say something, but his voice wouldn't work. Moving only his eyes, he saw the white-coated surgeons working as fast as they could with other wounded men. Martin passed out again.

It was three weeks before the plaster was removed for the last time, and Martin was handed a mirror. He was sick. His life was ruined. He'd be a freak for as long as he lived. The sutures had pulled down the corner of his left eye and the corner of his mouth. A red scar ran from the top of his head to his chin. He was the ugliest human he'd ever seen.

A surgeon tried to make him feel better by joking. "Your skull must be made of rubber, the way that ball put a dent in it without puncturing it. Ha, ha. It was a freakish thing. You're lucky to be alive, ha, ha."

After six months of severe headaches, Martin went to the well-equipped Citizen's Volunteer Hospital in Philadelphia where a doctor advised against further surgery. It could possibly relieve the pressure on his brain, but more than likely it would kill him. The odds were bad, very bad.

Even now, thirteen years later, Martin could feel the small depression in his skull with his fingers. There'd been times, many times, over the past thirteen years when he wished he'd taken a chance with the surgery.

Daylight was slow in coming, but Martin stayed awake, listening, always listening. Every time a horse shuffled its feet he imagined it was the robber-killers. Daylight at first was a dim glow on the east. The glow gradually brightened until he could see the silhouette of Pikes Peak. And then finally he could make out the horses and the wagon. He skipped breakfast, knowing he would be a good target cooking and eating. Leading the four horses to water, he tried to keep at least one horse between him and the trees and boulders, places where a bushwhacker could be hiding.

Harnessing the horses was the worst part. He felt as if he had a target pinned to his shirt, and he half expected a bullet to slam into his back or chest. He wouldn't even hear the shot. It would just hit him and kill him, and he wouldn't know where it came from. It seemed to take forever, but finally, he got the harness buckled on and got the team hitched to the wagon.

He climbed to the seat, kept the Winchester rifle beside him, gathered the driving lines, and said, "Come on, boys, let's strike a trot and get down there in the open country. Gee-up, there." The wagon bounced over the rocks and rattled its way back to the road.

In a half hour they were off the steepest part of the pass and in rolling hill country, green and pretty. He could see the Platte River just a short distance north, and the high mountains beyond that. Martin let the tension drain from his body, feeling lighter, breathing easier. Boy, oh boy, that was as scary as any part of the war.

As the wagon rolled along behind slow-trotting horses, he tried to guess what the thugs had done. They'd either taken the man he'd shot to a doctor somewhere or they'd buried him. Or left his body behind a boulder or in a ravine to rot. Either way, they'd decided not to come back.

His stomach reminded him he'd had no breakfast, but he kept going until the sun was straight overhead. When he spotted a line of willows, which he believed hid a small creek, he turned the team and wagon in that direction. There he broke up a downed aspen, got a small fire going and some bacon frying. While his meal cooked, he led the horses to water, then let them rest and graze with the harness on for an hour. He reckoned he'd get to Florissant before dark.

At midafternoon they forded a shallow part of the Platte, and just before sundown, the wagon rattled and rolled into the lumber town of Florissant.

There was no livery barn, but Ray had told Martin where he could find a family who owned a half-dozen corrals and kept a supply of hay, who supplemented the family income by boarding horses. The Wentworth Freight & Wholesale office was closed for the night. There was no hotel, either, but there was a boardinghouse where the unmarried sawmill workers and timber cutters lived.

The overweight middle-aged woman who owned the place and her teen-aged hired girl put another plate on the table for him, seating him between two broad-shouldered timberjacks. Something about cutting timber—using a crosscut saw and an axe, maybe—built big shoulders and muscle on a man, and Martin was glad they were friendly. Eight men gathered around the table, men in baggy clothes, suspenders, and heavy lace-up boots. Some had full beards and some were smooth-shaved. They were hungry men, but there was no grabbing and hogging. They were polite.

Unlike a crew of cowboys who ate silently, these men talked. They talked about the likelihood of a railroad being built from Colorado Springs over the divide to Florissant, and how that would create a new market for the lumber from Florissant. The cities of Colorado Springs and Colorado City were buying lumber faster than the sawmills there could produce it.

"How come they named that new town Colorado Springs?" a man asked. "There ain't no springs around there. All the springs are west of it. They call 'em soda springs 'cuz they bubble and taste funny."

" 'Cause it sounds good," answered a gray-haired gent around a mouthful of cabbage and beef. "They wanted a name that sounds good and draws the rich folks. I hear they don't sell no likker in that town. I hear the town's full of foreigners that don't want to dirty their hands on likker."

"They're callin' it Little London 'cause of all the rich Englishmen that're building big houses there."

"They can pass all the laws they want to, but they can't stop men from buyin' booze. If they can't buy it the legal way they'll find another way."

"Say, Martin—is that what you said your name is?— you got acquainted yet with the king fisher of Vega? C. C. Vance?"

Martin swallowed quickly so he could answer, "No. I'm not acquainted there. I'm staying with my brother and his family, and I only got there a couple nights ago."

"Mossman? That'd be Ray Mossman. Yeah, I seen 'im around. I usta muck in the Buckskin mine, and I remember him as being' one of the bigshots in town. Seems to be a fair and honest man."

With a grin, Martin said, "He has to be. He's my brother."

The house had only two bedrooms for boarders, with four cots to a room. Martin spent the night in a room with three other men, but at least he had a narrow cot to himself. He'd been in roominghouses where strangers—total strangers—had shared beds. Often, the boarders didn't know what kind of men, clean or dirty, they were sleeping with.

Lying on the cot with a headache, Martin recalled what one of the boarders had said about buying whiskey. The gent was right. No law could keep men from drinking if they wanted to drink. Towns that had tried to outlaw it had turned a lot of men into outlaws. That's what would happen in Vega if Ray and three other county-board members had their way. They couldn't stop the drinking, and as long as men outnumbered women about five to one in the west, they couldn't stop the whoring either.

That was a lesson Ray would have to learn the hard way. Martin could only hope there would be no killing. He could only hope that his brother wouldn't be killed.

Chapter Seven

Rather then wait his turn at one of the two washpans and shaving mirrors, Martin skipped shaving that morning. He didn't like shaving every day anyway. He wiped his eyes with his fingertips and went in to breakfast of sausage and hotcakes. At the corrals where he'd left his horses, he splashed water from a horse trough over his face, and harnessed his team.

It was around seven A.M. when Harold Wentworth opened his office at the Wentworth Freight & Wholesale, a long, low wood-frame building with a string of freight wagons parked nearby. A paunchy man with a high-crown hat and a round face, Wentworth looked over the list Martin handed him, carefully read the signed note from Ray Mossman, and allowed, "Take 'bout an hour to fill this order. I ain't sure we got enough of this here airtight canned stuff, though. Them oysters're sellin' like flapjacks aroun' here. They look like spit to me, but most folks like 'em. Got plenty of dried fruit."

Two hired men went to work loading the wagon while Wentworth totaled the bill. He had a scarred wobbly-legged desk in the small room he used for an office, and he had to roll his eyes up and touch the lead pencil to his tongue as he recalled the price of everything. Finally, he got Martin's signature on Ray Mossman's note, and Martin was on his way with a wagonload of groceries covered with two heavy tarps. As soon as he was out of town he uncapped the whiskey bottle and took two long swallows.

With the goal of reaching the top of Wilkerson Pass by dark, he kept the four horses trotting steadily until they started the long climb. Then he had to let them slow to a walk. By noon he realized he wasn't going to make the top by dark if he stopped for a noon rest, so he kept the horses going.

"Sorry, fellers. You'll get a good feed and rest tonight. Tomorrow it will be downhill."

While he sat the bouncing seat, eyes trained ahead, he remembered some of the tough towns he'd been in, towns like Georgetown in the Territory of New Mexico near the Black Range where he'd prospected for silver. Every man carried a gun in Georgetown and in the Black Range. Thieves, cutthroats were everywhere, and so were the marauding Apache. A man needed eyes in the back of his head and a quick trigger finger.

Martin had practiced with the Remington until he could draw it and thumb the hammer back in one motion, and hit a tomato can at twenty-five feet.

Cimarron in the northern end of the Territory of New Mexico was even worse. Cimarron was in the middle of the Maxwell Land Grant, and one wrong word was all it took to have the grant men and the antigrants shooting. There was a killing a day in Cimarron.

But the worst was California. The killers, backstabbers, and bushwhackers had come to California from everywhere. They'd come overland, by sailing ship around the Cape, and even from overseas. They'd cut a man's throat for a dollar. Hell, a half-dollar. Men like Martin worked their placer claims with their eyes open for danger.

Martin had killed two men in the Sierra Nevadas. He'd built a sluice box and was working his claim by himself, and when he'd come back from the settlement with a net sack of groceries one day he found two other men ransacking his tent. He'd put the groceries down, drawn the Remington, and approached the tent cautiously. But he hadn't seen the third man until the man barked, "Stop in your tracks, mister, or I'll blow another hole in your skinny ass."

He had no choice, he had to stop. Out of habit, he holstered the Remington instead of dropping it. Two men came out of his tent with six-guns pointed at him.

"I reckon," said a bearded gent through a slit of a mouth, "that you think this is your claim."

"It is," Martin said.

"Nope. It's our'n. We just claimed it. Haw, haw."

Martin knew that if he tried to make a fight of it he'd be killed. He shrugged, trying to put on an act. "Well, if you want it, it's yours. I never got a dime's worth of color out of it anyway."

"You're lyin'. We done found a good four ounces in your wigwam, and I'll bet you got some more hid aroun' here. Whar is it, you ugly sumbitch?"

Martin said, "There is no more."

"You're lyin'." The one behind Martin had stepped around in front of him, a nickel-plated revolver in his hand. He spat a stream of tobacco juice through a wild brown beard at Martin's feet, and demanded, "Whar is it?" With his left fist he hit Martin in the mouth, staggering him.

Martin wiped his mouth with the back of his right hand. The bearded one haw-hawed. "Somebody done busted up your mug. Wal, I'll bust up the other side." He drew back a big fist. That was his mistake.

When the robber drew back his fist, he allowed the barrel of the nickel-plated pistol to point down. Martin dodged the blow, and in two seconds he'd grabbed the thug around the throat with his left arm and spun him so he was facing his partners. In another split second, Martin had the bore of the Remington at the hoodlum's right temple.

He hissed, "Drop that pistol and tell your partners to drop theirs or I'll drop you."

The bearded one dropped his gun as if it were hot, and he squawked, "Do like he said, fellers. For Christ sake, don't let 'im kill me, for Christ sake."

Two six-guns hit the dirt.

It took only a moment for Martin to decide what to do next. There was no law in the Sierra Nevadas. No courts. The only justice was six-gun justice. Men had been bush-whacked working their claims, shot down by killers who had no right to live. These three had no right to live.

He released his hold on the bearded one's throat, gave him a hard push away, and shot him in the back. Then he shot one of the others in the middle of the chest. The third one ran around behind the tent, jumped into a gully, and disappeared in the thick willows.

There was no arrest, no inquest. Other miners had seen Martin working his claim, had seen the three ransacking Martin's tent. A man had a right to defend himself and his property. But Martin left the Sierra Nevadas a few days later and went back to New Mexico. He'd had enough of prospecting and breaking his back placer-mining. He'd always liked horses and he liked working with cowboys. The huge Ladder Ranch at the foot of the Black Range was hiring, and Martin was added to the payroll.

There'd been saloon brawls. And he was shot at once by four cattle rustlers he caught moving a small herd toward Mexico, but the shots had missed. Martin had been too far away to do any accurate shooting with the Remington, but he fired two shots anyway to warn three other Ladder cowboys who were gathering cattle nearby. The four rustlers rode off on a high lope with the cowboys giving chase. Shots were fired, but they were fired hastily from running horses. When the rustlers rode over a low pinon ridge, the cowboys reined up.

"They're just a layin' up there a waitin' fer us," said an older hand wearing brush-scarred chaps. "Prob'ly got us in their sights right now."

"Wal, we didn't hit any of 'em, but we put the fear of God into 'em."

"They'll be back, and some poor dumb cowprod'll ride up on 'em before he knows it and get the shit shot out of 'im."

It happened. It happened many times in the frontier west. A man had to be armed and ready. Always ready.

That was something Mary Mossman didn't seem to understand, and Martin wasn't sure Ray Mossman understood it either.

The sun was sitting on the jagged, purple line of mountains and the tired team was pulling the heavy wagon near the top of Wilkerson Pass when Martin spotted two men on horseback ahead. They'd just come over the crest of the pass and they stopped immediately when they saw the four-horse team and wagon. Then they wheeled their horses and disappeared back the way they'd come.

Martin didn't need a warning blast from a steam whistle. He didn't need a painted sign telling him of danger ahead. They were waiting for him up there. At least two and probably more. They wanted the horses and the wagon and whatever the wagon was carrying. They wanted him dead.

"Whoa," he said quietly. The horses were more than happy to stop. Looking around, Martin spotted a shale-stone bluff two hundred yards off to the south, and he got the team going again in that direction.

"Better to let them come to us than for us to go to them," he muttered.

While the horses plodded and the heavy wagon bounced, Martin kept his eyes busy, watching in all directions. His only hope now was to make it to the bluff before they attacked. If he could get there, the bluff would protect him and the horses from one side, and he'd have a little better chance. He tried to whip up the horses, but they were too tired, the wagon was too heavy, and the ground was too rocky. "Keep going, fellers," he muttered. "Maybe we'll make it." He half expected to see armed riders pour off the top of the pass, shooting as they came. But it didn't happen.

At the bluff, he quickly unhitched the horses and tied all four of them to the side of the wagon, between the wagon and the bluff. Looking for cover for himself, he spotted a waist-high boulder that had rolled off the pass maybe five hundred years ago. It was no more than fifty feet from the wagon, a good spot. The ground was littered with rocks, some the size of bushel baskets, but no other as big as this one. Carrying the Winchester rifle, he got behind it, watched, and waited.

Why didn't they come? Were they hiding up there waiting for him? Were they so dumb that they didn't see him turn off the road? Did he confuse them, spoil their plan by turning off? The answer had to be affirmative to at least one of the questions that were going through his mind.

One thing was sure. They'd come.

Chapter Eight

The more he thought about it, the more he was convinced they planned to bushwhack him somewhere near the top of the pass. From up there they could see the road in both directions to be sure there were no witnesses. Now they'd have to change their plan. Now it wouldn't be so easy. Maybe they'd give up.

Nope. Two of them came down the road to where he'd turned off, sat their horses, and looked in his direction. Only two? Now they were riding toward him, riding at a walk.

"Hey," one yelled when they were closer. "We mean you no harm. We're friends of Ray Mossman, and we come to see if you needed any help."

"I don't need any help," he yelled back.

Closer still, the other yelled, "Well, Ray asked us to meet you in case you had some trouble."

"Yeah," the other said, "we're friends. We're comin' up."

"Stay back," Martin yelled. "Don't come any closer. Stop right there."

"Why? Like I said, we're friends."

The last one to speak was a short, wide-shouldered

man with a high-crown, wide-brim hat. The other was average-size with a blond beard and a bill cap with ear-flaps tied over the top. The short one glanced off to his left. It was a furtive glance. Goddamn, Martin thought, they've got partners trying to come up on me from the west. And probably from the east too. That would make four of them. He pulled his head down so only his hat and eyes showed over the top of the boulder. "Don't move. Come closer and I'll shoot."

The gent in the bill cap glanced to his right, then to his left. Martin squatted on his heels and took a good look in both directions. Yep. He caught a glimpse of a man on foot ducking into a shallow, rocky gulch off to the west, uphill from him. The two ahead got off their horses, carrying lever-action rifles.

No doubt about it now. They intended to surround him on three sides and kill him.

What he ought to do, he thought, was shoot the two in front of him. Just shoot them. That would narrow the odds. It would be plain stupid to just sit here and wait for one of the gunsels on either side of him to shoot first. Could he just shoot and kill without warning? Hell, they weren't about to give him any warning.

Raising up enough to get the rifle over the top of the rock, Martin aimed and fired. The short one dropped with a rifle slug in his chest. Then hell opened up.

Bullets spanged off the boulder from two sides, off the rocks behind him. A lead slug ricocheted from the top of the boulder and smacked into the bluff. Another went whining away to the east. Squatting on his heels, Martin made himself as small as possible. Instinct told him to cover his head with his arms. But that wouldn't do. He had to shoot back. Look, find a target, and shoot.

A slug hit the boulder near his head. Granite chips stung his face.

Goddamn, he muttered, this is dangerous.

Out of the corner of his eyes, he saw a man running at him from the east, trying to get into a better position. Martin drew the Remington and snapped a shot at him. The man hit the ground on his belly, hugged the ground for a moment. Then he raised a rifle barrel, trying to get Martin in his sights without showing more than his head and shoulders. Martin took aim with the Remington, fired, and saw a bullet kick dirt in the man's face. The man started crawling backward, away from Martin's gun.

The other two were firing, their bullets smacking the ground and the rocks so close that Martin was afraid to move. He had to move. Move where? Think.

The rifleman on the east had backed away to a safer spot, but he wasn't out of the fight. The gunsel ahead couldn't get to him as long as he was behind the boulder.

All right now. Their scheme from the beginning was to get a shooter on each side of him. The bluff kept them from getting behind him, and the boulder protected him from the front. So the man in front had to get around to the east or west. He'd seen that the east wasn't safe, so he'd try to work his way uphill to the west.

That's what Martin guessed. It was only a guess. Well, hell, he had to do something.

Still squatting, Martin duckwalked around to the east side of the boulder, head swiveling, eyes trying to see in all directions. A bullet ricocheted off the top of the boulder. He didn't see where the bullet came from, but he did see the blond-bearded one running, bending low. Without taking time to put the Winchester to his shoulder, Martin fired the Remington six-shooter.

The gunsel fell, dropped his rifle, and grabbed his left

leg below the knee. Martin could see his teeth bared as he rolled onto his back and grimaced in pain.

A hush fell over the country. All was calm.

For a long moment, nothing happened, nobody moved. The short man was lying over there no more than sixty feet away, dead or near death. The wounded man was on his back, holding his left leg with both hands, rocking and grimacing.

There were two more shooters, and Martin didn't know where they were. Still duckwalking, he made his way to the opposite side of the boulder, eyes trying to spot movement, anything. Nothing else moved.

Then a man came out of a shallow gulch uphill and ran toward the wounded man. Martin put the Winchester to his shoulder. But the man ducked behind the wounded one, got his hands under his partner's armpits, and started dragging him backward, keeping his partner between him and Martin. Martin watched them until they dropped into another rocky gulch, then turned his attention to the shooter on the east. Whereever he was, he was well-hidden.

It was quiet again. Glancing at the horses, Martin saw they were all standing, nervous at the gunfire, but not fighting to get loose. "You old boys are big targets," Martin muttered. "I wouldn't want to be in your place."

Where were the shooters? The healthy one to the west could be busy rescuing his partner. He could be giving up the fight. That left one over east somewhere. Watch for him, Martin reminded himself.

The sun was behind the crest of Wilkerson Pass now, its light reflecting off a haze in the western sky, creating a bright red glow. The east side of the pass was in shadow, while the low hills farther east were still in sunlight. But the shadow was moving on as the sun sank lower. Dark wasn't far ahead. If he could hold out until dark, he'd have won. They wouldn't try to sneak up on him in the dark. They, or somebody like them, had tried that once and lost. Maybe he'd have won. Maybe not.

A bullet screamed off the boulder not far from Martin's head, and Martin got a glimpse of the shooter. He was over there behind a slight rise in the ground, no doubt lying flat. He'd raised up long enough to snap a shot, then hit the ground again. Martin was sitting on his boot heels, and the bullet screamed off the boulder over his head.

Missed, Martin said under his breath, but if he takes time to aim, he won't miss again. Got to watch him. Can't let him take aim.

Quiet. The sun had gone completely behind the horizon, and the whole country was in shadow. When it turned dark, he'd move, Martin decided. Make them guess where he was. Move where? To the wagon. They might try to steal the horses in the dark. The horses were standing tied to the wagon with the harness on. They could sneak up, keep the horses between them and this boulder, and lead the horses away. Yep, when dark came he'd have to go over there and guard the horses.

Oh, oh. That yahoo over there raised up again, a rifle to his shoulder. Martin fired a hasty shot at him with the Remington. The shot missed, but was close enough to make the rifleman take cover again.

Keeping an eye on the rifleman's position, Martin punched the empty cartridges out of the Remington and refilled the cylinder with cartridges from his belt.

Dammit, wasn't there any other traffic on that road? There had to be other travelers. There had to be a stage line going to Vega from the east. But Martin had seen none, nor had he seen a stage relay station. He'd seen wheel tracks leading off the road, however, and they could

have been coach tracks going to a relay station somewhere in the timber out of sight of the road. They probably were. If so, the stage probably ran only twice a week,
and these last two days weren't the days.

And hell, suppose a stage did come by, what could
Martin do? Stand up and holler and wave? No. He was
pinned down here.

Come on, darkness.

Knees cramped, tired of squatting, Martin shifted onto
the seat of his pants with his legs straight out in front of
him and kept an eye on the land swell over there. Now
and then he took a look behind him. The four horses were
quiet, so calm they were trying to get at the hay under one
of the tarps on the wagon, pushing at the canvas with their
noses. Darkness was settling fast. The rise over east was
invisible now. The shooter behind it could come out without being seen. It was time for Martin to move.

Standing, he took a long careful look in all directions.
The moon hadn't shown itself yet, and everything was
black.

Then a rifle shot split the quiet. A horse squealed in
pain.

Anger surged through Martin like an electric shock.
"Son of a bitch," he said aloud. "The goddamn son of a
bitch."

Another shot, and Martin heard it smack into horse
flesh.

So angry he couldn't stand it, Martin started running
toward the muzzle flash. All he wanted to do was get that
son of a bitch. Kill the sorry, bloodthirsty pile of shit. He
ran, firing the Remington. Fired until it clicked on empty.

Holstering it, he fired the Winchester rifle as fast as he could lever the cartridges in.

Suddenly it occurred to him that this was dumb. The shooter could hide in the dark. He hadn't fired a shot in the past ten seconds and was probably running away. Martin stopped and listened. Sure enough, running footsteps were headed for the road. Squinting, eyes straining, Martin tried to see him. He would have been happy to make a target of himself just to get a clear shot at that one man.

Too dark. It was hopeless.

Grinding his teeth in anger and frustration, Martin turned back toward the wagon to see how much damage had been done.

Chapter Nine

He could tell by feel that one horse was down, and another was buckling at the knees and about to go down. The rattle in the downed horse's breathing told him it was near death. The other two were standing, and as far as he could tell in the dark they weren't hurt.

Still cursing under his breath, he untied the halter rope of the wounded horse and tried to lead it away. At first, the animal couldn't move, but by pulling on the halter rope, Martin got its head away from the wagon and then got it to take a few steps. Then its knees collapsed and it fell over on its side.

Muttering "Son of a bitch, son of a bitch," Martin ran his hands over the two animals still standing and found no wounds. He remembered then that only two shots had been fired, so no more than two horses could have been hit. One of the two downed horses had stopped breathing. The other's lungs were gurgling. It was doomed.

Groping, Martin felt blood on its side, just behind the elbow. It had been shot through the lungs. "Sorry, feller. I'm real sorry," Martin said, drawing the Remington. He remembered that the gun was loaded with nothing but empty cartridges, and, working by feel, he punched out the empties and reloaded.

Repeating "Sorry, feller," he located the horse's ears and eyes and imagined an X between the ears and eyes. He put the bore of the gun a few inches from the spot where the imaginary lines crossed and squeezed the trigger. The horse's body jerked, its legs stiffened, and it died.

"Goddamn. Christ. Goddammit."

Anger and frustration had every muscle in Martin's body so tense he had to lean against the wagon a while, arms crossed on top of the sideboard, head down. "Goddamn son of a bitch. God-almighty damn."

Finally, he realized he'd have to calm himself and think. He forced each limb, one at a time, to relax. He was sorry for the two dead horses. Too bad they had to pay with their lives for the greed and cruelty of the human animals. He'd felt sorry for the horses in the war. In some battles there were as many horses killed and crippled as men, and it was the men who'd started the damned war.

Martin had been accused of liking horses better than people, and that was never more true than right now.

"Goddamn, greedy, grubby, bloodthirsty, sons of bitches. They ain't nothing but shit. They're not fit to live. I wish I'd killed every goddamned one of them. I hope that pile of crud I shot in the leg suffers the rest of his life. If that son of a bitch lives, I hope to hell I see him again. I'll drop him on the spot. Son of a bitch."

It occurred to him that he was tense again, not thinking clearly. He had to think.

So what's next?

There was nothing he could do in the dark. Come daylight, he'd have to try to get the wagon to the top of Wilkerson Pass with only two horses. With that in mind, he untied the two, led them around to the other side of the wagon, and pulled back the tarp that covered the hay. The two animals began munching.

"In a way," Martin mused aloud, "you brutes are lucky. You're so dumb you don't know what's happened. Yeah, you're lucky there."

It was another sleepless night, though Martin didn't believe the shooters would come back. Like the attackers of two nights before, they had wounded to take care of, and they'd either headed for the nearest doctor or put the wounded one out of his misery and left him. He wondered if the survivors of two nights before were among the four who'd tried to kill him last night. With a wry grin, he figured they had to be getting pretty discouraged by now. Two tries, and at least one dead and two others shot.

The only thing they'd accomplished was to kill two of his horses. That son of a bitch who'd shot the horses no doubt wanted to kill all four, but Martin's rapid fire had driven him away. Why did they want to kill the horses?

At first it didn't make sense. If they'd killed him they would have stolen the horses and groceries, and they'd have had something to show for their dirty work. Then, when they gave up that plan, they'd tried to kill the horses. Come to think of it, Ray had said something about some folks wanting to put him out of business. Was that what these gunhands wanted to do? Was that what they had on their minds as well as robbery? Was this their idea or somebody else's? If somebody else's, who?

If they'd killed the horses, Martin would have had to leave the wagon while he walked back to Ray's ranch to get another team, and while he was gone they'd have ripped open the grocery bags and scattered everything over this side of Wilkerson Pass, everything they didn't want themselves. And they'd have wrecked the wagon.

Yep, that would have been bad, very bad, for Ray's business.

Around midnight, the two surviving horses had eaten their fill and were quiet. Some horses, Martin mused, didn't like the smell of blood and wouldn't go near it. Others paid it no mind. Horses could get used to anything if they had to. Like the horses in the war.

"Rest easy, fellers," Martin said aloud. "You've got a hell of a job to do in the morning."

He didn't even think about breakfast. All he could think about was getting the wagon to the top of the pass. While the morning light was no more than a glow on the east, he fed the two standing horses their morning ration of oats. As they ate, he unbuckled and unsnapped the harness on the dead ones. He tried, but it was impossible for a man to pull the harness out from under them. He untied the gray gelding, hitched a singletree to its tug chains, and tied the singletree to the hames on the harness of the closest dead horse. Instead of trying to drive the gray with the long lines, he led it, and it easily pulled the harness free. After tossing that set of harness in the wagon, Martin got the other set free. Not until then, after daylight had brightened the countryside, did he notice that the short man he'd shot was still lying over there.

"Aw, for cryin' in the road. Didn't the sons of bitches care enough about their partner to pack his carcass away? What a sorry bunch of bastards."

Looking around, Martin saw no water. He and the horses would have to wait until they got to the top of the pass to get a drink. Well, it sure wasn't the first time Martin had gone without grub or water. And the horses wouldn't die of dehydration that soon, either.

He got the two horses on either side of the wagon tongue and hitched to the singletrees which were hitched to the doubletree which was bolted to the wagon tongue which was bolted to the front axle. The gray had been a lead horse while the bay was a wheel horse. They'd have to be both now.

"All right," Ray said, gathering the lines and climbing to the high seat, "let see if you can do it. Gee-up, there."

At first the two big horses couldn't move the wagon. The gray lunged into its collar and slacked off, then the bay lunged. "Whoa. Whoa now. Just stand quiet a minute. If you old boys are gonna move this load, you're gonna have to pull together. Quiet down now and let's try again."

Two minutes later, in a conversational tone, Martin said, "Gee-up, now. Easy." With expert handling of the lines he got the two horses leaning into their collars, then he hollered, "Hit up, there. Hit it." Huge muscles bulged as the two horses pulled together. The wagon moved. "Hit in there. Hit it, boys, hit it . . ."

Martin got the team moving toward the road, and when they came to the dead man, he said, "Whoa." He didn't have to holler. The animals heard him and were glad to stop.

Climbing down, Martin knelt before the body. The rifle slug had hit the man squarely in the heart, and he'd died so suddenly that he'd bled very little.

"Ought to leave you here for the coyotes and magpies," Martin muttered. "You're no better than those dead horses. Either one of those horses was worth more than a hundred jaspers like you." He got one arm under the dead man's shoulders and the other under the knees, then straightened and carried him to the tailgate of the wagon. The dead limbs could still be bent, but they were beginning to stiffen. Dead eyes stared straight ahead. Laying the body just inside the tailgate, Martin tried to close the eyes, but could only get them half-closed. "Well, go ahead and gawk, then," he muttered. He put the man's big-brim hat over the face, then covered the body with the tarp that had been used to cover hay.

Back on the wagon seat, he gathered the lines and said, "All right, fellers. It's going to be damned hard work, but you can do it. Let's go."

The ground was fairly level from there to the road, but rocky. Every time the front wheels rolled over a rock, the wagon tongue jerked and the horses could feel it in their collars. Three times before they got to the road, Martin "Whoaed" them and let them blow. Back on the road, he said, "Here's where the hard work begins." Then, with two horses doing the work of four, he got the team moving again, uphill.

It was slow going. Martin let the team stop to rest and blow every fifty feet. Once, stopped and looking back, he saw another team and carriage coming from the east, traveling at a trot, raising a small cloud of dust. His two horses and wagon went on another fifty feet, stopped. Looking back again, the rig behind him had gained enough that he could make out four horses and a coach. "That," he said to himself, "has to be the stage that runs from Colorado City to Vega and probably somewhere beyond."

After two more stops, he looked for a wide spot in the road where he could pull over and let the stage go by. There was no wide spot, and one of the two rigs was going to have to leave the road. At a place where the ground was level with the road, Martin stopped again. The stage team was alternately walking and trotting, and soon caught up. The teamster pulled his horses down to a careful walk to get alongside Martin's wagon, then stopped.

"You wouldn't consider gettin' over and lettin' a faster outfit go past, would you?" The stage teamster was a skinny man with a trimmed gray beard and a wide-brim black hat. Sitting beside him was a husky gent with a thick mustache, a bill cap and a double-barreled shotgun. Both squinted at Martin's face for a moment, but only for a moment.

"If I did," Martin drawled, "I might not get back on the road again."

"I c'n see you got a heavy load and not 'nuff horse-power. How'd yu git this fur?"

Martin took the makings out of a shirt pocket and started rolling a smoke. "Well, you see, it was like this: I started with four good big horses, but a few gents decided they wanted them, and started a shooting match. I saw them coming and forted up, and when they couldn't get me they shot two of my horses."

"The hell you say." The shotgun messenger put the gun across his lap and started rolling his own smoke. "Right up here's a good place for road agents. We got robbed twicet up here, and we learned this's not the place to stop and let the hosses rest."

The coach was the kind with two seats facing each other. Three passengers were inside. One, a plump man in a business suit and a derby hat, opened a door and stepped out. "What's this about a robbery?"

"Best git back inside," the teamster said. "We'll be movin' on in a minute."

"Where's your relay station?" Martin asked.

"Few mile ahead and to the north. It's out of our way a mile or so, but there's good water and grass there for a bunch of horses. Can't be seen from this road."

A message painted on the side of the coach read South Park Stage Co. Below that was U.S. Mail.

"How often do you make this run?"

"Three times a week gen'ly, but skipped a day cuz of a wreck on Ute Pass. Took most of a day to git ever'thing untangled."

"I've been over that road. Getting two wagons past each other has to take some time and a lot of careful breathing."

"We try not to breathe. One little whisper is all it takes to lock wheels or shove one wagon off the road and down into the crik."

"I reckon you'll get to Vega about the middle of the afternoon."

"Expect to, yeah."

"Would you send the sheriff back this way? I've got a dead man under that tarp there."

"The hell you say."

"What's this about a dead man?" Derby-hat had stuck his head out the stage door.

"Didja shoot one of them road agents?"

"Yeah."

"That's the thing to do with 'em."

"We'll tell Sheriff Little, but don't wait up for 'im. I never knowed 'im to hurry hisself."

"Well, tell him I'll be at Ray Mossman's ranch."

"We'll tell 'im."

By careful maneuvering, the stage teamster got his four horses and stage ahead of Ray's horses and back on the road. There he yelled at his team, and with a wave of his hand the stage was going up the road at a trot.

"Well, fellers," Martin said to his two overworked horses, "let's make a few more yards. Someday we'll get to the top."

Chapter Ten

The sun was straight overhead when at last they topped Wilkerson Pass. "Just a few more yards, fellers, and that's it for a while." Up here was a wide flat spot where wagons had pulled off many times before. Smoke-blackened rock rings meant many travelers had camped here. A creek— Martin guessed it was Granite Creek—ran out of the high hills to the north and along the top of the pass. Water was plentiful.

Martin swung the team off the road and stopped. He unhitched and led the horses to the creek where they sucked water up between their broad lips until their thirst was quenched. The gray horse's ears moved every time he swallowed. Martin lay on his belly with his face in the water upstream and took a long drink himself.

"We're just about out of hay, old boys, but it's easy going from here and you'll get a good feed tonight."

Eating stale bread and dried ham with a dead man for company wasn't exactly a picnic, but it was the first food Martin had had in twenty-four hours, and he managed to chew and swallow. Looking back, he had to admire the scenery: green hills, tall timber to the south, high, steep hills to the north, and Pikes Peak away off in the distance.

"Pretty country," he mused. After a half hour he hitched up the team and got back on the road.

"You won't have to pull for a few miles, fellers. All you have to do is keep this wagon from running over you. Hope the brakes hold out."

Two miles from the top of the pass the road leveled onto the prairie, and now that the sun was overhead and the sky was clear, Martin could see the Mosquito Range away over west. A few low ridges led out of the timber country to the north, but the land south was flat. Heat waves danced across it. The two horses had to pull again, but the road was level, and they walked right along, knowing they were going home.

Late in the afternoon, Martin and a rancher driving a light spring wagon in the opposite direction had to ease their rigs carefully past each other on the narrow road. They both "Whoaed" with their wheel hubs no more than a foot apart.

"You're Ray Mossman's brother, ain't you?" the rancher asked. He wore a dirty gray Stetson, and had a two-day growth of whiskers.

"Yessir, I am."

"Ray said he sent you to Florissant to fetch some staples. I wish I could buy some from you right here and now, but I don't reckon you'd sell."

Shaking his head, Martin said, "I would if I could, but this is not my stuff and I wouldn't know how much to charge."

"Well, I'll have to make another trip to town in a few days."

"Did you pass the stage back there?"

"Yep. They was comin' down First Street when I left town."

That meant, Martin thought, that this rancher hadn't

heard about the gunfire and the dead man. "Well, I hope to get to the Mossman Ranch in time for supper." He flicked the lines and got his team moving again.

It was dark when he turned the tired horses into the ranch yard. A lighted lantern was hanging from the front porch, and two more were hanging over the door of the barn. Martin didn't have to holler. His brother had been watching for him.

Carrying still another lantern, Ray Mossman stepped off the porch, and said, "You can unhitch right here, Mart. In fact, I'll unhitch and take care of the horses while you go in the house and eat. We just finished supper."

"I guess you heard about what happened, why I've got only two horses."

"Yeah, the stage driver told somebody who told somebody else who told me. I hated to lose two good horses, but I'm damned glad you're all right. If I'd known . . . Dammit, Mart, I should have known. I shouldn't have put you at risk like that."

Stepping down from the high seat, using a wheel hub as a step, Martin asked, "Has the sheriff been told?"

"Yeah, he was here waiting for you, then went home to supper. Said he'd be back in an hour."

The boy Joshua came out onto the porch, but his dad sent him back inside.

The two brothers unhitched the team, and Ray said, "Go on in the house and eat, Mart. I'll put these animals up."

"Does Mary know?"

"Yeah, she knows."

"How much should I tell her?"

"Just answer her questions. She knows you had to defend yourself and my property."

"How about Josh?"

Ray's face was in shadow as he wrapped the driving lines around a hame. "Well, none of us know the whole story, the details, and I wouldn't want my son to be the first to know, but use your own judgment."

Martin knew he was a sorry sight. He hadn't shaved in four days, and his clothes were dirty, but Mary said only, "Thank God you weren't hurt, Martin. You must be awfully tired and hungry. Come on in the kitchen."

Apologetically, Martin said, "I'll shave in the morning, Mary, and I should have a clean change of clothes at the laundry in town." He followed her into the kitchen and dropped wearily into a chair at the table.

"I have some potato and beef soup, and some fresh bread and butter—thank goodness for our cow—and I baked some pies today with canned peaches."

Grinning wryly, Martin said, "Just what the doctor ordered."

"Uncle Martin, did you really shoot a robber?" Josh had kept quiet until then, but he could contain himself no longer. Martin looked to Mary for guidance. She answered for him.

"Yes, Joshua. Some men tried to rob your uncle Martin and he shot one of them. Now let him eat and rest."

"Boy, oh boy. Did they shoot at you? Poppa said they shot two of our horses."

"Yeah, Josh. That's what happened."

"I heard about them robbers up there. I wish I'd of been there with my rifle. Bennie's too little to shoot a gun."

"*Those* robbers, Joshua, not *them* robbers. Now let your uncle eat in peace." Mary set a large bowl of steaming soup on the table and half a loaf of fresh warm bread.

"Momma said it's bad manners to blow on your soup, but Luke does it, and you can too."

"Your mother is right. It is bad manners." Martin wished the soup would cool.

He'd eaten two bowls of meaty soup and two thick slices of bread, and had his eye on a slab of pie Mary had set before him, when Ray came in. "Sheriff Little is here, Mart. We'll wait for you outside. Take your time."

"I'll be there directly, but"—Martin grinned—"nothing can keep me from that pie."

Finished, he said, "That was exactly what I needed, Mary. I appreciate it." He tried to think of a way to apologize to her for what had happened, but the proper words wouldn't come to mind. "I, uh . . . I wish . . ."

She was tight-lipped, as if she had a bad taste in her mouth, but she managed, "I'm just glad you're not hurt. Raymond was so worried about you. He would never have forgiven himself if you'd been killed or hurt."

Grinning a one-sided grin, trying to joke, Martin said, "I'm glad I wasn't hurt too." He picked up his hat from the floor in the parlor and stepped outside.

In the lanternlight, Martin couldn't make out Sheriff Bert Little's features, but he looked to be average height and build with a smooth-shaved face. he wore a high-crown, flat-brim gray hat, and carried an ivory-gripped pistol in a double-loop Mexican holster.

After being introduced and shaking hands, Martin asked, "Do you recognize that gent?"

"Yessir. I don't know him or his name, but I've seen him around town, mostly in the saloons. I need to get a statement in writing about what happened up there with all the details."

"Well, you ask the questions and I'll answer them. I hope you like to write."

"Come over to my office in the morning, and I'll get the county clerk to do the writing. Meanwhile, I've got to get this corpse to town. Doctor Hanley's got a shed he keeps corpses in, but not for long. He refuses to do any embalming, and we have to have a funeral in a few days."

"I was wondering if you've got a doctor in Vega. Did he fix any gunshot wounds in the last couple of days?"

"I don't know. I'll ask him."

Sheriff Little talked with short, clipped words like some city men Martin had met, and Martin wondered where he'd come from. Vega was a fairly new town, and everybody there had come from somewhere else.

"I'll be in your office in the morning. Any particular time?"

"Oh, make it around ten. I'll talk to the doctor first thing, then get some of the denizens from the saloons to view the corpse and see if they can identify it."

The three men carried the rapidly stiffening body to a buggy pulled by two horses and laid it in the back. Ray donated the canvas tarp it had been covered with. "I don't think I want to cover groceries with it anymore," he said.

Sheriff Little said, "Folks will be glad to see you unload your wagon. Mr. Pritchard is getting low on supplies too, and he's going to have to send a wagon to Florissant, but you can bet he won't send a man alone, not after what happened to your brother here."

"I won't make that mistake again," Ray said.

After the sheriff had clucked to his team and driven out of the yard, Ray said, "I can't apologize enough, Mart. I knew there was a chance something like this would happen, but I didn't really expect it to. I owe you a great deal."

Standing in the pale lamplight, Martin grinned a weak grin. "It ain't the first time I've been shot at. But you know, Ray, there's something sort of strange about all this. We need to talk and do some thinking."

"Believe me, I've been thinking. But right now I expect you're about dead yourself."

"To tell the truth, I could use some shuteye." Martin rubbed the left side of his head and frowned.

"Headache again?"

"Yeah, it comes and goes."

"Don't you have any laudanum or anything?"

"I sort of gave up on laudanum, but don't worry, I've lived with it a long time."

Martin was pleased to see that his brother had picked up his laundry and had laid his one change of clothes out on the narrow bed in the small room off the kitchen. First thing in the morning he'd shave and try to find a way to take a bath.

As tired as he was, sleep didn't come immediately. For a while he lay awake, his mind going over the two gunfights he'd just had. The first one could be explained; they'd planned to sneak up on him in the dark, kill him, and steal everything he had. It was the second attack that didn't fit the usual pattern.

He wondered if Ray had any idea who was trying to wreck his business. Whoever he is, Martin thought, he's one dangerous hombre.

Chapter Eleven

Sheriff Bert Little was a harried, worried man. He leaned back in a wooden chair in his cubbyhole of an office in a two-room clapboard shack on Grant Street, one block from First Street. The other room was the office of the Prairie County clerk and recorder.

"This county is going to pieces. Before I even had a chance to investigate the attempted robbery on Wilkerson Pass, I hear about a murder here in town, and no one knows who did the murdering."

Ray had left his hired clerk to manage his mercantile after the wagon was unloaded, and had accompanied Martin to the sheriff's office. Martin had waited until after breakfast that morning to buckle on the Remington, not wanting Mary to see him carrying it. Ray asked, "I heard it was one of the, uh, ladies on Second Street who was murdered."

"That's who it was, and that's what makes it difficult to investigate. Too many men come and go over there. She was stabbed through the heart instead of shot, so no one heard anything."

"That's the second woman of, uh, doubtful virtue murdered this year, and nobody seems to care," Ray said.

"Yeah. One of the prettier and cleaner ones got her throat cut."

"As undesirable as they are," Ray went on, "they are human, and the murderers should be found out and arrested."

"You just put your finger on my main problem—no one cares."

Martin had been listening quietly, but now he asked, "Is there a justice of the peace or anything like that in Vega?"

"None," the sheriff answered. "A district-court judge is supposed to come around when we need him, but we haven't had a trial yet. When anything of any significance happens, I make out a written report and send it over to the district attorney's office in Fair Play, but they don't seem to care either."

"Fair Play?" Martin asked.

"It's about forty miles northwest of here," Ray answered. "It's the county seat of Park County. The only time Judge Hawthorn came here, he complained about the lack of a local justice of the peace and about having to deal with misdemeanors. So far everyone the sheriff has taken to court has pleaded guilty. All the judge has had to do was levy fines."

"Have you got a jail?"

"A log shack down the alley a ways, but the county doesn't have enough money to feed prisoners, so unless the judge is handy Sheriff Little fines the miscreants himself and sends them on their way."

Tilting his head up, looking at Martin, the sheriff asked, "Have you ever been in a place like this, Mr. Mossman?"

"Huh," Martin snorted. "I've been places where there was no law at all. Every man was jury, judge, and executioner."

"Must have been a lot of innocent men convicted," the sheriff commented.

"Not so many. I've noticed that where there is no law, the thugs, robbers, and killers don't try very hard to cover their tracks. Prosecution is easy."

"Well"—Sheriff Little heaved himself up from his chair—"I'll get the clerk in here and you can tell everything while he writes it down and we listen."

"Then what?" Martin asked.

"Then I'll have a better idea of what to look for and where to look."

It took an hour. The county clerk was in his mid-sixties, with a few strands of white hair combed straight back and a thin, slack-jawed face. He wore a gray striped shirt with no collar buttoned to his throat, and a green eyeshade. Every few minutes he had to say, "Stop," and flex the fingers on his writing hand. Martin told the story in so much detail that the sheriff had to ask only a few questions.

"No," Martin said, "I wouldn't recognize any of the three who tried to shoot me the first night, but one of them was shot. He's either dead or hurt so bad he'll need a doctor. The one I shot in the leg has got a blond beard trimmed short. He wore a bill cap on his head. He'll need a doctor too."

"He doesn't fit the description of anyone I know, but men come and go around here. He could be in one of the mining camps or one of the cow camps, but from his description I'd say he's not a cowboy. I'll go over to see Dr. Hanley right away. Maybe he's doctored both of them and has learned something about them."

"They'd lie about how they got shot."

"Of course, but maybe they let something slip."

Outside on the two-block-long plankwalk, Martin

looked up and down the street, wanting to see as much of the town as he could. He nodded at a hand-painted sign that hung over the walk a block away. "That's what I need," he said to his brother. "I could take a bath in your bunkhouse, but this ought to be better. Will your team be all right in the alley?"

"Yeah, they've been tied there before. All but the filly on the wheel team. But the other horses will keep her from misbehaving."

"I'll drive them back to your ranch as soon as I get a bath."

Martin walked to the board-and-batten one-story building with a false front and a sign hanging over the walk. The sign said simply, BARBER SHOP   BATHS. He opened a screen door with a squeaking spring and stepped inside. The barber was a plump middle-aged gent with long sideburns and gray-streaked hair. He was snipping at the dark hair of a young man sitting stiffly in a straight-backed wooden chair. The young man had riding boots and spurs on his feet, and a face that had been browned by the sun from the eyebrows down and was lady white from the eyebrows up. Both frowned at the sight of Martin's face, then looked away.

"You'll be next," the barber said.

"What I need," Martin drawled, "is a bath. I'm so dirty I can't stand myself."

"Ain't fired up the water tank yet this mornin', but I'll do that soon's I finish with this gentleman here. Come back in an hour and I'll have plenty of hot water ready."

"Good enough," Martin said, turning to leave.

"Say"—the barber was studying Martin's face now—"your name wouldn't be Mossman, would it?"

With his lop-sided grin, Martin said, "How'd you guess?"

"Word gets around. Almost ever'body knows by now how you shot it out with some road agents up on the pass."

"You wouldn't happen to know who those road agents are, would you?"

Grinning, showing two overlapping teeth, the barber said, "Naw."

"Well, I'll be back in about an hour." Martin went out onto the plankwalk.

For a short while he stood on the walk, watching the traffic go by: a lumber wagon coming from a sawmill somewhere and a one-horse buggy. Two cowboys rode by, their eyes taking in the sights. Martin guessed from their ragged clothes and long hair that this was their first trip to town in a couple of months. One spoke to the other, and they reined their horses over to the hitchrail in front of the barber shop.

"Morning," Martin said when they dismounted. After a one-second stare at Martin's face, they both nodded and said almost in unison, "Mornin'." They opened the squeaking screen door and went into the barber shop.

With time to kill, Martin walked up one side of First Street and down the other. Businesses lined each side for only two blocks. The sidewalk ran along the front of the businesses and no farther. Pedestrians had to walk on dirt paths from there to the scattering of houses. Most of the houses were wood frame, three or four rooms, but a few were of logs. The roofs were split shingle from the sawmill. Martin walked past a hardware store, a gunshop, a land office, and the Silver Tip Gaming Palace with its small glass window. A short distance farther on was another saloon with a sign over a plank door that identified it as the Ore Bucket. All that separated the two saloons was a weed-grown vacant lot and the Vega Cafe.

Walking back up the other side of First Street, Martin passed the laundry, a small grocery store, another saloon, the Mossman Mercantile, a two-story wood-frame building identified by a sign painted on a large glass window as the South Park Hotel, next to it the Denver Steak House, and then a sign that said HARD TACK SALOON   FINE SPIRITS.

Martin could have used a drink of whiskey, but he didn't stop. Turning his steps to Second Street, he saw immediately why Ray and some others wanted to clean up the town. Second Street was shantytown, a one-block row of clapboard rooms with dirty windows and hog weeds growing in the yards. The windows were covered on the inside with dirty blankets, and each room had a cardboard sign hanging from a doorknob that said Stay Out. Martin counted six of the cribs. He knew from experience what they were: one-woman whorehouses. The Stay Out signs meant they had customers or were not ready yet for the evening's business. By midafternoon the signs would be turned over to read Come In."

Yep, Martin mused, same story all over the West. The men outnumbered the women by at least five to one, and the women were either married or homely as sin. That left the whores for the single men. He knew from experience too that most of the crib women were dirty, bad-tempered, foul-mouthed, and would cut a man's throat for a few dollars. That's why no one grieved when they were murdered themselves. As repugnant as they were, they managed to make a living whoring because of the difference between the sexes.

Men needed it, had a powerful urge for it, hell, had to have it. A lot of women cashed in on it.

Shaking his head, Martin reckoned that even the most polished gentlemen would patronize the cribs if there was nothing else. Sure, he admitted to himself, he'd done it.

With his face there was no other way. And he'd do it again. But not here, not in Vega. He'd die before he'd have his brother's wife even suspect him of such a disgraceful act.

Hastily, he walked the length of crib row and turned back to First Street, wishing he could get onto the sidewalk without anyone seeing where he'd come from. No such luck.

Two women pedestrians in long dresses, button-up shoes, and poke bonnets saw him, looked him up and down like he was the filthiest specimen they'd ever seen, then stared straight ahead. Martin had an urge to do something smarty and cocky, like tipping his hat, but he didn't.

He reckoned he still had time to kill and was wondering how to do it when his steps led him to the front of the Silver Tip Gaming Palace. A shot of whiskey would feel good. Naw. Mary had a nose like a bloodhound. Beer? He might get by with a mug of beer. Surely, she wouldn't smell that, not after he'd had a bath and everything. He stepped through the open door.

And before he'd even had a chance to look around, he was challenged to a fight.

Chapter Twelve

"Hey, Scarface. Who let you in here?"

To Martin's left was the bar and standing at the bar was the first man he'd ever talked to in Vega. Young, red-bearded, gray hat tilted to one side, cocky, carrying that Navy Colt in a fast-draw holster on his right hip.

"Aw"—Martin shook his head sadly—"cut it out, will you? I don't want any trouble."

"Trouble is what you're gonna get. I got no use for you Mossmans."

Shrugging, Martin drawled, "Mister, I don't know who you are or why you're trying to pick a fight with me, but if it's all the same to you I'll just leave." He started to turn around and go back outside. It just wouldn't do to get into another fight. Mary would scold him and make him feel like a dirty dog.

But with a few quick steps the cocky one beat him to the door, got between him and the door. "I heard about some fancy shootin' you done up yonder. Way I heard it, all the shootin' was done in the dark. How'd you like to do some shootin' in the daylight?"

He carried that Navy Colt as if he knew how to use it. Martin was good with a gun, but he knew a lot of men were better. But scared? Naw. He'd been in spots like this before.

"You're just itchin' for a fight, aren't you?"

"Like I said, I got no use for a Mossman."

"Well"—Martin shrugged again—"'fraid you're gonna have to fight somebody else. That ain't what I came in here for."

A sneer twisted the cocky one's mouth. "Scared? That fightin' you done up yonder, I bet you just got lucky. I bet you shit your drawers. I bet you—"

He didn't get to finish what he'd started to say. Suddenly another man was between them. "Gentlemen, what seems to be the trouble?" He was well-dressed in creased wool pants, boots with a shine, a brocaded vest, and a short, square necktie. His face was smooth-shaved. His dark hair was parted on the right side and carefully trimmed and combed. "Unless I'm mistaken, you two gentlemen were about to settle a difference the hard way."

"No sir, Mr. Vance." The young man wasn't so cocky now. "We, uh, this here is Ray Mossman's brother, and he thinks he's tough. I was just about to, uh, show 'im he ain't so tough."

Shaking his head again, Martin said, "Naw, that's not the way it was at all." Then he knew why the cocky one had suddenly turned meek. On one side of the dandy was a wide-shouldered, square-faced gent with a neck as thick as one of Martin's thighs. One ear was twisted into a shapeless mass, and white scar tissue was spread over one eye. He looked like he could outwrestle a bear and had done it many times.

On the dandy's right was another man who was the opposite. Slender, hipless, narrow in the shoulders, weak in the chin, a slit for a mouth, and eyes that looked like death about to happen.

And that double-action Colt in a cut-away holster on his right hip, just above his fingertips, told the world he didn't have to be big and strong. The man had gunfighter written all over him.

Smiling, the dandy held out his right hand. "I heard about what happened up there on the pass, Mr. Mossman. I admire you for successfully defending yourself and your brother's property. My name is Vance, C. C. Vance. I own this establishment, and you are very welcome here."

Martin shook with him and grinned his crooked grin. "I wasn't altogether successful, you know."

"But you completed your mission, and that is admirable. May I buy you a drink? We have some very fine imported scotch whiskey."

It was good whiskey. C. C. Vance stood beside Martin at the bar with one polished boot on the brass rail that ran along the floor. "I don't drink this time of day myself, or I'd join you," he said, "and not much any time." The two watchdogs stood back, but appeared to be ready for anything.

Smacking his lips, Martin said, "Scotch, you said? It's good stuff. I drink a little all the time, but I seldom get drunk."

The dandy's smooth face turned serious now. "You know, your brother and I don't always agree on everything."

"I could have guessed, yeah."

"But that doesn't make us enemies. I never met the man I agreed with on everything."

"But you are against his hopes of cleaning out some of the crud in town." It was a statement, not a question.

"Mr. Mossman—may I call you Martin?—I've known some towns that outlawed drinking altogether. Colorado Springs, for instance. If that happened here I would lose this." Vance waved at the surroundings, the fine mahogany bar, the walls papered with a roses design, crystal chandeliers. A small dance platform took up a piece of the back of the big room, but on either side of the platform were gaming tables, a roulette wheel, a faro layout, a dice table. There was a ricky-tick piano and space beside it for more musicians. Carpeted stairs along a back wall led to a second floor. One of the tables was occupied by five men playing cards. A thin man in sharp clothes, slicked-back hair, and a handlebar mustache stood behind the roulette wheel, waiting for business.

"As you can see," Vance said, "I've got a lot invested here."

"I know what you're talking about," Martin said, setting the empty whiskey glass on the bar. "I'm not sure exactly what Ray and the other county-board members want, but I doubt they'd try to shut down a place like this."

"Have you read the ordinance they are proposing?"

"No, can't say I have."

"It would give the county government control over everything. Most folks don't want to be controlled by the government."

"Well, I've been told it's gonna be put to a vote of the citizens. Ray is my brother, and I'm on his side."

"Of course. But like I said, we don't have to be enemies." Vance stepped back, his thumbs hooked inside his vest pockets. "I have some business to attend to. Have another drink on the house, and remember you are always welcome here."

* * *

On his way to the barbershop-bathhouse, Martin tried to figure a way to get the smell of whiskey off his breath. Gargle with saltwater, maybe. Keep his distance from Mary.

"Water should be pretty warm by now," the barber said when he came through the squeaking screen door. "Right through that door there. Just turn the spigot. If it's too hot, there's a barrel of cold water and a bucket. That'll be two bits." He was trimming around the ears of a nearly bald, wrinkled man. Martin wondered if he charged the old man as much as he charged a thick-haired man.

A long, narrow tin tub nearly filled the small room, with a pipe coming in from outside over one end of it. A spigot was on the end of the pipe. Sure enough, a water barrel sat near the door, and there were nails in the door for customers to hang their clothes on. While the tub was filling with lukewarm water, Martin latched the door, which didn't look very strong, then peeled off his clothes. He put the Remington on the floor beside the tub.

Soap. Where was the soap? And a towel? Aw, shit.

Opening the door a crack, standing there naked, he yelled, "Hey, barber, where's the soap."

"Soap? Oh, yeah, I forgot, didn't I? Coming right up. Within a minute, the barber handed a smelly, yellow bar through the crack in the door. "Here y'are."

"How about a towel?"

"Towel? Oh, yeah, I forgot. I'll fetch one." In another minute he handed a clean flour sack through the crack in the door.

Martin latched the door again, climbed into the tub, and settled back. "Ahh." The tub wasn't long enough that he could stretch out, and he had to sit with his knees bent.

But soon he was wet. Then he got on his knees so he could put his head underwater and wash his hair. While he was scrubbing his head his fingers went over the small indentation on the left side. Hair washed, he sat with his knees bent again, and lathered himself all over.

Finished, he stood and wiped himself with the slick excuse for a towel. Only time would dry his hair.

The barber was sitting in his own chair reading an old copy of the *Rocky Mountain News* when Martin came out of the water closet. "A cup of water and some salt? Well, yeah, I can get it from the kitchen. My wife won't mind."

"Wife?" Martin said. "There's a woman back there?"

"Sure, but she stays in the kitchen. She ain't a-tall interested in seeing any nekked cowboys."

Martin was handed a tin cup of water and a salt shaker. He said, "Tell your wife thanks. Do I owe you anything more?"

"Nope, two bits. No charge for the salt and water."

Holding a mouth full of salty water, trying not to swallow, Martin handed the cup to the barber and hurried outside. With quick steps he quit the plankwalk and went around the corner of the building. There he tipped his head back and gargled, then spat. "Gaah." If that doesn't kill the liquor on my breath, nothing will, he thought. It damn near killed me.

Ray was busy selling groceries. He had as many men customers as women. There were bachelor ranchers, timberjacks, miners, and a few housewives. The clerk was finding groceries and piling them on the counter as Ray read the grocery lists. One list filled, Ray totaled the bill, collected the money in U.S. greenbacks, and made out the change in silver. Glancing up at his brother, Ray said,

"I might have to skip lunch, Mart. That wagonload you brought is going fast. Mary will fix you something."

"See you tonight," Martin said, and went through the back door, through a storeroom, and on into the alley. The bay filly had stepped over the outside tug and had skinned her lower leg a little, but she let Martin pick up the left hind foot and put it back inside the tugs.

"That will heal," Martin said. "You're young, but you'll learn and you'll be a damned good horse."

It was a little past noon when the empty freight wagon rattled into the ranch yard and up to the barn. The two boys were in the barn. They came out when they heard the wagon. "I'll help you unhitch, Uncle Martin," the older boy said. "Bennie's too little."

"Be careful of the bay filly," Martin warned. "She just might kick when you reach behind her."

"Naw. I know her. Her name is Lulu. She won't kick if she knows it's me." Boldly, but talking quietly, the boy unhitched the tugs from the singletree. "Whoa, Lulu. Behave yourself, now, Lulu." The filly stood quietly, and Martin was pleased to see that the boy knew how to handle young horses.

"There was a man here," Joshua said, unbuckling the hame straps on a lead horse. "A stranger. I never seen him before. He scared Mama. She won't say so, but I can tell."

A sick feeling of fear climbed into Martin's throat. "Where is he now?"

"He's gone. He got on his horse and left."

Hurriedly, he finished pulling harness off the horses and turned them out to graze, then he walked with quick steps to the kitchen. Mary had seen him coming, and had placed bread, butter, and plum preserves on the table, and was warming a pot of stew.

Removing his hat as he entered, Martin said, "Joshua told me a stranger was here, Mary. Did he want anything in particular?"

"He, uh, it was nothing important."

With his gray eyes fixed on her face, Martin said, "Listen, Mary, maybe it's none of my business, but you-all are my brother's family, the only family I've got. If you're in any kind of danger I want to help."

She turned her back to him and stirred the stew, then she faced him again. "He, uh, he wasn't friendly. He made me understand he doesn't like the proposed ordinances."

"Is that all?"

"No. He, uh, he threatened me."

Chapter Thirteen

Ray Mossman, when he got the news, was suddenly quiet, morose, worried. The family ate supper with little conversation. Luke was always quiet. He'd been working on a fence and doing some irrigating a mile from the house and hadn't seen the visitor. Only Joshua was talkative.

"I seen two coyotes today. I came to get my rifle, but Mama had the bullets hid."

"Saw two coyotes, Joshua, not seen."

"It was them goshdurn coyotes that got our chickens. We usta have eggs for breakfast and some fried chicken, but the coyotes ate our chickens."

"Those coyotes. You know better than that, Joshua. Please try to use better grammar."

"Yeah, but if I'd a had my gun there'd be two less coyotes."

Mary shrugged with resignation.

After supper, after Luke had gone to the bunkhouse, the boys were sent out of the kitchen and Ray, Martin, and Mary sat at the table and talked. Mary described the visitor as about thirty, five feet ten, with a badly trimmed brown beard, brown hair showing from under his wide-brim, shapeless hat, flat-heeled boots, and duck pants held up with suspenders. He carried a pistol butt-forward in a holster on his left side.

Ray frowned at the table, trying to remember whether he'd ever seen the man, and finally shook his head. "I could have seen him around town, but he doesn't stick in my memory."

"Sounds like a hundred men I've seen in my wanderings," Martin said.

"The question is," Ray said, "did he do this on his own, or was he part of the conspiracy?"

Mary said, "There is obviously a conspiracy."

"I'm convinced of that. The two attempts up on the pass. The second bunch had destruction on their minds as much as anything else. If they had succeeded they would have struck a blow to my mercantile business. It wouldn't have been a fatal blow, but it would have hurt, and it would have been a warning that more was to come."

"That's someone's way of defeating you." Mary said. "But who?"

With a sigh, Ray said, "It could be the saloon owners, one or all of them. I wish I knew and could prove it."

Martin kept quiet, only listened as they talked.

"Perhaps," Mary said, "once the election is over, all this will end."

"Hopefully. If we win, they will have lost. They would have nothing to gain by continuing this."

Mary stood and poured more coffee, using the bottom of her apron to protect her hand from the hot pot handle. "Anyway, I don't think this man today was part of a conspiracy. I think he acted alone."

Martin took the cup she handed him. "I sort of agree. Those four up there did have destruction on their minds. But one gent alone? It could be he happened along, knew we were both in town, saw Luke working a mile from the house, and just couldn't pass up a chance to throw a scare into somebody."

Sitting again, Mary picked up her coffee cup, put it down. "One thing we do know, those proposed ordinances have generated a lot of opposition."

"We expected that. But if they're approved by the voters, we'll feel justified in putting them into effect. And if they're not, well," Ray shrugged, "so be it. We tried."

"Yes," Mary sighed, "someone has to try."

Martin had a strong urge to blow on his coffee to cool it down, but he knew Mary would frown at that. He took a quick sip. "You know, out of curiosity, I'd like to see those ordinances. I keep hearing about them but I've never read them for myself."

"Sure, Mart." Ray pushed his chair back and stood. "I've got copies in my desk upstairs. I'll get one."

While he was gone Mary spoke quietly, sincerely, to her brother-in-law. "You know I abhor fighting, and at first, when this whole thing started, I tried to talk Raymond into giving it up. Why start a dispute that could turn violent? Just give it up. But then I remembered how this nation was started by men who refused to give up. I know the frontier west will eventually be civilized by men who refuse to give up. The United States of America will one day be the greatest nation in the world, and all because the people didn't give up. I, uh, I will stand by whatever my husband decides."

Martin only nodded in agreement, but in that thirty seconds he'd learned something about his sister-in-law. She was a gentlewoman, a lady. She hated violence so much that she'd persuaded her husband to move west rather than go to war against his own countrymen, a war she didn't believe in. But she was no quitter. His admiration for Mary went up a couple of notches just then.

Ray came back downstairs, hard heels thumping on the steps. Handing Ray one of two white sheets of paper, he said, "We have no print shop in Vega yet, so we had to send to Colorado Springs to have copies printed. We ordered two hundred copies and posted them all over town and handed them to everyone we met. The whole county knows about these proposals and the special election by now."

Martin turned up the wick in the lamp on the center of the table, scooted his chair closer to it and read:

Be it known by all citizens of Prairie County in the State of Colorado that a special election will be conducted in the town of Vega on July second, 1878, to decide whether the following two ordinances shall become law:

An ordinance giving the county Board of Commissioners authority to regulate the sale of alcoholic beverages in the county, to place restrictions and regulations on those who gamble for a livelihood and on those who practice prostitution. To wit: Those gamblers who have no other means of livelihood shall register with the county clerk and recorder and shall be required to pay a license fee of ten dollars per week. Proprietors of gambling establishments shall post the names of licensed gamblers in a prominent place inside their establishments.

Any woman who sells her sexual favors shall be considered a prostitute. All who practice prostitution in Prairie County shall register with the county clerk and recorder and shall be licensed. To qualify for a license, prostitutes must provide proof that they have been examined by a qualified doctor of medicine within the past week, and shall be examined by a doctor of medicine once each week thereafter.

All officers of the law in Prairie County shall have the authority to demand proof of licensing, and all violators of these ordinances shall be punished by a fine of no less than fifty dollars and no more than one hundred dollars.

Putting the paper down, Martin smiled a wry, lopsided

smile. Ray said, "We know these papers are not written in legal terminology, but we think they are unmistakably clear. What do you think?"

Shaking his head, still smiling, Martin said, "It's clear enough for anybody to understand. Some of the legal writing I've seen is so full of whereases and wherefores you have to read it five times forward and backwards to figure out what it means."

"We know we can't drive out the gamblers and prostitutes, but this will give us the power to regulate them instead of just letting them take over the town."

"It will do that, all right. I like that part about posting the names of the gamblers. I've learned, most of us have learned, to recognize the slicks when we see them. We also learn by word of mouth who is a professional and who is not. But it's a lesson the youngsters have to learn the hard way, and it's an expensive lesson."

Ray handed Martin another sheet of paper. "This is the second proposal."

Martin read: *The Board of County Commissioners of Prairie County in the State of Colorado shall have authority to levy ADDITIONAL taxes to pay for county government services. To wit: A tax of one dollar shall be levied on each barrel of beer brought into the county for sale at retail. A tax of two dollars shall be levied on each case of whiskey, wine or other alcoholic spirits stored in the retail establishments. Proceeds from the tax shall be deposited into a special fund to (a) build a county courthouse (b) pay the salaries of a Justice of the Peace and a deputy sheriff (c) build an addition to the Prairie County school house and employ an additional teacher (d) make improvements to the town public water system.*

"Notice," Ray said, "the word *additional* is in capital letters. We already have a small tax on the livestock, the lumber and mining industries. Enforcing it is something else. That's why we need a deputy sheriff. The justice of the peace will probably collect enough in fines to pay his and the deputy's wages. What do you think?"

"Government has to be paid for. At least this isn't a hardship on anyone. Nobody has to drink."

"The thinking people," Mary said, "realize that government services cost money and have to be paid for through taxes. Yet there are those who strenuously object. People on the frontier aren't accustomed to paying taxes."

"Yes, they will object," Ray said, "but we're hoping the thinking folks will outnumber the nonthinkers."

Martin's headache was back. He needed a drink of whiskey. And he needed a cigarette. Wanting to end the discussion so he could go outside and smoke, he said, "Well, the whole thing will soon be resolved, one way or the other."

"Yep," said Ray. "We're just doing what we think is best. We can only hope the voters agree." He stood. "Must be time to hit the blankets." Grinning, he added, "I feel like it is."

Martin didn't want to wear out his welcome, so he suggested after breakfast that he saddle his horse and ride on. "I like the New Mexico Territory," he said. "There's all kinds of country and climates in New Mexico. There's some big cow outfits, there's timber cutting, and mining. I can always find a job in New Mexico."

What was different about Ray this morning was the walnut-handled revolver he carried in a deep holster, belt high, on his right side. It looked to be a double-action six-gun, and Martin guessed it was either a Colt or Smith & Wesson. Ray and Mary were taking the threat seriously.

"You can find the same things here," Ray argued. "If the mines peter out like they did in Buckskin, we still have ranching and lumber production. The county has some of the most productive hay meadows in Colorado, and we're right on the east-west route through the middle of the state. A railroad is coming. We won't dry up and blow away."

"Yeah, but . . ."

"I don't want to sound like a nagging woman, Mart, but you really ought to settle somewhere, and this is a good place."

"I know you're right, but . . ."

"If you want to go into a business of some kind, start an enterprise, I'll help with the financing."

"Well, uh, I'm no businessman. You think business, but I never did." Martin started rolling another cigarette.

"You don't want to work for someone else the rest of your life, and growing hay can be very profitable. There is some good hay land available."

"Well . . ." Then Martin thought of something he hoped would end the discussion. "You know, the older I get, the more I feel the cold. This is a damned cold climate. When the snow starts flying I get homesick for southern New Mexico, or even Texas."

"Sure it gets cold here, and we know it's going to snow. Some winters it snows a lot. But we've learned how to prepare for it and live comfortably with it. The main thing is to be prepared."

"Yeah, well, uh . . ." His mind racing, trying to think of another excuse, Martin used a new tactic. "You know I like to drink and carouse. Mary wouldn't like having me so close and setting a bad example for the boys."

"Hmm." That had Ray stumped for a moment. He frowned at the ground between his boots. "You can abstain when you want to. But anyway, I wish you would stay at least through the election. And Pritchard and I—Pritchard owns the other general store—we're going to have to send some wagons to Florissant again. This time we'll send at least four wagons and six men, two for outriders. The problem is, like I said before, finding enough idle men that we can hire and trust. We could sure use a man like you."

While Martin mulled it over, Ray added, "With six armed men along, the road agents won't dare attack. You won't have to fight them again."

"Well, when are you planning to get this trip started?"

"In two days. We got word from the stage driver that a twelve-wagon train delivered enough supplies to Wentworth's warehouse to fill it up. It will be another four-day trip for us. What I'm thinking is, you can scout ahead on horseback, keep an eye out for bushwackers, and stop trouble before it starts. I really don't believe there will be any trouble, however. What do you think?"

"Six men with repeating rifles will have a lot of firepower. No, I don't think there'll be any danger. I'll go."

"Fine. I knew I could count on you. Luke will go over every inch of my two wagons to be sure they are sound, and I wish you would take a good look at the eight horses I'm using. Luke can show you which eight. Me, I've got to go open the store."

Sure, Martin thought as his brother walked toward the corrals, I can scout ahead. But there's a lot of hiding places on that pass, and any road agents won't shoot me and sound a warning to the teamsters. They'll just get the drop on me and then cut my throat.

Oh well, I've had worse jobs.

Chapter Fourteen

He saddled his own horse and helped Luke round up the Mossman Ranch's small horse herd. Luke pointed out the eight big horses that were to pull two heavy wagons, and they herded them into a separate corral. Six of the horses were familiar: the two survivors from the first trip to Florissant and the four he'd driven to the Mossman store the day before. They included the bay filly—a four-year-old, he was told. The other two were a bay gelding and a sorrel mare. Both had collar marks on their shoulders and looked to be experienced harness horses. Luke pointed out which were the leaders and which were the wheel teams.

While Martin caught and haltered them one at a time, Joshua climbed to the top rail of the corral and talked. "I know all their names. I got to name some of 'em. Want me to tell you?"

Glancing up at him, Martin said, "Well, no, I've got enough to remember without trying to remember eight names."

"Horses don't know their names anyway. We usta have a dog that knew his name. He died. Papa said dogs are smarter than horses."

Martin was picking up the horses' feet one at a time. None of them were shod, but the road was clear of rocks most of the way and the horses shouldn't get sorefooted.

"Is there some nippers and a rasp here?" he asked the boy.

"Yeah, in the barn. I'll fetch 'em."

When the boy returned, Martin trimmed a hoof where the wall was cracked then rasped off the sharp edge. He did the same to another horse. Then came Lulu's turn. She let Martin pick up a forefoot, but when he began rasping on it she jerked her foot away from him.

"Whoa, young lady," Martin said. "This is something you have to get used to." He picked up the foot and tried again. The filly jerked her foot, but Martin managed to hold it between his knees.

"She's a goshdamned, hammer-headed, contrary sumbitch, ain't she, Uncle Martin."

"No, she's just young. She'll get used to it." He let the foot down and scratched the filly's neck. "Where'd you learn to talk like that? You'd better not let your mother hear that."

"From the blacksmith that came out here to shoe some saddle horses. He sure could cuss."

Shaking his head sadly, Martin knew Mary had a hopeless task, trying to keep her sons from learning how to swear. "Well, I'll tell you, Josh, you're bound to hear some bad words, but don't you repeat them where your mother can hear, or your brother, or women or girls. Not even me. I don't like to hear kids cuss."

"I hear cussin' at school, but one time Mrs. Harrison made one of the big boys stay after school and she marched him home and told his mama on him."

"I hope his mother gave him what for."

"I don't know if she did, but he didn't cuss no more."

At that, Martin had to grin his lopsided grin.

Ray came home for lunch, riding a sorrel mare. He turned her loose in a corral while the family finished last night's stew, warmed over, served with warm bread and butter. The boys had a glass of milk apiece.

"Luke tells me Grandmaw, our milk cow, is going dry, and she's bulling. I'm in the market for another cow to supply us with milk and butter till Grandmaw comes fresh again."

"What's bulling?" Joshua asked.

"I'll explain it to you sometime, son. Right now I've got to get back to the store."

Martin and the boy followed him out to the corrals, where he tightened the latigo on his A-fork saddle, mounted, and rode off toward town.

"Uncle Martin, what's bullin'?"

"That's something your dad will have to explain."

"Goshdarn it, I'm big enough to know. Bennie's too little, but I'm big enough."

"Well, I'll say this much, it means Grandmaw wants to have another calf."

"Huh?" The boy's mouth went slack. "Well, what . . . what?"

Martin knew then he'd made a mistake. He shouldn't have tried to satisfy the boy's curiosity. "Let's open the gate and let these old ponies out. They're ready to go to work any time."

Right then Mary came out of the house, wiping her hands on her long white apron, squinting in the bright sunlight. The younger boy, Benjamin, followed her. "Joshua, I need some firewood. Will you please carry some into the kitchen."

"Yeah." Glumly.

"How do the horses look, Martin?" Her dark hair was

combed down over her ears and fastened behind her neck with a long sterling silver comb. A pretty young woman.

"They're in good shape."

"Raymond has often said he wished he knew horses as well as you do."

"He knows a lot of things I don't."

"Momma, I know what bulling means, it means Grandmaw wants to have another calf."

Frowning, Mary spoke in quick harsh words, "Martin, what did you tell him?"

Oh-oh, thought Martin. Here it comes. "Why, I, uh, that's all I told him."

"It's his father's place to explain things like that."

Feeling like a spanked puppy again, Martin said, "You're right. I should have kept my mouth shut."

She continued frowning at Martin a moment, then said, "I have some dough about to rise in the oven." She turned and walked away. Benjamin stayed.

"Say, Bennie," Joshua said, "Momma wants some stove wood. Go fetch her some."

Looking over the boys' heads, Martin saw an axe and a chopping block next to a pile of dead tree limbs. "Tell you what, you fellers carry it and I'll chop it."

"Here's the plan Pritchard and I cooked up, Mart, but you can change it if you want to. With your experience in the war and in your travels you know more about this sort of thing than we do. We're putting you in charge. You'll be the boss, and the other men will be instructed to follow your orders."

They were standing outside in the dark after supper. Martin was smoking, wishing he had a drink of whiskey to dull the headache. He decided he'd take a drink from his nearly empty bottle before he went to bed. A man had to have some relief. In the morning, he'd have to keep his distance from Mary.

"What we're thinking," Ray went on, "is you and a cowboy named Joe Jackson, borrowed from Ted Wilson's Flying W Ranch, will be horseback. You two can scout ahead and warn the teamsters if you see anything suspicious. That way you won't be caught by surprise from ambush. What do you think?"

"Sounds all right to me. What about the other four men, are they men you can trust?"

"We think so. They include Harlan Longacre, a blacksmith who is also a member of the county board, and Hugh Williams, who runs what passes for a livery barn. Harlan doesn't always have enough work to keep him busy, and Hugh's got three strapping sons to do the work at his livery business. I tried to hire them to go with you last time but they had other work promised."

Martin finished his smoke, ground it into the dirt with a boot heel, and started rolling another. "That's three who ought to be trustworthy."

"The other two aren't what you could call responsible citizens, but able-bodied men who have time on their hands are not easy to find. One is a miner who was laid off when one of the mines at Buckskin shut down and the other is Jed Oaks, a handy man about town. The miner's name is, uh, Evetts Haskell. He swears he can handle a four-up. Jed is a boozer and a gambler, but he's a good worker when he's sober, and he's handled a team for us before."

"Will they all have rifles?"

"Harlan and Hugh will carry pistols and shotguns. The others will have Winchester repeating rifles."

"Other than being escorted by the Army," Martin said,

"I don't know of a better way to do it. It would take an organized gang to rob six well-armed men."

"We haven't heard of any organized gangs in this part of the country."

Lifting his hat, massaging the depression above his left ear, Martin allowed, "Well, sounds like you and Pritchard have got everything worked out. Where are we all gonna meet?"

"At Hugh's livery at daylight day after tomorrow. You and Luke can drive my two wagons and teams over there tomorrow and leave them where they'll be ready."

"Good enough." Martin's head was throbbing. No matter what, he had to get some relief.

"There is one more thing, Mart. We're sending cash to pay Wentworth. He'll accept some notes, but he wants cash most of the time. I deposited some money in a bank in Colorado Springs, and I could send along a bank draft, but I've got the cash on hand and I don't like to keep that much on hand. You'll be carrying four hundred dollars. That will pay for this order and the last order you bought from Wentworth. I don't know who will carry Pritchard's cash."

Martin reset his hat and repeated, "Good enough."

Finally, he got to go to the little room off the kitchen, uncap his whiskey bottle, and drain it in two gulps. He sighed with relief as it burned its way down into his stomach and up into his brain. Now he could think better, and what he thought was worrisome.

At least seven hundred dollars cash and sixteen big sound horses. That would be a good haul for a robber gang. The bunch who'd tried to rob and kill him wouldn't try six men, but word of this trip had been passed around by now, and more robber-killer types could be rounded up.

They had plenty of time and a hell of a strong motive.

Chapter Fifteen

Harnessing eight horses took a while, even with two men, and Joshua was watching it all with bright-eyed interest. "Who's gonna drive our teams? What're you gonna do, Uncle Martin, look for robbers? Are you gonna shoot 'em if you see 'em? What if they shoot some more of our horses? When are you gonna get back? Can you make Lulu behave herself? Bennie's too little, but I wish I could go."

"Everything is going to be fine, Josh. We'll have a small army with us."

Martin tied his saddle horse behind one of the wagons so he'd have something to ride back. Luke allowed he'd walk back. Luke studied the western horizon, and said, "Them clouds gatherin' over yonder ain't gonna dump on us today, but I'm bettin' it'll rain afore you git back."

Joshua said, "Luke's good at guessin' what the weather's gonna do. Papa said so."

"Nah," Luke said, "this durn Colorado weather cain't be predicted. Back in Kansas where I come from, a feller can make a purty good guess." Glancing at the sky again, he added, "Wish it would rain. It'd save irrigatin'."

Hugh Williams's barn was one-story, built with rough-sawn lumber. The lumber had shrunk, leaving cracks between the boards. The roof was boards nailed on top of two layers of tarpaper. It was far from being weathertight, but it was at least a break from the cold winter winds, which was all horses really needed. The four plank corrals looked strong, and water was piped from Granite Creek slightly uphill from the corrals. Williams was a big-bellied man who moved as though he was arthritic. He wore a bill cap and bib overalls. The stack of hay he had behind the barn had shrunk considerably by the time sixteen big horses had been penned and fed.

"Gonna be hayin' time in a couple a weeks or so, and it's about time. My boys and me, we work for your brother to help pay for a few loads of hay."

Work done, Martin mounted his saddle horse and rode up First Street to see what there was to see. There wasn't much. The blacksmith, Harlan Longacre, was making some horseshoes though there wasn't a horse anywhere near. He'd have them handy when they were needed, Martin mused. He nodded, and the blacksmith, a man of average size with big hands and a shirt with the sleeves cut off, nodded in return.

The country west and south of Vega was flat sagebrush prairie. To the north, more timber-covered fingers stretched down out of the mountains. Martin couldn't help frowning at the sight of a stump-covered narrow valley up there where the timber had been clear-cut. "Takes thirty years to grow a tree," he said to himself, "and ten minutes to cut it down." He rode past a sawmill where he counted eight men working hard at cutting logs into lumber. The big circular saw was powered with a steam engine with a boiler that hissed steam from a safety valve on top.

Turning back, he rode down a street two blocks south

of First Street, and thought Vega was a typical frontier settlement, with houses built of whatever materials could be had, lumber, logs, rocks. Most were one-story, three or four rooms, but a few were two-story and whitewashed. Most had lacy curtains in the windows and flowers growing in the yards. They did have a look of permanancy, Martin thought. On farther, another block south, was a two-story whitewashed house standing alone in the middle of an acre of sagebrush. Hitchrails had been built for ten or more horses in front of the house. Out of curiosity, Martin turned his horse in that direction.

"If I didn't know better," he said to himself, "I'd reckon that's a whorehouse. A fancy one. The kind where the ranch owners and mine owners and businessmen go. Probably priced too high for the working stiffs. Probably draws the money class from fifty miles around."

Martin had known men to ride all day to get to a whorehouse like this one and all day to get back, just for a couple of fifteen-minute sessions with a woman.

The thin clouds on the western horizon had turned pale red as Martin tied up in front of the Mossman Mercantile. "Thought I'd ride back with you," he said to his brother inside. "Be just a few minutes," Ray said. "Ready for a long day tomorrow?"

Grinning his lopsided grin, Martin allowed, "Ready, willing, and able."

Only a pale light glowed in the east as eight men gathered at the Williams barn. Horses were bridled, harnessed, and hitched to wagons. Ray Mossman and the merchant named Pritchard were there, helping. Martin was introduced to the men one at a time, and each man was told to follow Martin's orders. The cowboy named Joe Jackson introduced himself. "Call me J.J.," he said. Freshly shaved and barbered, he was a small, wiry young man, the size that made good bronc riders. Martin guessed it would take a hard-bucking horse to throw him off.

When they lined out, four wagons and two riders going east on the narrow prairie road, Martin and J.J. took the lead. Glancing at the young cowboy now and then, Martin took a liking to him. For most of the day they could see for miles, and the two riders stayed on the road and talked. Though they'd never worked for the same cow outfits they had a lot in common.

"I've heard of the Ladder brand," J.J. said, "but I ain't never been that far south."

"I'd guess from your saddle and all," Martin said, "that you've always ranged in the north, Colorado and Wyoming."

J.J. carried his six-gun on his left side, butt forward, where it was out of the way when he mounted and dismounted a horse, or led a horse or dragged a calf from horseback. His saddle had a high cantle, wide fork, and a three-quarter rigging, while Martin's saddle was shallower and narrower with a rimfire rigging.

"Ever hear of the Iliff outfit?" J.J. asked. "Up north of Denver? Now there's a big outfit. They keep two or three wagons out nine months of the year."

"I've heard of it," Martin said. "I keep hearing the free range is coming to an end, and it's gonna take a corporation to own as much land as old Iliff grazes on."

Shortly after noon, after they'd stopped long enough to gobble a sandwich apiece and drink from canteens, they began the long climb to the top of the pass, and the horses were allowed to slow from a shuffling trot to a walk.

"Right about here," Martin said, "is where you and I ought to split up. You go south and I'll go north. Stay within sight of the road, but keep your eyes open. If you see anybody, anybody at all, fire a shot, and I'll come on a high lope."

"You betcha." J.J. reined off the south side of the road.

"Don't let anybody drop a loop on you and drag you off your horse before you can get off a shot," Martin yelled.

"I'll keep my finger on the trigger of this here Winchester," the cowboy yelled back.

Martin motioned for the teamsters behind him to keep coming, then reined off the road too, angling for the tall timber and big boulders to the north. He kept the rifle in its boot under his right leg, thinking he could draw and fire the Remington six-gun faster than he could aim and fire the rifle.

The higher he climbed, the rougher the country became; short scrubby oak, tall pines and granite boulders as big as horses. No wonder the stage drivers squirmed on their seats when their horses climbed this pass. This was a perfect place for an ambush. Martin rode at a walk, right hand near his gun butt, stopping now and then to take a careful look in all directions. He rode around boulders, through a patch of scrub oak, and up a steep hill.

It was near the top that he spotted a man.

The gent was crouching behind a waist-high rock and he'd already seen Martin. He jumped up, ran to a horse tied to a pine branch, mounted, and rode away at a gallop. Martin touched spurs to his brown gelding and took after him.

Drawing the Remington, Martin fired a shot in the air to warn the teamsters and to attract the attention of J.J. He urged his brown horse to greater speed. "Like to catch that jasper," he muttered. "He's up to some meanness, you can bet on that."

The race went on for nearly two miles, and when he saw his man ride out of a ravine two hundred yards ahead, Martin knew he wasn't gaining. "Damn, damn."

Then the man disappeared. Just disappeared.

Martin reined up suddenly. This didn't look right. That jasper had to be forted up behind those big rocks over there, just waiting for Martin to come within easy gun range.

Stepping down from his winded horse to make a smaller target of himself, Martin studied every tree, rock, and bush. Yep, the son of a bitch had to be over there behind that handful of boulders that seemed to grow out of the ground like giant mushrooms.

Hearing hoofbeats behind him, Martin looked back and saw the cowboy, J.J., coming at a gallop, a rifle in his hand. "What'd you see, Mart?" he asked as he reined up.

"There's a man over there behind those big rocks," Martin said. "He's pretty well forted up."

"Can we get around 'im?"

"I don't know. When he sees us trying to circle him, he'll run again."

"Maybe we can catch 'im."

"Maybe." Then a cold, fearsome thought popped into Martin's mind. "Something about this ain't right." Quickly he stepped into his saddle. "Could it be he wanted us to chase him? Draw us away from the road?"

"Goddamn."

"We've got to get back. Let's lope."

They rode back toward the road as fast as they'd ridden away from it, then Martin brought his horse to a stop, and got down, lifting his Winchester from the saddle boot. The young cowboy did the same. Walking carefully, as quietly as they could, they got within sight of the road. Just in time to fire the first shot.

Chapter Sixteen

The three riflemen were lying low behind a line of small boulders, waiting for the wagons. The first wagon was almost even with them, coming slowly, the horses leaning into their collars. One of the three raised up on his knees, put a rifle to his shoulder.

Martin's hasty shot smacked into a boulder near his right knee and ricocheted on across the road. The rifleman jumped as if he'd been kicked in the pants, whirled. J.J.'s first shot missed too, but his target was so surprised he dropped his rifle and threw his hands up.

"Don't shoot, don't shoot."

The third man spun, snapped a rifle shot that whistled past J.J.'s head. Martin fired at the third man. The lead slug knocked him down. To the first one, Martin yelled, "Drop that gun. Right now." He was standing spraddle-legged, holding the Winchester in his left hand and the Remington in his right, straight out at eyeball level, with the rifleman in the sights.

The man was on his knees, his rifle pointed at the ground. He hesitated, trying to decide whether to try to shoot it out or give up. Another slug from Martin's Remington burned his right shoulder. He dropped the rifle.

"Stay put," Martin yelled. "Move and you're dead." No one moved.

"I'll cover them, J.J. You pick up their guns."

Not wanting to get between Martin and the gunman, the young cowboy circled, then carefully, pistol ready, picked up three rifles. He dropped them on the ground away from the three. The first one Martin had shot was sitting up, holding his hands against his right side. J.J. got behind him and lifted a six-gun out of a holster near his hands.

Looking down the road now, Martin saw that the wagons were stopped, the teamsters looking up this way, trying to see what was happening. Then a shot came from across the road, and Martin swore.

"Goddamn. I should of known there were more than these three. Hit the ground, J.J."

The young cowboy was on his knees behind the same boulders the two riflemen had been hiding behind. Martin ran up and joined him.

Then two of the riflemen ran, just put their heads down and ran off into the woods, leaving their guns and their wounded partner. J.J. turned and snapped a shot at them, missed. Martin said, "Don't worry about those two. We've got trouble over there."

"See anybody?" J.J. asked.

"No, but we've got to keep them down. Can't let them pick off the teamsters."

For a moment, all was quiet. One of the teamsters yelled, "Hey, what's goin' on?"

Martin yelled back, "Get out of the wagons, get on the north side, keep hold of the lines." The four teamsters spilled out of the wagons immediately.

J.J. said, "I still don't see anybody over there."

"They're there. I think maybe we spoiled their scheme, but they're still over there."

"Oh, oh," the young cowboy muttered. He put a rifle to his shoulder and fired. "Shit. The son of a bitch jumped back."

"I saw him. You can bet he ain't alone. But I think the drivers are safe now."

"There's another'n." J.J. fired again. "Don't know if I hit 'im."

"That makes two over there. At least two."

Martin saw a gunman across the road in time to drop to the ground a split second before a lead slug sang like an angry bee over his head. J.J. fired again.

"I think they're leavin', Mart. I got a quick glimpse of two of 'em, runnin' like barrel-assed apes."

"There's another one. Over there behind that big pine. Keep your sights on him. I'd sure like to get some of the sons of bitches."

Two more rapid shots came their way, but the bullets didn't come close. "He's leavin' too."

Both Martin and J.J. fired at the running man across the road, but they got only glimpses of him as he ran through the trees and around a rocky knoll.

"Damn," J.J. swore. "Goddamn. Think they're gone now, Mart?"

"I'd say they are, but we can't be sure. Let's sit tight a couple of minutes, then get on our horses and go over."

With no more then their hats and eyes showing over the boulders, Martin and the young cowboy studied the terrain across the road. Now and then Martin glanced back at the wounded man. The man got to his knees, then to his feet, swaying drunkenly. "You," Martin yelled, "sit down. Sit down or I'll shoot you down." The man sank to his knees, then onto the seat of his pants.

"Hey, up there." It was Hugh Williams, liveryman, yelling. "What's goin' on?"

"Stay put," Martin yelled back. "I think they're gone, but we're not sure yet."

"Think we could get on our horses now, Mart?"

"All right. We can't stay here all day."

They found their horses grazing on bunch grass, and also the wounded man's horse tied to a tree. Leading the third horse, they rode across the road, around the boulders, through the pines and brush. They found cigarette butts where men had smoked while they waited, and they found a few empty cartridge casings and plenty of boot and hoof prints.

"They went down off this hill and across the crick," J.J. said. "They're long gone."

"I saw three. How many did you see?"

"Three over here. Three over there makes six and the one you chased makes seven."

"Yeah, and six of them got away."

"How do you picture it, Mart?"

"Looks like the one I took out after was a decoy. We were both supposed to chase him and leave the teamsters to take care of themselves. With us gone, the other six would have had the teamsters in a crossfire."

"Yep. That's the way it looks to me."

"They had it planned, all right. The one I chased had a good fort picked out, and if I'd chased him any farther he'd have shot me right off my horse."

"Was you in the war, Mart?"

"Yeah."

"Then you've had a lot of experience. That's what spoiled their scheme."

With a lopsided grin, Martin said, "I'm sure glad you came along. I couldn't have handled it by myself." After a moment, he said, "Well, let's get the wagons up here and make camp."

The wounded man could walk, although his steps were unsteady. "I'll be damned if I'll carry 'im as long as he can walk a-tall," the young cowboy said. "Keep movin', mister. Fall, and we'll leave you here. And with no horse you wouldn't go far."

The gunman had left his hat behind, and thick dark hair stuck out in all directions and hung over his forehead. He had a thick-lipped mouth, colorless eyes, and a nose that had once been broken and healed crooked.

"Let him take his time," Martin said. "I'll go on over to the wagons and see if we've got anything to patch him up with."

Their prisoner hadn't spoken a word.

The teamsters had the wagons parked side by side with enough space between them to tie horses. They were leading the horses to the creek when Martin rode up. He wished they'd camped farther downhill, in the open, but dark was coming on fast, and he guessed they wanted to make camp while they had enough daylight to see. Too, there was no water for the horses down in the open country.

So many travelers had camped up here that firewood was scarce. Martin rode in a half circle until finally he found a small dead pine. Knowing that pine trees had shallow roots, he got off his horse and pushed on it, put a shoulder to it. Grunting and gritting his teeth, he finally got it to fall over with a crash. Then he tied one end of his catch rope to the bottom of the trunk, got on his horse, wrapped the other end of the rope around his saddle horn, and dragged the tree to the wagons.

By then the others were back and had the horses tied to the wagons and fed. The wounded man was sitting with his back against a knee-high boulder, looking weak. "Anybody recognize this gent?" Martin asked.

"Nope."—"He's nobody I ever saw before."—"He ain't from Vega."

Squatting in front of the man, Martin asked, "Where are you from, mister?"

The colorless eyes turned Martin's way, but the lips didn't move.

"I said, where are you from?"

The lips moved, barely. "I ain't tellin' you nothin'."

Martin tore open the man's shirt and studied the bullet hole. The wound was just above the hip bone, bleeding only a little. Three inches farther to the right, and the bullet would have missed. But there was no exit wound. The bullet was still inside."

Trying a lie, Martin said, "That's a nasty hole you've got there. You're probably bleeding in your guts. It'll be a miracle if you last through the night."

No response.

"Some men, when they're dying, like to confess their sins. Who planned your scheme?"

No answer.

"Well, I don't think there's a doctor at Florissant, and we won't get back to Vega for three days at least. You'll be dead by then."

"I ain't sayin' nothin'."

J.J. walked over, spurs ringing, and squatted on his boot heels beside Martin. "I seen a killer once that wouldn't talk till he was hung by the neck a few times. It was up in Wyoming. Ever'body knew he killed and robbed a merchant, and ever'body knew he had partners, but he wouldn't name 'em. Not until they put a rope around his neck and threw the other end over the top of a barn door, and pulled 'im up by the neck. I didn't take no part in it, but I watched. They pulled 'im up and let 'im hang till he was 'bout strangled to death, then let 'im down. They done that three times, and after the third time he talked his fool head off. He brayed like a jackass. He wouldn't stop talkin'."

The four teamsters had gathered around now, standing, looking down at the wounded prisoner. "Him and his pards was plannin' to make coyote bait out'n us," somebody said.

"That's what we oughta do to him. Just put 'im out of his misery."

"We c'd pull his boots off and put a burnin' stick to his feet, and he'd tell us ever'thing he knows."

Looking up at the gathering, Martin said, "Mr. Longacre, you're on the county board, would you torture a prisoner?"

"Naw." Big hands shoved into baggy pants pockets, the blacksmith said, "We're tryin' to build a civilized county, and we can't do things like that."

"I agree." Martin stood. "Anybody got anything to make a bandage out of?"

"Nope."—"Didn't think to bring anything."—"If I had a bullet hole in me I'd use my shirttail, but I ain't givin' him my shirt."

"Well, I'll have to use his shirttail. Wish it was clean. Anybody got any whiskey?"

Jed Oaks, the handyman answered, "Now, that I have got, but I hate to waste good likker on a man that tried to kill me."

"I'll pay you for it," Martin said. "I'll do as much for him as I can. Within reason, that is."

"Well, in that case, I'll fetch it."

Dark had settled in, but a fire the men had built was putting out enough light that Martin managed to pull the wounded man's shirttail out, cut off a piece, splash whiskey on it, pour whiskey on the wound, then tie the piece of shirttail in place with the prisoner's gunbelt. "Don't move more than you have to and maybe it'll stay put," he said.

"What're we gonna do with 'im now?" J.J. asked. "Tie 'im up?"

"Just watch him, I reckon." To the prisoner, Martin said, "Don't stand up, don't move at all. Make one wrong move and we'll tie your hands so tight gangrene will set in before we get you to town. Savvy?"

"Uhnn."

A pot of stew was warming over the fire, and a teamster was slicing bread. "We'll eat good," someone said.

"I'm gonna get up there on that knoll and keep watch," Martin said. "Soon's you gents get your bellies full, one of you can spell me."

"If anybody comes sneakin' around they won't come before daylight."

"Unless they're already around. I'll keep watch up there a while, then we'll have to take turns standing guard. You men keep your rifles handy."

After a half hour, the young cowboy made his way to the top of the knoll, whispering, "It's me, J.J. Where are you, Mart?"

"Over here. Straight ahead."

"Darker'n Old Coalie's ass. Say somethin' again."

"Over here."

Soon J.J. found him, and hunkered down beside him. He whispered, "If you'd a seen or heard anything you'd a said so."

"I don't expect to see anything, as dark as it is, but if anybody is around I ought to hear them."

"There's a purty good stew down there. Go feed your face. I'll do the listenin'."

"I don't think we need to stay up here all night. If anybody comes calling it will be right after daylight."

"Then I'll stand the first guard at the wagons."

"We'll all take a turn at it," Martin said. He grinned in the dark. "Seems to me I've been here and done this before."

Chapter Seventeen

During the night the wind came up, whooshing through the pines. Martin lay awake awhile, listening and worrying. The sound of the wind could drown out the sound of men getting into position to attack. He relieved Evetts Haskell, the miner, and took the last watch, wanting to be wide awake at dawn. Men were covered with their blankets, some under the wagons, and some in the wagons. The wounded prisoner was lying on his side, knees drawn up. Someone had given him a blanket. The cooking fire was nothing more than dead ashes.

Martin's head was throbbing as he groped his way back to the knoll, south of the camp, trying to make no noise. Up here, the wind was stronger, making hearing more difficult. And the wind was cold. He wished he'd brought a blanket. Not a star was in sight, and the sky was black. He picked a spot where he believed he could see in all directions when daylight came, knowing he would be a good target.

There was no pink horizon. The coming daylight was a slow brightening. Clouds hung so low he couldn't see Pikes Peak, couldn't see very far in any direction. Moisture was in the air. Martin stayed where he was until after the men had a fire going and bacon sizzling. J.J. climbed the knoll. "Go get some chuck, Mart. My ass'll keep this spot warm till we're ready to move on."

"I'll stay a little longer. They'll save some bacon for me."

"Yeah, well, look what I've got." J.J. showed Martin a bottle of whiskey. "Gave ol' Jed a couple bucks for it. He wanted four, but it's only half full. Want a swig?"

"J.J., there's nothing I want more right now. I get a headache sometimes, and whiskey helps."

" 'Cause of that war wound?"

"Yeah."

"Have a long drink. Two or three or four. If I was you I'd prob'ly be drunk on my ass all the time."

Grinning on one side of his face, Martin said, "I might turn out that way yet."

He ate two thick slices of bacon wrapped in a lukewarm pancake, drank a tin cup of coffee, then watched the prisoner while he emptied his bladder. By then the light was stronger, and the teamsters were harnessing horses.

A rifle shot came from up on the knoll.

All heads swiveled in that direction. Martin yelled, "Pull out as fast as you can. Get down off this mountain. I'll go up there and see what's to see." As an afterthought, he said, "If it looks like we're about to be attacked, I'll holler and you-all drop everything and take cover."

"What about him?" A teamster nodded at the prisoner.

"Put him in the back end of a wagon. Keep an eye on him. Don't, for Christ's sake, let him get his hands on a gun. If he gives you any trouble, kill him."

Martin grabbed up his Winchester, then half ran, scrambling over rocks, to the top of the knoll. J.J. was on his belly, but his head was up and his rifle was ready. "You hit?" Martin asked.

"Naw. It was me that fired. There's a man down there. I seen 'im over yonder in the buck brush. Where there's one there's more."

"They'll have the horses hitched up in a few minutes and they'll strike a trot and be down out of the timber in a half hour. They didn't take time to water the horses. We'll have to do that later."

"We gonna wait up here till they get down on the flats?"

Martin had to think it over a moment. "Maybe what we ought to do is wait here till they get going, then get horseback and scout ahead of them a ways, on both sides of the road, like we did yesterday."

"You're the boss."

They waited, squatting on their heels, eyes scanning the terrain in all directions. Then J.J. said, "The wagons are movin'. They're back on the road."

"All right. Whoever is down there knows we're up here watching. It's time for us to move."

They found their two saddle horses tied to a tree where the teamsters had left them. The wounded man's horse was tied to the back of a wagon. Mounted, J.J. asked, "Which side of the road you want me to take?"

"Wait a minute. Let's give this some thought. Let's see, the man you just saw was south. If they're gonna attack, they'll probably come from the south. Maybe we both ought to prowl along this side, stay a little ahead of the wagons. Tell you what, I'll go on uphill a couple hundred yards and you stay closer to the road.

"You're the boss."

"If you hear shooting, don't come to help me. Get to the wagons on a high lope, get the drivers out of the wagons and ready to fight."

"Yessir, I'll do 'er."

Reining his brown horse uphill, Martin rode to the top of the knoll, scanned the terrain, then turned downhill. The morning fog had cleared, but the sky was filled with dark clouds, moving clouds. Eyes busy, Martin went on, keeping about two hundred yards from the road. The Winchester was in the boot under his right leg. His hand was on the butt of the six-gun. The brown horse picked its way over the rocks, around boulders and tall pines. Martin half expected to see men with guns on the other side of every boulder he rode around. But the farther downhill he rode, the better he felt.

Then he spotted a man.

The man was on horseback, riding along a ridge. He was too far away to be part of an attack force. What was he doing? Was there a trail up there? Martin watched him, puzzled. Then the rider turned downhill, toward the road. He'd seen Martin and the wagons, that was certain. If he had partners, they were well hidden.

Studying the country ahead, Martin calculated the rider would come out to the road right about where he'd meet the wagons. Alone, he couldn't be a threat. But was he alone? Martin had to decide whether to hang back and see what the rider did when he got to the wagons, be ready to counterattack from up here if necessary, or spur on ahead. The wagons would soon be in the open. In fact, only one line of scrub oak and cedars came within two hundred yards of the road up ahead, and it was open country from there on. The only place men could be hiding was in those scrubs.

He didn't know whether he'd made the right decision, but Martin spurred his horse downhill, angling toward the road, hoping to intercept J.J. Rounding a shalestone outcropping, he saw the young cowboy ahead. He yelled and waved. J.J. saw him and stopped. Martin rode to him at a lope.

"There's a rider coming down to meet the wagons," he said. "Either he's alone or there's more men in those scrubs up there. If he's alone he's harmless. If he's got pards in those scrubs, we'd best get to the wagons and be ready to fight."

Squinting ahead, J.J. allowed, "Those scrubs are in rifle range of the road, but if somebody was gonna ambush us they passed up some better spots."

"That's right. This gent's got me puzzled. Do you know if there's a trail up there?"

"I don't know this country, but I heard there's horse-back trails over this pass, and some men would rather take them than follow the wagon road."

"Maybe he's just a harmless traveler. Well"—Martin touched spurs to his horse—"let's get on over to the wagons and see what he does."

They rode at a gallop, horses dodging small boulders, running into and out of shallow gulches. They rode under the shale bluff where Martin had camped before, where he'd shot it out before, where he'd killed a man. The decomposing carcasses of two horses were there, which made Martin swearing mad again. When they reached the wagons, Harlan Longacre said, "Somethin' about to happen?"

"Don't know," Martin said, bringing his horse down to a trot. "There's a rider coming from over there." He pointed. "Maybe he's harmless and maybe he ain't. Keep your eyes on those scrubs." He rode along the line of wagons and said to each driver, "I don't know that anything's gonna happen, but be ready to bail out of your wagon with your rifle cocked." That done, he waited and watched.

The rider was in plain view now, coming at a fast trot. He waved his hat, and kept coming. He had a rifle in a saddle boot and a six-gun in a cross-draw holster on his left side. He wore a wide-brim hat and a brown beard. He reined up a hundred feet from the first wagon.

"Hello," he yelled. "I'm goin' to Florissant. If you don't mind, I'll join you."

Martin yelled, "Come on over." He studied the rider carefully. The rifle had a long barrel, but was hidden in the scabbard so Martin couldn't see what kind of gun it was. A blanket roll was tied behind the cantle, but there were no saddlebags. Either he was eating damned little or he was no traveler.

"Seen youall from up yonder," the rider said when he drew up at the wagons. "I took the horseback trail 'stead a the wagon road 'cuz I heard there's road agents that like to bushwhack wagon travelers."

He sat his horse beside Martin and they let the wagons go by. The wounded outlaw was in the last wagon, lying on a tarp-covered pile of hay. He rose to a sitting position at the sound of voices. Watching closely, Martin thought he detected a glimpse of recognition in the wounded man's eyes, but he wasn't sure. He motioned for J.J. to go on up to the head of the wagon train.

"Yessir," the strange rider was saying, "I hear there's men in this territory that'd shoot you out'n your wagon, steal ever'thing you got, and take your team and wagon and leave you to die with a bullet in you. But now that we're out of the hills, I reckon we're safe from here on."

Martin said nothing, just watched the man.

"Yessir, I'm goin' on down to Colorada City. I hear a man can find anything he wants down there. I heard that new town called Colorada Springs is full of furriners."

Still Martin said nothing.

"I'm a workin' man and I want nothing' to do with them furriners. Ain't that the way you see it?"

Martin shrugged.

"Say, you don't talk much do you? Maybe you don't want me ridin' with you."

When Martin only shrugged again, he talked on, "Well, hell, I don't havta stay with you. I can git back up there on that trail and git to Florissant quicker anyhow."

Martin thought, No, you can't. This road goes almost straight to Florissant from here. There is no shortcut. He kept his right hand close to the Remington six-gun.

"If I see you in Florissant, don't bother to say howdy or nothin'." With that, the stranger turned south, and rode at a lope toward the scrubs.

Martin watched him a moment, then looked back at the wounded outlaw. He was on his knees, also watching the rider leave.

"What did he want?" Longacre asked.

"Don't know. There's something about him I don't like."

"He's stopped over yonder."

Martin looked to the south just in time to see that the stranger was off his horse, kneeling with a long-barreled rifle in his hands. A puff of smoke came from the rifle. A bullet smacked into something. Then the rider was on his horse again, spurring hard for the scrubs.

J.J. started to ride after him, but Martin yelled, "No, J.J. Stop. Come back." The young cowboy brought his horse to a stop and turned around. Martin motioned for him to come back to the wagons, then let his eyes rove, trying to see what the bullet had hit. Within seconds, he picked out the target.

The wounded outlaw was on his back, one leg folded

under him, his eyes and mouth open, a bullet hole in the side of his head.

Longacre swore, "Well, I'll be goddamned."

Riding up at a gallop, J.J. said, "What'd he shoot?"

"Him," Martin said quietly.

"Son of a bitch. What in hell did he do that for?"

"I don't know, but I can guess," Martin said.

"Well," Longacre said, "guess out loud."

"I'm guessing he came over here to do one of two things." Martin wrapped his reins around his saddle horn and started building a cigarette. "One, to find out if this gent was alive, and two, to kill him if he was."

"And I can guess what for," J.J. said.

The wagons were standing still and other teamsters were walking back to see what had happened. Longacre said, "To shut his mouth, huh?"

"Yep. Keep 'im from spillin' the beans about his cohorts."

"No doubt about it," Martin said. To the teamsters he yelled, "Our prisoner was shot by one of his pardners. Let's get going. We'll stop at noon at the river down there."

When the wagons were moving again, and the dead man's head was covered with his own saddle blanket, J.J. said, "He's a good shot, whoever that jasper was, to hit a man in the head from that distance. And if I'd a kept after 'im, he'd a picked me off from those bushes."

With his twisted grin, Martin said, "We can't afford to lose you, J.J."

"Well, anyhow, we got 'er whupped now, Mart. We'll make Florissant before dark, easy."

"Yeah," Martin said.

But under his breath he said, "Then we have to come back."

Chapter Eighteen

By noon thunder was grumbling, and lightning was flashing to the west. Riding beside Martin, J.J. looked back, said, "That hill we was on, I'll bet that lightnin's got them rocks sizzlin'."

"I was warned once about lightning in the high country. You don't want to be on a ridge and you don't want to be sitting on a granite rock."

"I know lightnin' kills folks, but there's been too many times I had no choice but to stay horseback and keep on ridin' and hope it didn't take aim at me."

"You can't just drop everything and hide your head." Eyes busy, Martin added, "Might be a creek over there where those trees are. Want to lope over there and see?"

"Shore."

"If there's water, yell, wave your hat or something, and we'll pull over there to water the horses."

The young cowboy was about three hundred yards away when he yelled and waved his hat. Martin directed the wagon train in that direction. By the time the horses were unhitched, led to the small stream and back, the rain started. Men sat under the wagons and ate cold bacon that had been fried that morning, and two-day-old bread.

Two of the teamsters had long yellow rain slickers. The rest of the crew had to endure the wet and cold. "I learned long ago you can't predict the weather in Colorado," Longacre said, "and I don't go nowhere without a slicker."

Rain turned to hail as the wagon train got moving again, and for two minutes or so small hailstones beat down on men and animals. Then the hail changed back to rain. Men shivered, and thought of their homes with warm stoves. To the horses, the rain was cool and refreshing, and it kept the flies off. They trotted along easily.

Gradually, the lightning, thunder, and rain moved on east. When the settlement of Florissant came into view, the late-day sun was shining.

They parked the wagons close to the big door of Wentworth's warehouse, and Martin wanted to start loading immediately. But the dead man had to be explained to a deputy sheriff of El Paso County. Martin ordered three of the teamsters to load wagons as Wentworth read the lists and pointed out the bags and boxes. Wentworth had two hired men of his own helping.

The deputy was a short man with big shoulders and wide hips. His Stetson was grimy and his face was round, but rock hard. "So you're the one that put a bullet in his side, but you think it was one of his own bunch that shot 'im in the head?"

Nodding, Martin said, "That's what we think."

"So he couldn't identify his pards?"

"That's our guess."

"Did he? Did he give you any clue as to who his pards was?"

"No, he wouldn't say anything, but you know, if he was locked up or if he thought he was gonna die, or if he thought he was gonna hang, he might have blabbed everything."

Nodding in agreement, the deputy said, "He might of at that. I've seen this gent here in town. I didn't like his looks, but as far as I know he didn't commit any crime." He sighed. "I'll get some of the rowdies around here to see if they can put a name to 'im, then we'll have to bury 'im. We ain't got no undertaker."

The boardinghouse in Florissant couldn't accommodate the six men who'd come to town with a wagon train, but the one cafe managed to feed them. They bedded down in their blankets under the wagons while the horses munched hay in one of the livery pens.

By sunup next morning, they had the groceries covered with tarps and the wagons on the road.

Just before noon, they stopped at the same place they'd stopped on the way down. The narrow stream had grown a little wider since the rain, and the grass was a little greener. On their way again, they looked back and saw the stage coming at a trot. When they came to a place where the ground was level with the road on both sides, Martin brought the wagon train to a halt. "We'll let the stage go by," he said. "Up there it could be tricky."

The stage driver slowed his four horses to a walk and steered them off the road and around the wagons. He didn't stop, but nodded and said "Howdy." The shotgun messenger waved one hand.

"Got any idea where to camp for the night, Mart?" J.J. asked.

"Up there under that cliff was a good spot, but not now, not with two dead horses. We'll go on and see how far we get before dark."

"If anybody tries again to bushwhack us, they'll prob'ly be waitin' on top."

Grimly, Martin said only, "Yeah."

It rained. Lightning streaked down too close for comfort and thunder cracked like gunfire. But it lasted only a few minutes, just long enough to get everyone wet, then the storm clouds moved on over Florissant, then on to Pikes Peak. "It'll do this ever' day now," Longacre allowed. "Well, on second thought maybe it will and maybe it won't."

"If I was a bettin' man," said Jed Oaks, "you'd have to give me odds. Sure as hell, if you bet it's gonna rain it won't, and if you bet it won't it will."

There was no water for the horses at their campsite, but the teamsters had filled their canteens at Florissant, and they had coffee. A big fire soon had everyone dry and warm, but it also had Martin nervous. At dusk, he said, "Gents, a warm fire makes a feller feel good, but you know, it makes us all perfect targets. I'd feel better if you all scattered, got under your wagons or someplace where it's dark. It might be all for nothing, but . . ."

Longacre finished the thought for him, "It's better to be careful than dead."

"Yeah. We'll have to take turns standing guard again."

Sitting back against a pine tree, Martin wished his head would stop thumping. Damn headache was going to drive him crazy one day. When he thought he couldn't stand it anymore, he found J.J. rolled up in his blankets, and whispered, "It's me. Is there anything left in that bottle?"

"Sure, Mart," J.J. said, sitting up. "Here, help yourself."

"I'll pay you back when we get to town."

"If you do, all right, and if you don't, all right."

Again, Martin took the last watch, believing the first hint of daylight was the most dangerous time of day. While the men boiled coffee and fried pancakes from three-day-old batter, he walked off in all directions, nervous. Not until the horses were harnessed did he help himself to some lukewarm pancakes and coffee.

"Are we gonna do it like we done before, Mart?"

"Yeah, we'll scout ahead on each side of the road." Turning to Hugh Williams, who was driving the lead wagon, Martin said, "If you hear shooting, stop and get down. Be ready. If nothing happens, stop at the top of the pass and water the horses. It'll be an easy haul from there on."

Nothing happened. The wagons reached the top shortly before noon. Martin and J.J. continued riding parallel to the road, downhill now, while the horses were being unhitched and led to water. Down out of the timber and boulders, Martin turned his horse back to the road. He sat his saddle, eyes scanning the terrain uphill, until he was joined by J.J.

"Didn't even see a rabbit," J.J. said.

"Me either. Let's go back the way we came, but maybe stay a little farther from the road this time."

With the rifle under his right leg and his hand on the butt of his six-gun, Martin rode slowly, his eyes on distant rock formations, pines.

When he saw a puff of smoke on a high ridge he reacted immediately, pitching himself off the right side of his horse. The animal wasn't used to being dismounted from the off side, and it wasn't used to having a man fall practically under its feet. It shied sideways with a snort, then trotted away dragging the reins. Even before he hit the ground on his back, Martin heard the angry whine of a lead slug pass just over the top of the saddle. He rolled over twice, making a moving target of himself and trying to find something to hide behind. His rolling came to a stop beside a tall ponderosa with long roots above the rocky ground.

The sound of the rifle shot reached him before the next bullet slammed into the ground no more than four inches from his left shoulder. Scrambling desperately, he got behind the tree, flat on his belly, head down.

Damn. Those shots came from way out there, too far for a repeating rifle. He remembered that the stranger who'd shot their prisoner had a long-barreled gun. It was him, had to be.

The clatter of hooves on rocks brought Martin's head around. He waved frantically at J.J., yelling at him to go back. J.J. reined up, but cupped a hand behind an ear, letting Martin know he couldn't understand. Martin pointed toward the hidden rifleman, and again motioned toward the road. Another heavy slug knocked chips off the ponderosa just above Martin's head. J.J. got the message then. He turned his horse around and rode at a lope for the wagon road.

Lying with his face in the dirt, Martin tried to figure out what to do. He turned his head enough to see that his horse had trotted too far away for him to reach him. His Winchester was with the horse. The .44–40 repeating rifle would have been no help anyway. The shooter over there had a heavy-caliber long-range gun, probably a buffalo gun. Martin's Remington six-shooter would do nothing more than make a noise.

Chancing a look back, the wagon road was over a quarter of a mile behind him. Was that far enough to be safe from the long gun? Martin estimated the distance between the gun and the road at three-quarters of a mile. Some of those damned buffalo guns would shoot a mile.

Another slug punched a hole in the big root that protected Martin's head. The root jerked with the impact, but stopped the bullet. A minute later, another shot hit the ground so close rock fragments and dirt peppered Martin's face.

If this kept up, a bullet would find him. What, Martin wondered, could he do?

Yet another slug hit the root and jerked it away from Martin's head. Jumping up, Martin stood behind the tree, turned sideways to keep any part of his body from being exposed.

What was that gunsel over there trying to do? It wasn't robbery he had on his mind. No, what he wanted to do was to kill someone.

He wanted to kill Martin.

Chapter Nineteen

Why me? That was the next question to pop into Martin's mind. Because he was Ray Mossman's brother? To scare Ray Mossman out of the country, or at least into giving up his proposed laws? Or because Martin had made it known he was not only a Mossman, he was a fighting Mossman? Or all of this?

Next question: Why wait until now to shoot from ambush? There were better spots back there to shoot from. With that long gun, all the shooter had to do was pick a good spot, wait until Martin came along, aim, and fire.

While he was running it through his mind, another slug smacked into the tree. The gun was a single-shot, but if the shooter had a handful of cartridges lying handy on a rock he could reload in ten seconds.

Why did he wait until now? The answer came easily. The gunsel had a problem. He didn't know which side of the road Martin would ride on. On the way up the pass two days ago Martin had scouted the north side of the road. The shooter had to make a guess and he guessed Martin would scout the same side on the way back.

Martin was alive because he'd guessed wrong.

Once the man realized he'd guessed wrong, he'd had

to wait until the wagons went past, then get across to the south side and hurry like hell to get ahead again, all without being seen. So he'd gotten ahead of the wagons somehow, quickly picked a spot to shoot from, and found out he was almost too late. Martin had gone on downhill.

But then he got lucky. Or thought he did. Martin turned and started back to the top of the pass, still on the south side.

The shooter knew he wasn't in the best spot for sniping, but he couldn't move again without being seen, so he'd done the best he could.

He was a damned good shot with that buffalo gun, and he'd almost succeeded. He might succeed yet.

So Martin had it figured. At least he'd made some sense of it. But that didn't help him out of the jackpot he was in. If he moved one foot in any direction he'd be hit with a slug that would drop a buffalo, and the wagons were just standing up there on top of Wilkerson Pass going nowhere. The teamsters were probably ready, as ready as they could be, for a possible attack, but how long would they stay there? J.J. had seen that Martin was pinned down. Would he come to the rescue? How?

One thing was sure, this couldn't go on forever. Now it was a waiting game, and waiting was hell. Goddammit, something had to happen.

Though he knew it was an old, old trick that didn't fool anyone anymore, Martin took his hat off and held one edge and the crown where it would be seen by the sniper. He moved it up and down, back and forth. It didn't work. So you're too smart for that, are you, you son of a bitch? Then Martin got another idea. He put the hat on, drew his six-gun, and put his head and gun hand around the tree just long enough to snap four shots in the direction of the shooter.

At first, the shooter thought it was another hat trick, and by the time he knew better, Martin had fired four rounds and ducked back behind the tree. Not that it mattered. The pistol bullets fell far short.

But it did bring another useless shot from over there. Still another. *Whop*. Ten seconds later another *whop*. As big as the tree was, it shuddered, dropping pine needles, when those slugs hit it.

That jasper must have started with a full box of cartridges. How many of those big cartridges did a box hold?

What next? Wait until dark?

Then another rifle opened up. Rapid shots came from uphill. Someone was shooting as fast as he could lever in the cartridges. It had to be J.J., doing what he could. But he was wasting ammunition. Martin couldn't see him, but he figured that J.J. was behind a boulder.

The big gun boomed again over there. The bullet didn't come near Martin. The shooter was popping away at J.J. "Duck, J.J.," Martin whispered. Knowing it was useless, Martin exposed himself long enough to empty the Remington at the sniper. Stepping back, he started reloading with cartridges from his gunbelt. A heavy slug whined past the tree, and ten seconds later another.

While the sniper was shooting at Martin's tree, J.J. opened up again, firing six rapid shots. About ten seconds after the young cowboy stopped shooting, the big gun boomed in return.

Now Martin got the idea. Bullets from the repeating rifle and the six-gun were no threat to the sniper, but he knew they were coming his way, and that made him cautious. And they were irritating him, harrassing him.

"Keep it up, J.J.," Martin whispered, "but don't forget to duck."

The young cowboy kept it up, and when he had to

reload, Martin fired. The sniper returned the fire, but only while his targets were reloading.

Grinning to himself now, Martin knew the sniper was no soldier. If he'd been smart he'd have drawn a bead on one of the two, waited his chance, and then fired. He could have done that without any danger to himself. But instead, he was instinctively ducking when shots were aimed his way and returning the fire after the shots ceased. He was getting frustrated. He was being foolish.

Again, the repeating rifle blasted away, one, two, three, four shots. "Don't get too bold, J.J.," Martin whispered. Six-gun ready, he waited for the return fire, planning to pump more pistol bullets toward the sniper. But there was no return fire.

Goddamn. The sniper finally got wise. He was playing it smart now, waiting until one of his targets couldn't contain his curiosity and took a look.

It was a waiting game again.

Then J.J. yelled, "Hey, Mart. You still there?"

"Yeah, I'm here," Martin yelled back.

"I think he's gone."

"Stay down. Don't take any chances."

"No, he's makin' tracks. I seen 'im lopin' over that ridge, packin' that smoke pole of his."

"You sure?"

"Sure enough. I'm comin' over."

Martin stepped far enough away from the ponderosa to get a clear view of the ridge. He kept his six-gun ready, eye level, knowing he wouldn't hit the sniper, but hoping his shots would cause him to shoot with haste.

The young cowboy walked up, grinning. "I know we didn't hit 'im at that distance, but we scared the hound-dog shit out of 'im."

Grinning too, Martin said, "We didn't scare him as much as he scared me."

"What in hell was he shootin', anyhow, a cannon?"

"Probably a buffalo gun, a fifty-caliber."

"Yeah, that's what it had to be. Damn, I thought it was gonna shoot right through that big rock I was hidin' behind. He must've shot up all his ca'tridges. He must've been scared somebody'd sneak up behind 'im."

"I hope to see that yahoo again somewhere."

"Yeah, someplace within shortgun range."

"Well," Martin said, "let's get the wagons moving again, see if we can finish this trip without somebody else blasting at us."

It was after dark when the wagons were pulled up to Hugh Williams's livery pens. Rather than spend half the night unloading by lanternlight, they parked the wagons there. The Williams boys came up, and promised to guard everything. Soon Ray Mossman and his competitor Pritchard showed up too. Pritchard went to get the sheriff, and Martin and J.J. had to tell their story again.

Sheriff Little's round smooth face scowled. "Even though you left the body at Florissant, I'd judge from what you said that the killing took place in my jurisdiction."

"The county line is just this side of Florissant," Ray Mossman allowed.

"Well, that sure puts me in a bind. I've got to leave here first thing in the morning and ride up to Buckskin and try to keep the citizens up there from hanging some cattle thieves. I got word they caught some rustlers in the act and they're in no mood to wait for a trial. I sure do need a deputy."

Ray Mossman said, "If the voters give their approval

you'll soon have one. The election is only two days away, you know. Surely, you'll be back before then."

"I expect to, but I don't know what I'm riding into up there."

J.J. wanted Martin to have supper with him at the Denver Steak House and then a few drinks at the Silver Tip Gaming Palace, but Ray said Mary was waiting supper for them at the ranch.

"I'll see you later, J.J.," Martin said. "We'll hoist a few."

The young cowboy was so disappointed his features fell into a puddle at the bottom of his face. Martin looked at Ray and asked, "Does Mary have supper cooked or anything? I would sort of like to stay in town for a while."

"She's waiting, Mart. She's expecting you."

Martin looked at J.J. and shook his head sadly. He said nothing more, but he couldn't help thinking, *That's one reason I never wanted to get married. A married man can't go where he wants or do what he wants.*

They left the Mossman horses at the livery pens and rode horseback to the ranch. Mary was waiting, two steaks ready to drop into a hot skillet for searing, beans and potatoes kept warm on the back of the stove. She'd fed the two boys and the hired hand earlier, but Joshua sat at the table with them, full of questions, until his mother sent him upstairs.

"Why can't I stay up? Bennie's too little but I'm old enough."

"Don't argue, Joshua. Do as you're told. Read the storybook that came in the mail yesterday. And read to Benjamin."

"Aww, Bennie don't wanta be read to."

"Doesn't want to, not don't wanta."

"Aww."

While the steaks sizzled, Ray told Mary about the new shooting. Mary sat with her elbows on the table and her chin in her hands, scowling. "Another killing. Another . . ." She shrugged, stood and went to the stove.

"It wasn't Martin's fault, Mary," Ray said. "He was strictly on the defensive."

"Yes, but . . . two trips and two men killed and at least two wounded, and . . ." Again she shrugged and said no more. But silently, Martin finished her statement.

Two killings and Martin was the cause of both of them. Many trips have been made over the pass with no one killed until Martin came along. Martin can't stay out of trouble. Martin is a bad influence on the boys.

Martin ate silently, afraid to talk, afraid he'd say something he'd regret later. After his meal, he excused himself and went outside where he could smoke.

Durn women. That was another reason he'd never wanted a wife. Always finding fault. Always blaming a man for everything that went wrong. Durn women.

Durn headache. Martin had a notion to get on a horse and go to town. Have a couple of drinks with J.J. They had stories to tell, and there would be plenty of listeners. Get rid of the headache. So Mary wouldn't approve. He wasn't married to her and he didn't have to dance to her tune.

But, aw hell, she was his brother's wife and he was staying in their home, and he wasn't going to be here much longer anyway. Time to move on.

Ray Mossman had to wait on customers in the Mossman Mercantile, so Martin and the hired clerk had to unload the wagons. It was noon when they finished, and Ray bought Martin's noon meal at the Vega Cafe. After they'd finished eating, Martin smoked and again said he believed he'd saddle his horse, pack his saddlebags, and ride on.

Again, Ray talked him out of it. "Stick around, Mart. Tomorrow's election day. History is going to be made tomorrow. Things are going to get darned interesting around here."

"Aw, it's none of my business. I can't vote here." Martin chuckled dryly. "Come to think of it, I can't vote anywhere."

"That's what I mean, Mart. You don't stay in one place long enough to establish residency. You can't vote. You're not even a full-fledged citizen."

"Aw . . ."

"Stick around. Things might get exciting."

Chapter Twenty

Martin didn't want to go back to the ranch yet. Ray's harness horses were unhitched and tied to the side of the wagons in the alley. They'd keep awhile. Besides, when he and his brother came out of the restaurant, he spotted the cowboy J.J. a block ahead on the sidewalk.

"I'll take the horses and wagons back to the ranch pretty soon, Ray. Right now I see J.J. up there and we've got things to talk about."

"Sure, Mart. Be careful."

Walking fast, Martin tried to catch up to the young cowboy, but J.J. ducked into the Silver Tip Gaming Palace. Martin went in two minutes behind him. Business was good for that time of day, but the saloon wasn't crowded. J.J. stood alone at one end of the long mahogany bar with one boot on the brass rail under it. He was sipping beer from a thick glass mug when he saw Martin coming.

"Well, by god, lookee here. They let anybody in here, don't they." He was smiling, but his eyes weren't quite in focus.

"Yeah." Martin grinned. "Even ugly mugs like mine."

"Well, step up here and let me buy you one." J.J. was slurring his words and his smile was rubbery.

"My turn to buy, J.J. Looks like you've been at it a while."

"Most of the night. Hell, Mart, when I started tellin' ever'body about ever'thing my money wasn't no good. They just kept settin' booze in front of me."

"Think you can stand another? I don't want to see you fall on your ass, but I owe you about a dozen. Maybe two dozen."

"I ain't gonna fall on my ass. I'm gonna have a drink with you and then I'm gonna go back to that fleatrap hotel and sleep like a dead man. No, not like a dead man, like a, like a drunk man."

"We've seen enough dead men. Is the beer cold?"

"Ha! Is hoss piss cold?" He shoved the beer aside. "I feel like somebody done shit in my mouth an' I thought a beer would help, but it don't. A shot of whiskey'd please my pa-pal-palate a lot better."

Motioning to the barman, Martin said, "Two shots of whiskey, good whiskey, bourbon whiskey."

"A buck," the barman said, looking at Martin's disfigured face.

"A buck? Why, thash, thash . . ."

"It's all right," Martin said. "I'll pay for it."

"It oughta be damned good—damned good stuff."

The whiskey was good. Martin sipped his, hoping he didn't carry the smell of it back to the Mossman ranch. "I take it," he said, "this isn't the usual workingman's saloon." His gaze took in the chandeliers, the floral walls, the clean glasses and imported liquor bottles behind the bar.

"Naw. The bosses of the goddamn world drink in here, but some of us workin' stiffs come in here once in a while just to see how the high mucky-mucks live. A gent name of Vance owns the place. He's the stud duck in here."

"I've met him. I don't know what to make of him."

J.J. took a small sip and put the shot glass down. "He keeps it peaceable. Him and his two hired goons."

"I've seen them too."

"Sh—say, Mart, I hear there's gonna be an election tomorra, and your brother Ray is right square in the middle of it."

"Yeah, he's on the county board."

"Whatta they wanta do, shut down the saloons?"

"Naw, I don't think so. They just don't want this town to be like Cimarron, or El Paso, or the Sierra Nevadas."

J.J. picked up his shot glass, put it down again. "Well, 'slong as they don't shut 'em down, I don't care. I been in s'loons where if you accidentally bumped into somebody they'd cut your throat or put a bullet in you."

"That's what they want to stop."

"An' I been in towns where if you stepped outside with booze on your breath, some lawdog'd slam you in the hoosegow, and some jackass thief of a judge'd fine you for ever'thing you got in your pockets." J.J. had taken only a small sip of his whiskey, and his speech was clearing up.

"I don't think Ray and the county board would stand for that either."

"And I been in towns where there wasn't no whores. A man's gotta get his socks washed once in a while. They wanta shut down the whorehouses?"

"Just the cribs, I think. And they want the whores that stay to be looked at by a doctor, try to keep out the diseases."

"I heard about the clap. They say it makes your pecker stick to your blankets, and hurts like hell when you pee."

"That's what they want to keep out."

"Well, I ain't been to them cribs no how. I don't wanta get the clap or the Chinese crud or any of that stuff."

Taking another sip of his whiskey, Martin said, "There's a house over on the south side, on the edge of town, a big house, whitewashed and all. That wouldn't be a whorehouse, would it?"

"Yep. Sis Able runs it, and she keeps them girls clean and behavin' theirselfs. I heard she sends 'em to the doctor ever' week."

"I'll bet it costs a week's pay."

"And then some. I been there twice, and both times I think I got my money's worth. Your, uh, the county board don't wanta shut down Sis Able, do they?"

"I don't think so. They just want to get rid of the cribs."

The conversation was interrupted—in a pleasant way. "Gentlemen." The dandy named Vance was standing behind them, smiling, thumbs hooked in the pockets of his brocaded vest. "I've been hearing stories about you two. Why, you're almost a legend in your own time. May I have the pleasure of buying you both a drink of good Scotch whiskey?"

Half turning, Martin quickly spotted the husky pug and the weasellike gunslinger. They were hanging back, but watching. "Why, uh, sure, I'll take a drink on the house."

"Fine. How about you, my good man?"

J.J. was hesitant. "Well, uh, I sure do appreciate the offer, Mr. Vance, but I'm, uh, tryin' to get my head on straight again. I'm thinkin' about goin' to the hotel and sleepin' till I'm sober."

Smiling widely, his thin mustache stretched across his upper lip, the dandy said, "That's very commendable. Only a fool keeps on drinking when he's had enough. You gentlemen are the kind of clientele I like." He motioned to the barman. "Scotch for my friend here."

Martin finished the bourbon in one gulp and reached for the shot glass of Scotch. Maybe he'd buy some peppermint candy to cover the booze on his breath.

"Mr. Mossman, your, uh, your brother must be excited about the election tomorrow. Are you expecting a large turnout of voters?"

"I don't know," Martin said. "I just flat don't know."

"Well, let's hope the majority rules. That's what democracy is all about, eh?"

Martin downed the Scotch. It was smooth and pleasing, but he decided he liked bourbon better. "That's what I hear."

"You, uh, are you going to be there, at the polling place?"

Shrugging, Martin said, "I don't know. I can't vote in this county, so I doubt I'll be there."

"I expect you'll be busy at the ranch, eh? Haying season is upon us, and the Mossman Ranch has the biggest hay-growing operation in the county."

"Well, I'm not much of a farmer. Down south, where I've worked mostly, they don't feed hay."

"I think . . ." And then the smile slipped. "I would suggest that the ranch would be a good place to be—for a nonvoter." Then the smile was back. "What I mean is, a nonvoter could get in the way, confuse things, don't you think?"

Confused was what Martin was now. He didn't know what to say, so he said nothing. The dandy's smile was gone again.

"Believe me, Mossman, you would accomplish nothing by being there. Absolutely nothing." Smiling again, he said, "Have a good day, gentlemen," and he turned on his heels and left.

For two or three seconds, the pug and the gunslinger

stayed and shot mean hard looks at Martin, then they followed their boss.

"Well, I'll be gone to hell," J.J. said, looking sober now. "Whatta you reckon he meant by that?"

"If I didn't know better," Martin said, "I'd take that as a threat."

"It could be. It sure could be. Me, I'm gonna catch some shuteye, eat a big meal, drink a pot of coffee, and get the taste of shit out of my mouth. Then maybe I can think straight."

"Are you going back to the Flying W?"

"Soon's I'm sober. I already told the boss my ass fits a saddle just fine and I ain't gonna ride no hay rake. I could be out of a job."

"Me too." Martin grinned a lopsided grin. "But then, hell, I wasn't looking for a job when I came here."

Ray told his clerk to mind the store while he helped Martin chain one wagon to the back of the other, tie four horses by their halters to the back of the rear wagon, and hitch four horses to the first one. When Martin turned the outfit into the ranch yard, the two boys were chasing each other near the kitchen door. They started to go over to the barn to meet their uncle.

"No, Bennie, you stay here," Joshua said. "You're too little." Then he hollered, "Hi, Uncle Mart. I'll help you unhitch."

Martin whoaed the team and climbed down from the wagon. "Be sure to talk to the horses, Josh. They've got blinders on the bridles, you know, and they can't see you. Let them know it's you behind them."

"I know how to do it, Uncle Mart. Whoa, boys, whoa."

He unhooked the tug chains from the singletrees of the lead team. Martin unhitched the wheel team, started stripping off the harnes.

"I've got something for you, Josh. On the seat of the first wagon."

"What is it?"

"Look and see."

The boy climbed up into the wagon, using a wheel hub as a step. "Candy. Peppermint. Boy."

"Share it with your brother." Martin didn't mention the peppermint he'd kept in his pockets.

Mary wasn't pleased when Martin went into the house. "I don't let them eat between meals. Candy is a treat that they get once in a while after dinner."

Feeling criticized, Martin said, "I'll wait outside for Ray." At the corrals, he crossed his arms on a top rail, rested his chin on his arms, and muttered under his breath, "Durn women."

Talk at supper was about the election. The polling place was to be the second floor of the Mossman store. It could be reached by an outside staircase or by an inside staircase, but Ray said the stairs inside would be closed to the public. "We painted a big sign on a strip of canvas so everyone will know where to vote," he said. "The poll opens at seven o'clock. We picked two elderly men who've lived in this territory for a long time to be the judges and to count the ballots. Coming over, Mart?"

"Oh, I'll probably mosey over that way some time tomorrow just out of curiosity. I've got to reset the shoes on my ol' pony's forefeet and get ready to travel."

"Come and watch civilization at work. It will be interesting."

Outside, rolling a smoke, Martin silently agreed. Remembering a veiled threat from a dandy at the Silver Tip Gaming Palace, he thought out loud, "Yeah, it could be interesting."

Chapter Twenty-one

Ray walked to the store that morning. Martin caught his brown horse, tied him to a corral post, and pried the iron shoes off the forefeet. The two kids sat on the ground nearby and watched. Setting a foot down, Martin went to an anvil just inside the barn and pounded the shoes flat again. Then he went back and picked up the left forefoot. The horse jerked his foot, jerking Martin.

Joshua said, "He's a goshdarn s—"

"Don't say that," Martin interrupted. "I told you I don't like to hear kids cuss."

"But I wasn't gonna cuss. I was gonna say son of a buck. That ain't a bad word, is it?"

"Some folks might think so." He had the hoof between his knees, trimming the outer wall with a pair of nippers.

"That's like your fingernails, ain't it, Uncle Martin. That's what Papa said."

"Yep. It grows and grows, and if you don't trim it now and then it'll grow until it breaks off."

"Indians don't trim their horses' feet, do they?"

"Naw. They don't have the tools."

"Are you gonna nail the old shoes back on?"

"Yep. They've got some wear left on them."

Standing, the boy said, "We got some nails made for horseshoes. I'll get some."

Martin let the foot down and straightened his back. "Bennie, you don't talk much, do you."

The boy was still sitting on the ground, leaning against a corral post. He shook his head. "Huh-uh."

"Well, I'll tell you something, Benjamin, nobody ever learned anything by talking." Martin grinned. "You just keep on listening."

Ray didn't come home for the noon meal, but Mary set out a good meal for the boys, Martin, and the hired man Luke. "Momma," Joshua said, "is son of a buck a bad word?"

Mary shot a glance at Martin and asked, "Now where did you hear that?"

"I don't know. Someplace."

Martin was relieved.

After eating, Luke went off to a hay meadow, wearing high rubber boots and carrying a long-handled shovel over his shoulder. Joshua followed Martin to the corrals and watched while Martin saddled his horse.

"What's your horse's name, Uncle Martin?"

"The feller I bought him from called him Crackers, but I call him Partner. I call most horses Partner."

"Horses don't know their names anyhow."

"No, but horses on a big cow outfit have to have names so the men will know which horses are being talked about."

"Oh. Well, we name all our horses."

The town of Vega was alive. There was more horseback and wagon traffic on First Street, and more pedestrians on the plankwalk. Riding down the street, Martin couldn't help noticing that the busiest places in town were the saloons. This was election day.

But while most of the men coming out of the saloons were laughing, boisterous, some of the men on the street wore tight, hard expressions. Inside the Mossman Mercantile, Ray Mossman was so angry he was snapping his words, his face was red, and when he walked he stomped.

"I can tell," Martin said, "that something's eating on you."

"It sure as hell is. Why . . . why . . . this is the worst outrage I've ever seen." Ray slammed a sack of coffee down on the counter so hard the sack split, spilling coffee beans.

"What? What's going on?"

"Just you go out there and take a look. Why, why, those bullies won't let folks vote. They . . . they're threatening anyone who tries to climb the stairs to the polling place."

"Where's the sheriff?"

"He's not back from Buckskin or wherever he went. There's no law. Those bullies are running roughshod over the citizens."

"Who is?"

"The bullies from the saloons. They don't want the measures to pass, and they are threatening everybody who doesn't agree with them."

"That's a hell of a note."

"I'm going to get the county board together and call it off. We'll have to reschedule the election for a later date."

Shaking his head, Martin allowed, "That's a damned shame."

"It is indeed. I'm sure there's something in the state statutes that gives us authority to void an election if it was obviously not conducted in a fair manner."

"If there isn't, there ought to be. Think I'll go outside and take a look."

"Be careful, Martin. Don't get into a ruckus on my account."

"I won't. It's none of my business. I'm just curious, that's all."

Outrage? It was bullyboy tactics of the worst kind. It was unabashed brutality. And right out in plain sight. There were three of them, armed with six-guns and clubs, standing on the deck at the top of the stairs in front of the door under the POLLING PLACE sign. They stopped and questioned everyone who came up, and when they didn't like the answers, they roughly shoved the would-be voters down the stairs.

Martin leaned against a corner of the mercantile building, rolled a smoke, and watched. Two voters who rounded the corner stopped when they saw the toughs at the top of the stairs. They talked in low tones with each other, then turned and went back onto the street. Another stopped at the foot of the stairs, looked up, hesitated as if trying to decide what to do, then climbed the steps. At the top, his way was blocked by a husky man in a derby hat, a stub of a cigar in his mouth, and a billy club in his hand. The voter tried to push past him, but was clubbed over the head and shoved so hard he fell backward and slid halfway down the stairs on his back. He lay there, head below his feet, only half conscious.

Martin ground his cigarette butt into the dirt with a boot heel, then went over and spoke to the man. "Are you hurt, mister? Want some help?"

The man's hat had rolled to the ground, leaving his nearly bald head bare. He groaned, and rubbed the spot on his head where he'd been hit.

"Can you stand? Let me help you." Martin got his hands under the man's shoulders and helped him to his feet. The man swayed unsteadily. "Let me help you down the stairs. Here, put your arm over my shoulder. Watch your feet, now."

On the ground, the voter managed to straighten to his full height. He was as tall as Martin. "You . . . ?" Faded eyes in a wrinkled face focused on Martin's scar.

"I'm ugly, but I'm not one of them. Can you walk?" Martin picked up the man's hat and handed it to him.

"Uh, yeah, uh, thanks, mister." He walked away on rubbery legs.

Martin looked up the stairs at the tough who stood legs apart, hands on hips, silently daring Martin to try to come up. Martin wondered if he could draw the Remington and outshoot the bully. He looked to be more of a club man or a knife man than a gunman. But there were three of them, all watching Martin, ready.

For a few seconds, Martin stood there, trying to think of a way to coax that cigar-chomping gunsel to come down and fight one-on-one. Finally, he said, "Hey, you. You with the billy club. Wanta come down here and try that?"

Around the stub of cigar, the pug sneered, "Why don't you come up here, shitface."

"I thought you might want to fight fair, for the first time in your sorry life."

"Where I come from, there ain't no fair."

"You scared? You afraid to fight man-on-man?"

"I ain't scairt of you."

"Yeah, you're yellow. You've got a yellow streak up your back."

The other two toughs stood beside the cigar-chomper, hands on gun butts. Now a growing sick fear was beginning to settle in Martin's stomach. He might have talked too much. He couldn't outshoot the three of them. If shooting started he'd be killed on the spot. But he'd be damned if he'd back down. His back stiffened. Damned if he would. "Well, you sorry pile of horseshit, are you coming down?"

The tough spat out the cigar and took a step down. One of the other two said something to him, and he stopped. "Why don't you come up here, you deformed son of a bitch, and let's see if you're as tough as you are ugly."

Two would-be voters had come up behind Martin, stopped, looked, listened, then turned and walked away. The bully wasn't coming down. He wasn't about to fight one-on-one. And it would have been suicide for Martin to climb the stairs.

For a long moment, he tried to outstare the three. Then an idea popped into his mind.

"You want me to come up there, huh? Well, maybe, just by God maybe I will."

Chapter Twenty-two

Martin backed to the corner of the clapboard building, then turned and walked to the front of the store. He wished he had some help. Was J.J. still in town? No, this wasn't the young cowboy's fight. Come to think of it, it wasn't Martin's fight either. So the county board wanted to have a special election and some saloon toughs were spoiling it. The world was full of bullies, and he couldn't fight all of them. The election was the county board's affair, not his.

Except that one of the board members was his brother. There was that.

Well, hell, he'd been in fights for a lot less.

"Say, Ray," he said as he approached the long counter inside the store, "suppose the voters didn't want to get up to the polling place by climbing the outside stairs, could they use the stairs in the back room?"

Ray Mossman was leaning over the counter, totaling some figures on a sheet of paper. He looked up thoughtfully. "Why, yeah. Sure. Why didn't I think of that? Next time somebody complains about what's going on outside, I'll send them up from the inside."

"That would save some sore heads."

"I've got the door locked at the head of the stairs. I'll go up right now and unlock it."

"I'll go with you, just out of curiosity."

Upstairs, Ray unlocked one door, went through a storage room, and unlocked another door. Martin followed him. In a small room, two men, both gray-haired and whiskered, sat at a table with a ballot box between them. Another table was a place for marking ballots. Ray spoke to the two. "Is everything peaceful in here?"

"In here, yeah, but not out there."

"I know. I'm going to send voters up here from inside, bypass those bullies."

"If you don't, we might as well go home." The elderly gent fingered a stack of folded sheets of paper. "Ain't had more'n twenty-thirty voters all day, and some of them couldn't read or write. I had to show 'em how to write yes or no."

Checking his pocket watch, Ray said, "We've still got five hours. I'm going down on the street and I'm going to tell everyone I see to come in the store to vote."

"When folks see what's goin' on out there, some of 'em will change their minds and vote yes."

"If we can just get them in here, we'll win this thing yet." Ray turned to leave.

Martin said, "Ray, a while ago you were madder than I've ever seen you. Are you fighting mad?"

After staring hard at his brother a moment, Ray answered, "Yes. What have you got in mind?"

"I've got an idea. It might be a dumb idea. You men, you get ready to hit the floor; there might be some shooting."

"Well, now, Mart, I'd rather not have any shooting."

Martin absorbed that, then shrugged with resignation. "You'll let them get by with it, then." He turned toward the connecting door. Nothing was more useless than trying to help a man who wouldn't help himself, not even his brother.

"No, now, wait, Mart. What have you got in mind?"

"Well . . ." Martin paused, then said, "Maybe . . . if it works the way I hope it will, there won't be a shot fired."

"What do you propose?"

"Well, it'll work like this, you open the door, then get ready to slam it shut when I tell you to. We ought to get at least one of them in here."

"What would we do with one of them?"

"Tell him we're gonna blow his damned head off if his partners don't get away from those stairs."

Ray thought it over, looked at the two election judges with a question on his face. The two gents looked at each other.

"I'm game."

"Me too."

"All right," Martin said, stepping over to the outer door. "Get ready." Ray took hold of the door handle, looked at Martin for a signal. "All right, open it."

Ray yanked open the door.

Martin moved fast. The three gunsels were watching two would-be voters at the foot of the stairs, and before they knew what was happening, Martin was behind the derby-hatted one, had an arm around his throat, had him turned half-around so he was facing his partners, had the Remington shoved into the small of his back.

"Wha . . . ?" was all the tough got out.

Hissing, deadly venom in his voice, Martin said, "Don't move a muscle. Move and I'll blow your spine in two."

The other two had spun on their heels, hands on their guns.

A strangling sound came from the tough. "Wha . . . ?"

"Tell your pals to throw their guns over the rail. Do it, goddamn it, or they'll have to bury you."

The other two stood still, surprised, not knowing what to do.

"Tell them," Martin hissed.

Another strangling noise.

Martin backed toward the door, dragging the gunsel backward with an arm around his throat. "We're going inside. If your pards shoot through the door, they'll hit you. If they don't hit you, I will. Get it?"

"Awwk. Wha . . . ?"

Looking through slitted eyes at the other two, Martin hissed, "Get down those stairs. Get away from this building. If you don't, this son of a bitch is dead. Get it?"

The two looked at each other.

"Git," Martin barked. "Right now."

They hesitated two seconds, then slowly, watching Martin, moved toward the steps. The first one took a few steps down. The other followed. Martin backed through the door. "Slam it, Ray." The door was slammed shut. "Get back. Get away from the door."

Expecting bullets to come tearing through the door, Martin waited, keeping the bully in front of him for a shield. "Better tell your pards not to shoot."

In a strangling voice, the tough yelled, "Don't shoot. For Christ's sake, don't shoot."

Martin waited a long moment. Nothing happened. The only sound was the strangling noises coming from the tough. Then Martin said, "Ray, get his gun."

Gingerly, carefully, Ray lifted the six-gun out of the tough's holster. Then Martin roughly threw the man down, kicked him in the side. The tough yelped in pain. Martin grabbed the two-foot-long club the man had dropped and clubbed him over the head, knocking the derby hat off.

"My god, Mart . . ."

"Did you see what he was doing to men who tried to come up here and vote?"

"Yes, I . . . I saw it."

"Do you feel sorry for him?"

"Why no, I, uh, it's just not the, uh, way . . ."

"Not the way civilized men do it, huh?"

"No. There are, uh, laws that deal with his kind."

The two elderly judges were standing behind the table. One said, "Hit the son of a bitch again. In my time we hung the likes of him."

"Think the men in town will hang him?"

"No," Ray said. "No, I can't allow that."

"What will you allow?"

"We have a jail. It's not a very good one, but we can lock him up and let the sheriff deal with him."

"All right. You've got his gun. Let's go." To the man on the floor, Martin barked, "Get up. Get your sorry ass up from there. Ray, get a piece of rope and tie his hands. You know how to tie a knot."

The three of them stomped down the stairs. Martin had a tight hold on the gunsel's shirt collar and the Remington at the back of his head. The prisoner's hands were tied. "If I was you, mister, I'd be damned careful, make no sudden moves. This pistol is on full cock and it only takes a twitch of my finger to blow your head off." The man was silent.

Downstairs, Martin said, "Have you got a better gun, Ray? A shotgun?"

"Well, yeah."

"Get it. Load it. Walk behind me, watch for anybody who might be dangerous. And try to look mean."

They went down the middle of First Street that way, Martin with the Remington to the prisoner's head, Ray walking behind, watching behind, walking backward at times, shotgun ready. Men in buggies and wagons whoaed their horses and gawked. Men on horseback reined up. Pedestrians stood like statues, trying to guess what was happening.

The Prairie County jail was two blocks away. It was a one-room log shack with iron bars in the only window, a plank roof covered with tarpaper, and a heavy plank door. The door was wide open. A big padlock in a hasp was wide open.

Martin shoved the prisoner inside, shut the door on its squeaky iron hinges and snapped the lock shut. "If we're lucky," he said, "nobody's got a key for this."

Stepping back, looking the building over, Martin shook his head. "Within two hours after dark, his pals will have him out of there."

But he was pleased to see that Ray had both hammers cocked on the double-barreled shotgun. "You can let the hammers down now, Ray. I think the danger is over."

"Whew," Ray said.

"You did fine, Ray. It took both of us to get those thugs out of the way and get this one in jail."

"I, uh, to tell the truth, Mart, I was scared."

"Hell, Ray." Martin grinned. "It's no disgrace to get scared. What's important is you watched my back. You were ready to fight, and you did what had to be done. Hell, you'll make a soldier yet."

With a weak grin, Ray said, "A soldier I'm not and don't want to be. I just want to be a businessman and raise a family."

"Well, because of your help, folks in your county can vote now."

"Yeah, Martin"—Ray had some pride in his voice—"you and I, we did it, didn't we."

Chapter Twenty-three

A lot of questions were asked of the two brothers on their way back to the store. Being an elected official, Ray stopped and answered, smiled, and shook hands. He handed the shotgun to Martin, who went on back to the polling place and climbed the outside stairs. In the room, he found the two judges explaining to three voters that all they had to do was write yes or no on the two-inch squares of paper, fold the paper, and push it through a slot in the ballot box. The voters had to answer only three questions: their names, which the judges added to a list, how long had they lived in Prairie County, and were they twenty-one.

This brought a cackle from one of the gray-haired judges. "By dang, you're older'n me, Dick, and I voted for Abraham Lincoln."

"Say, Mossman, what'd you do with that feller? Shoot 'im?"

"Naw. Locked him up in that excuse for a jail."

"Ha! Any kid could bust out'n there."

Martin only shrugged.

Two more men came in to vote, answered the questions, and went to the table to mark their ballots. While

Martin pretended he wasn't watching, both men slipped two-inch squares of paper out of their shirt pockets, marked them along with the squares the judges had given them, and stuffed them all in the ballot box. They left looking as innocent as Sunday-school children.

"I guess you gentlemen know everybody in the county," Martin said.

"Purt' near ever'body's that's been here very long, and I got a good eye for faces, and nodamnbody's gonna vote twice."

"Do you recognize all the names?"

"Purt' near."

"But not all of them?"

Another cackle. "There's a few things that even I don't know. Not many, mind you, but a few."

With a lopsided grin, Martin said, "Then I could vote."

"If you claim to be a resident of the county. Are you?"

"Naw, and I don't plan to be."

The polls closed at seven o'clock. The two judges, Ray Mossman, Commissioner Isaac Clausen, owner of the butcher shop, and two ranchers made up the official board of canvassers. It didn't take long to count the ballots. Ray was glum, so glum that he counted them again.

"Forty-eight nos and thirty-six yeses. It comes out the same no matter how many times I count them."

While Ray was counting ballots for the second time, the two judges were counting the names on their lists and comparing figures. "Wait just a goshdamn minute, here. If I can add right, that comes to, uh, eighty-four ballots."

"Correct," Martin said.

"Then how come we got only seventy-six names on these lists?"

"What? Let me see." Checking off each name on the lists with a lead pencil, Ray counted. "Well, by George, that proves it. There was some ballot-box stuffing here."

Isaac Clausen, bald, plump, chin whiskers, said, "We're gonna have to register voters, Raymond, and have ballots printed. It's too easy to cheat this way."

Ray was walking in a circle, face red, stomping. He stopped and faced everyone, hands out in front of him, palms up. "I know, I know, this is not the way to do it, but what else could we do with the money we have? If these ordinances had passed, we'd soon have enough revenue to do things the right way."

He resumed walking in a circle, scowling, hands shoved deep inside his pockets. Then he stopped and faced everyone again. "It's not hopeless. We'll void the election and try again in a few months. Next time, by George, we'll do it right if I have to pay for it myself."

"I b'lieve the state law says only a judge can declare an election void."

"Then we'll get the district judge over here and let him see these lists himself. Let him listen to people who were scared away from the polling place. Even beaten because they wanted to vote."

One of the ranchers, thin, hipless, pant legs stuffed into high-top boots, said, "The judge'll insist that we register all voters long before the next election, and check their names when they come in to vote. Our county clerk's already got as much work as he can handle."

"I'll pay another clerk out of my own pocket," Ray said. "This election was a fraud, and we can't let it go unchallenged."

"You're right." Isaac Clausen pulled at his chin whiskers. "The judge can't help but declare this election unvalid. I was thinkin', if the yeses had won, the nos would've bellyached to the judge."

Ray hooked his thumbs inside his belt. "That's what

we'll do, then. I'll write a letter to the judge tonight and get it on the mail coach tomorrow. The sooner we get this resolved, the better."

"Meantime," said the rancher, "there's a crowd of folks outside that want to know how it all comes out."

With a resigned shrug, Ray said, "I'll have to go down and explain it to them."

"I'll go with you," Clausen said.

Supper at the Mossman Ranch was quiet. Even Joshua, sensing that no one wanted to talk, asked fewer questions. But Martin was puzzled about something, and he had to ask, "Ray, you were elected. What kind of an election did you have then?"

"The same. But no one cared much and no one complained."

Ray told his wife about bullies keeping voters away, but he didn't say how he and his brother had handled the problem.

"That reminds me," Ray said suddenly. "I forgot. I have to feed the prisoner."

"Prisoner?" Mary asked.

"Yeah, we, uh, Martin and I arrested one of the bullies."

"But you're not supposed to arrest anyone."

"Well, the sheriff was out of town, and someone had to."

"But that's not one of your duties. We pay an officer of the law to do that."

"Mary"—Ray held his wife's gaze without wavering—"there are times when we have to do something we'd rather not do. That's the way it is."

She said no more, but she shook her head to let everyone in the kitchen know she didn't approve. And Martin wondered whether she blamed him.

He had to leave, drift on, before she got to hating him.

But Mary did fix a thick beef sandwich for the prisoner, and Martin pumped a jug of water for him. Horseback, the two brothers rode to town, to the jail. "Well," Ray said, when they saw the jail door wide open, "we might as well have stayed at home."

"I'm not surprised," Martin said, dismounting. "That feller has pals." He examined the door long enough to see the lock was still shut, but the hasp had been pried off. "All it took was a crowbar."

"No doubt he has pals," Ray said, sitting his horse. "And something else is obvious."

Martin guessed what his brother was about to say, but he asked anyway. "What?"

"Those hoodlums aren't from around here. They were hired."

"You've never seen them before?"

"No, and I would have if they'd been here long."

"Well, we both know that somebody is working to beat you and everything you stand for, somebody who doesn't want to be known."

"And it's someone who will stop at nothing, not even murder."

"You'll have to figure out who he is. Or they are. Me, none of this is my concern, and it's time I moved on."

They turned their horses around and rode back toward the ranch. "Don't leave, Mart. Stake a claim, get some roots down, be a part of the democratic process." Ray chuckled. "I sound like a nagging woman, don't I."

"Well . . ."

"I won't mention it again. I promise. But I wish you would."

They rode silently awhile, then Ray said, "Aside from your own good, Mart, I wish you'd stay awhile for me, for my family." Before Martin could comment on that, Ray continued, "This whole thing is . . . whoever hired them wants to stop the political process. First, he, or they, tried to ruin me financially. And now this."

"Yeah. He thinks ruining your business would force you to leave the territory."

"That's what he's thinking. Without me, he would have his way."

They rode silently a moment, then Ray added, "What worries me the most, though, is because attacks up there on the pass failed he is now resorting to other measures. I'll take my risks, but I don't want to put Mary and the boys in danger. We really need you."

"How would Mary feel about that?"

"She hates violence and she has a strong distaste for violent men. But Mary is sensible. She's reasonable. And she's no coward. You could easily get that impression, I know, but I've lived with her a long time, and I know she's no coward and she's no quitter."

"Well, you for sure know her better than I do."

"So what do you say? Will you stick around awhile?"

"It could take a long time, Ray, to hold another election and resolve this thing. I can't just loaf, and if I helped with the haying I'd be away from the house most of the day."

"Maybe it won't take so long. If we could find out who's behind all the violence . . . I haven't tried to find out yet. I'll start asking questions. This is a small county, population-wise, and word gets around. If I ask enough questions I'll learn something. And Sheriff Little will question folks. With his authority he'll surely learn something, and he has the power to make arrests."

They rode silently again. Martin didn't want to stay. He had no wish whatever to be a bodyguard. But, he asked himself, how could he say no to his brother? Or his brother's family?

As they rode into the ranch yard, Ray asked again, "What do you say, Mart? Will you stay a little longer?"

Martin answered reluctantly, "Well . . . I won't leave right now. I'll think about it."

Mary had sent the boys upstairs to bed, but she was still up, peeling and dicing potatoes for tomorrow's beef hash. Ray handed her the sandwich, and said, "Too late. The prisoner has escaped."

She glanced up from her work. "Is the sheriff back yet?"

"We didn't see him."

"Making arrests and keeping jail prisoners is his job, not yours."

Cracking a grin, Ray said, "He certainly knows more about it than I do. Well"—he stretched—"I've got to go upstairs to my desk and write a letter to the district judge. Are you coming up soon?"

"As soon as I put these potatoes in cold water so they'll keep."

At the sound of hoofbeats, hoofbeats of several horses running, Martin quickly blew out the kitchen lamps and yelled, "Get down. Get down on the floor."

As before, gunfire shattered glass in the parlor, and bullets drilled splintery holes in the walls. A lead slug clanged off the kitchen range.

Then the hoofbeats were gone.

"Stay down a minute," Martin said.

"But the boys . . ." Mary was up and running in the dark for the stairs.

"The boys are all right," Ray said, picking himself up.

"They're in a room on the other side of the house. But I'm going up to be sure."

While they were gone, Martin slipped out the kitchen door, stood there in the dark, wishing he could have seen who fired the shots. Luke's voice came from the direction of the bunkhouse.

"Hey. Anybody shot? It's me, Luke." He hadn't seen Martin standing near the kitchen door.

"I think everybody's all right, Luke. We heard them coming."

"Oh. Thank God." When he came closer, Martin saw the rifle in his hands.

"Tell me something, Luke, have you ever shot at a man?"

"No. Why, uh, no, I ain't. I've shot deer and a elk, but I ain't never pointed a gun at a man."

"Do you think you could if you had to?"

"Why, uh, I don't know. I reckon I could."

Martin said no more aloud, but thought, Sure, you reckon. But you'd hesitate and that hesitation could cost you your life. Or somebody else's life.

"Are you out here, Mart?" Ray's voice came from the kitchen door.

"Yeah. How are the boys?"

"They're not hurt." Ray chuckled dryly. "They're not even afraid. At least Josh isn't. He wanted to get his thirty-two breech loader and shoot back."

Martin chuckled too, and started rolling a cigarette.

"In a way we were lucky," Ray said, continuing his dry chuckle. "After the last shots were fired at the house I ordered some new window glass. It has to come from Denver, and it hasn't arrived yet."

A lamp was lighted in the parlor, illuminating the broken window. Mary scolded her sons, "Go right back up those stairs. I told you to stay in your room." Another lamp was lighted in the kitchen. Then Mary screamed.

Ray and Martin whirled and ran through the kitchen door. Mary was standing by the table, near the lamp, holding a torn sheet of wrapping paper. Her face was white in the lamplight, and her hands were trembling. "Raymond," she said in a cracked voice, "Raymond read this."

Ray took the paper and read aloud, "Mr. Ray Mossman—No More Elections—Next time we will get you and your wife and kids. We Mean Business."

Mary was near hysteria. Her voice was high, wavering. "It . . . it was on the parlor floor, under the window, wrapped around a rock."

Silently, Ray read the note again, then dropped into a kitchen chair. He groaned, "Oh, my god. My god, my god." For a moment he was in shock. Then he looked up at Martin, pleading with his eyes.

Jaws tight, Martin said, "You betcha. If you want me I'll stay."

Chapter Twenty-four

He'd promised, and he couldn't go back on his promise, but the whole idea of being a bodyguard had Martin unhappy and worried. He wasn't about to sit outside every night with a rifle across his lap, and he wasn't about to just loaf around the house during the day. And he might fail. A shooter could pick off Ray or Mary without being seen. This could be an impossible job, and if he failed he'd hate himself for the rest of his life.

And this damned headache.

Martin was out of bed before Ray and Mary were up, prowling behind the barn and probing every place a gunman could hide. Luke was up shortly after Martin was, calling the cow, feeding her grain and milking her. After breakfast, Martin and Ray went outside and talked.

Rolling a smoke, Martin advised his brother to take a different route to town every morning and come back by a different route every night.

"Whether you go afoot or horseback, stay off the road. If they know where you're going and which way you're going and what time, they can't miss. You can find your way in the dark without following the road. Take the east side of the road sometimes and the west side sometimes."

Ray had buckled on his gunbelt and was carrying his double-action six-shooter. "In other words, be unpredictable."

"Exactly."

"I understand. Uh, Mart, it's not me that I'm worried about, it's Mary and the boys. I can't expect you to always be on sentry duty, but I just don't know how best to protect them. We'll do whatever you suggest."

"I could fail, Ray. I can't see in all directions at the same time, and I can't outshoot an army. Hell, there are men alone I can't outshoot."

"I've already told the boys to stay close to the house and to do exactly as you tell them. Mary will constantly remind them."

"I could tell at breakfast that Mary is worried."

"Yes, she is. We talked after we went to bed last night, and I offered to sell out and move to Denver. Mart, would you believe she doesn't want to? I mean, she probably wants to but she knows I don't, so for my sake she's pretending she wants to stay. She's smart enough to know that if I give up and run away, like I did during the war, I'll always feel bad about it."

Martin took a deep drag on his cigarette, exhaled, blowing smoke through his nose. "Well, that note says to forget another election. Probably none of you are in any danger until it's known that you're going to call another election."

"I can't speak for the other board members, but I do intend to conduct another election." Ray took an envelope from inside his shirt and showed it to his brother. "This is a letter to the district judge in Fair Play. It will reach him tomorrow. He should set a date for a hearing in the very near future."

"The sooner you get all this over, the better."

"Yes. Meanwhile, I'm going to carry my revolver everywhere I go and I've told Luke to keep the rifle handy at all times."

They went to the corrals where Ray caught and saddled his horse. Mounted, he asked, "What do you think? Should I stay off the road?"

"I doubt they'll bushwhack you before something new happens, before the judge rules. Until then, go on about your business like always."

Ray rode away at a slow trot, right down the middle of the road.

Within half an hour, Martin was bored and restless. This just wasn't to his liking, this standing and sitting around with nothing to do. When the boy Joshua came outside, Martin was happy to have someone to talk to. Together they went to the open-sided shed where the wagons and haying machinery were parked.

Nodding at a mowing machine with an iron seat, a doubletree, singletrees, and a tongue, Martin said, "Do you know how this thing works?"

"Sure, horses pull it."

"But how does it cut hay?"

"With this." The boy put his hand on the cutter bar, a five-foot flat length of iron with short teeth. It stuck out on the right side of the seat. Martin felt the edge and found it about as sharp as an axe.

"But there has to be more. This alone won't do it."

"Over here." Josh pointed out the sickle standing against a wall. It was the same length as the cutter bar, and was fitted with an equally long row of wedge-shaped blades. The blades were bolted in place. The sickle was made to fit on top of the cutter bar.

"Uhm." Martin found a long wooden pole and a block of wood which he used as a fulcrum to pry one of the wheels of the machine off the ground. He turned the wheel by hand and discovered how the mower worked. The wheel was also an orbital gear which worked a wooden pitman shaft which moved the sickle back and forth across the cutter bar teeth.

"Papa said he's gonna have Luke sharpen the sickle blades on the grindstone," the boy said. The round emery stone was mounted on the front of a pony with a seat and a foot pedal. Working the pedal turned the stone.

And that gave Martin something to do. "If you see anybody, anybody at all except Luke, holler at me and run to the house." Martin spent the rest of the morning sharpening the sickle blades one at a time on each side. After the noon meal, he soon figured out how the horse-drawn hay rakes worked. They were sulky-type rakes with seats and a row of long curved tines behind the seat. The operators could raise the tines by pulling an iron handle. This allowed them to rake the hay into windrows.

Other machines were parked under the roof and behind the long shed. One had long wooden teeth and was designed to scoop up the windrows and carry the hay to another machine fitted with a series of pulleys, which, Martin guessed, piled the hay into stacks.

"Takes a lot of machinery to harvest hay the modern way," he mused.

By midafternoon, he was restless again. Sundown was a relief. He sent the boys into the house with their mother, then sat on a wagon seat near the barn to watch for his brother.

Ray came home riding down the middle of the road, but Martin remembered saying he doubted he was in danger just yet.

After supper the two brothers went outside where Martin could smoke, and talked. "I asked everyone who came in the store if they'd ever heard or seen anything that might point to the man who is giving the orders," Ray said. "I learned exactly nothing."

Taking a deep drag, blowing smoke, Martin said, "Do you know anything about a gent name of Vance? C. C. Vance, I believe his name is. They say he owns the Silver Tip Gaming Palace."

"That's about all I know. He seems to be a pleasant fellow who wears good clothes and keeps himself well-groomed. I've never been inside his establishment, but I've been told it is tastefully furnished and orderly. Why do you ask?"

"Well, I think he tried to warn me to stay away from the polling place on election day. In fact . . . I don't remember his exact words, but they could have been taken for a threat."

"Uh-huh." Ray nodded in the dark. "But it was either a warning or an outright threat?"

"Sounded like it to me."

"Then he knew somebody was planning to disrupt the election. Hmm. Of course he could have merely heard a rumor. I'm told he has two bodyguards who no doubt are good listeners."

"Somebody ought to ask him how he knew. He told me himself he stands to lose if the ordinances are passed."

"Yes, but so would the other saloon owners. But they wouldn't really lose anything. The taxes they'd have to pay would be passed on to their customers, and the ordinances wouldn't stop the gambling, only give us some control over it."

"Nobody likes to be controlled."

"That's true, but to have an orderly society there has to be some regulation. The problem is where and when to regulate and when to keep hands off."

"That's the problem, all right. Some government honchos, when they get started regulating, they don't know when to quit. Is the sheriff back yet?"

"Yes, he rode in this afternoon. He had to take a prisoner to the Park County jail at Fair Play for safekeeping. One of two rustlers caught up near Buckskin was shot to death, and that had to be reported to the district attorney. Sheriff Little really does need a deputy."

"Yeah, I reckon so. Too bad he had to be gone on election day, though."

"Well, I'll ask him to question Mr. Vance at the Silver Tip, try to find out where the rumor originated."

"That could be important."

Another day of nothing to do. Martin found some harness that needed stitching, and Josh showed him where to find a stitching awl and some heavy thread. Martin sewed, he oiled leather with neatsfoot oil, he chopped wood. And repeatedly, he studied the terrain around the ranch buildings. The headache was back, pounding his brain. How much of this could a man stand?

Ray had learned nothing new. He'd asked the sheriff to question C. C. Vance, but the sheriff hadn't reported back to him.

"I'm going to saddle up and go to town," Martin said after supper. "With you here, you won't need me. I'll nose around a little, and to be honest, I'm going to have a shot of whiskey. Whiskey gives me some relief from this headache."

"If it gives you relief, then I don't blame you," Ray said. "Be careful."

In the Silver Tip, he gulped a shot glass of whiskey, felt its warmth in his stomach. C. C. Vance and his two bodyguards weren't in sight. Martin decided to find out what the other saloons were like, so he untied his brown horse from the hitchrail and led him down the street a block to another hitchrail. A big sign painted on the false front of the wood frame building read Hardtack Saloon. It wasn't fancy. Wooden walls and a wooden floor. Table and chair legs made of sections of peeled aspen trunks, seats made of rough-sawed pine wood, and tabletops covered with linoleum. Two walls and the pinewood bar had been painted a bright red. Martin no more than stepped up to the bar when he was met by the first man he'd talked to in Vega.

"Still in town, drifter?" The cocky young man with a beard that matched the color of the bar had moved up beside Martin. He still wore his big hat and the Navy Colt in a holster made for a fast draw.

"Aw for . . . Are you everywhere?" The long narrow room held some fifteen customers, four at the bar and the others seated at tables.

Leaning on the bar, his left elbow on top of it, the gunsel faced Martin. "How'd you like the election? You Mossmans got your asses whipped, didn't you."

Martin ordered a shot of whiskey from a husky barman and tried to ignore the man beside him.

"I coulda told you how it'd turn out."

Martin turned his head and looked over at him. "How did you know?"

"I hear things. They ain't gonna let you win."

"Who are they?"

A sneer spread across the man's face. "Wouldn't you like to know."

Martin had no doubt the gunsel had heard rumors, and it was possible he knew all about it. But he wasn't going to tell. Martin looked away and again tried to ignore him.

"I know things you Mossmans'll never know."

"Well," Martin said, "do you know who owns this saloon?"

"Newt Haley. And he ain't no friend of you Mossmans either." He half turned and yelled across the room, "Hey, Newt. This here is one of the Mossmans. He wants to make your acquaintance."

A short, husky man with thick brown hair and a thick mustache came over on short stumpy legs. He was smoking a ready-made cigarette, and he had a walnut-handled six-gun in a worn holster. "You gotta be the brother." His voice was gravelly, as if he needed to clear his throat.

"Yep. You the owner of this place?"

"That's what it says on the papers."

"What papers?"

There was a second's hesitation before the saloon man answered, "In the county clerk's office. So what? You wanta make somethin' of it?"

Something pulled at Martin's mind, the way Newt Haley's jaws tightened at the question, the way his eyes shifted. He mulled it over a few seconds, then said, "I reckon the papers say you're the only owner?"

The gravel-voiced answer came through tight jaws: "They say what they're s'posed to say. What's it to you?"

"Want me to get rid of 'im, Newt? I never liked his ugly mug the first time I saw 'im and he gets uglier all the time."

"Do what you wanta do. I don't care." Newt Haley turned, and his short legs carried him away.

Then the young tough's voice rose two octaves so it would be heard across the room. "Say, listen, mister, you can't talk to me that way. That's a goddamn insult, and I don't take no insults." He stood, facing Martin, feet apart, right hand near the butt of the Navy Colt. "Take it back or I'll plug you right here."

Martin knew he was being prodded into a fight. He didn't want to fight. He was in enough trouble with his brother's wife already. He started to say something in defense of himself, but he knew it would be useless. Instead of wasting words, he moved.

His left fist came around in a roundhouse blow that connected squarely with the gunsel's right eye. The young man didn't go down, but he staggered back a few steps. When he stopped staggering he was blinking and squinting his right eye and looking up the bore of Martin's Remington with the other.

Martin said nothing. Instead, he shoved the bore under the punk's nose and used his left hand to lift the Navy Colt from its holster. The punk knew he'd die on the spot if he moved, and he stood like a statue. Martin felt like saying something insulting, but decided against it.

Eyes going over the other customers, mouth drawn in a tight straight line, he backed to the door. Outside, he mounted his brown horse, threw the Navy Colt across the street, and rode around a corner of the building, away from the front. Then, riding at an easy walk, he made his way out of town.

Chapter Twenty-five

He went in through the kitchen door, and to be sure everyone in the house knew who'd come in, he went to the bottom of the stairs and said, "It's me, Ray. Everything's quiet."

In the morning, he stayed as far from Mary as he could, fearing she would smell whiskey on his breath. Before breakfast, while Ray was shaving outside the kitchen, Martin said, "I heard something last night that might mean something and might not. It could be my imagination. I met a gent name of Newt Haley who owns the Hardtack Saloon. Says he does. There was something about the way he said it. I can't explain what. But it makes me wonder."

"You suspect he might not be the real owner?"

"Well, it's . . ." Martin shrugged. "It's probably nothing."

Ray splashed water from a tin pan over his face, wiped his face with a towel. "It's easy enough to check. The county clerk keeps records of who owns most of the real estate in Prairie County. Of course he hasn't yet recorded every inch of the county, but I'm sure he has records of who owns the business buildings in Vega. I'll check on it."

Finishing his first smoke of the day, Martin said, "It's probably nothing, but maybe . . . if it isn't much trouble."

"I'll check on anything that's the least bit suspicious."

Another day of tinkering, killing time, watching. Joshua asked questions and Martin answered them, carefully. When Ray came home, Martin met him at the corrals.

"I don't suppose you learned anything interesting?"

"No." Ray shook his head and pulled the saddle off his sorrel horse. "I asked the county clerk about who owns what property, and he showed me the papers. Newton Haley owns the Hardtack Saloon, John Gilberts owns the Ore Bucket Saloon, and C. C. Vance owns the Silver Tip."

"How about the big house on the south side, the whorehouse?"

"I checked on that too. Margaret Able is recorded as the owner of the lot and improvements. I've heard her referred to as Sis Able."

"Do you know how she feels about the ordinances?"

"I haven't talked to her, but I doubt she's on our side. The ordinances would put her to some inconvenience. Of course she would raise the price of her, uh, services to cover any extra expense."

"I heard she sends her girls to a doctor every week."

"I've been told the same thing. If that's so, the ordinances would have little or no effect on her."

"Well, damn. Has the sheriff questioned C. C. Vance?"

"He has, but he didn't learn anything either. Mr. Vance told him he'd heard some saloon rumors, but he has no idea how the rumors got started."

Martin grumbled, "Sure, sure."

After supper he saddled his horse and rode into town

again. Inside the Silver Tip, he spotted C. C. Vance and his two goons, but the dandy ignored him. He downed a shot of whiskey, then went outside, mounted, and rode to the whorehouse.

A half-dozen horses were tied to hitchrails next to the whitewashed house. The gate in the picket fence was open. Martin stepped up onto a wide porch and twisted a knob which rang a bell inside. The door with its etched-glass panes was opened by a woman who was as wide as she was tall. But breathtaking.

Her face was as round as a ball, but with clear smooth skin. Her eyes carried so much makeup she reminded Martin of a racoon. But she smelled like heaven and her clothes were silky, hanging in many folds, billowing around her fat body. Dark hair was coiffured in curls that came to just below her ears. Diamond earrings dangled and sparkled in the lamplight, and a long pearl necklace hung between huge breasts.

Wide blue eyes stopped for a moment on Martin's scarred face, and a rouged mouth turned up in a small smile. "Let me guess, your name is Mossman."

With a crooked grin, Martin said, "I'm easy to recognize, ain't I?"

"You're the bachelor brother."

"Bachelor is right."

Stepping back, she said, "Well, come in, Mr. Mossman. Your money is as good as anybody's."

He stepped into a parlor that was as lavish as any room he'd ever seen. A thick rug covered the floor and crystal chandeliers hung from the ceiling. A handcarved mahogany bar filled one side. Plush deep chairs squatted on the other. And there was a curved staircase with a polished oak bannister. Four girls. Pretty. Dressed like fashion models in fine linen, silk, and ruffles. All designed low on top, revealing half moons of creamy flesh. Smiling girls.

"For twenty bucks, Mr. Mossman, you can take your pick."

"Well, uh . . ." He stood with his hat in his hand, tempted. He hadn't had a woman since he'd stopped in Denver on his way to Vega. "Uh, well . . ." Mary would know. Somehow she'd see it in his face. She'd know. "Well, what I want is to palaver. Talk."

"Talk?" Sis Able was incredulous. "Just talk? Whoever cut your face, did he cut off your gonads too?"

Shifting his weight from one foot to the other, Martin stuttered, "No, uh, I'm, uh, sometimes I just feel like talking."

For a long moment, she studied his face, trying to guess what he had on his mind. He looked away, embarrassed. The four girls were sitting demurely, ankles crossed, wearing puzzled expressions. A customer at the bar turned toward him, curious. Another man was coming down the stairs with a brown-haired girl holding his hand.

"Well, now," Sis Able said finally, "the price is the same, talk, fornicate, or whatever you want to do. Pick a girl. They all speak English."

"How about you? You look like a good listener."

"Me? I don't . . . well, all right if all you want to do is talk. Come with me." She led the way into a room that opened off the parlor. The room was sparsely furnished with a couch, a soft chair, a table, and a lamp. "Sit down here." She plopped herself down on the sofa and patted the seat beside her. He chose the chair.

"I, uh, just wanted to ask you how you feel about the ordinances the county board wants to get passed."

"Oh. Now I get it. You want to ask questions."

"Well, I am trying to learn more about this town, and you probably know more than most folks."

"Hmm. How do I feel? Hell, I don't care one way or the other."

"You don't? But, uh, wouldn't it cost you?"

"Cost me?" She laughed a deep-throated laugh. "Not hardly. I already send my girls to the doctor every week. As a matter of fact, this town can thank me for that. If it wasn't for me and my girls, Doctor Hanley wouldn't collect enough money to keep him here. Without us, this town wouldn't have a doctor. As for costing me, I can add a dime or a quarter dollar to the liquor I sell and sell just as much. As a matter of fact, I was thinking I might add more than necessary, and tell my customers to blame the county board."

"Then you could profit from the ordinances?"

"In more ways than one."

"What other way?"

Sis Able glanced around the room as if to be certain they were alone. She opened her mouth to speak, then clamped it shut.

Martin said, "Is there something you're afraid to talk about?"

Finally, she spoke again, "You were right when you said I might know things most folks don't, but I can't tell you."

"Like what?"

She stood suddenly, silky folds swirling. "Pay me twenty dollars, Mr. Mossman, and we'll be even."

Martin kept his seat. "You're afraid to tell." It was an accusation. As an afterthought he asked, "Is somebody shaking you down?"

For a moment a shadow passed over her face and her features went blank. But only for a moment. Her lips tightened, and she said, "You keep asking questions around town, Mr. Mossman, and maybe you'll learn. If you do, maybe you'll be doing me a favor. Forget the twenty. Just don't mention my name. You have to go." To be certain the conversation was over, she went to the connecting door and opened it.

Standing, Martin put his hat on and said, "Thank you, ma'am."

A lamp was burning in the front upstairs room when Martin rode into the ranch yard. He stopped a moment, looked up at the broken window, and decided with some satisfaction that a bullet fired from the ground wouldn't hit anyone sitting or lying down up there. A small cool breeze was moving the lacy curtains in the window.

Ray came downstairs when Martin entered the kitchen, wearing a long nightshirt. "I was going over my books. Glad to see you're back early."

"I'm glad you're still up. Can we talk without Mary hearing us?"

"If we keep our voices down. Did you learn something?"

"Yeah, Ray. I know for sure now there's something going on in Vega that you don't know about. I, uh, went to the whorehouse and asked questions of Sis Able. She knows more than she's telling. She's afraid to tell everything she knows."

Pulling out a chair, Ray sat at the kitchen table. "What did she say?"

It was imprinted on Martin's mind, and he related every word. Ray said, "Hmm," and rested his chin in his hands.

"Know what I think, Ray? When I was in El Paso a couple of years ago, I heard the merchants there were paying what they called protection money to a gang of cutthroats. They paid or they got beat to pieces or killed, or their businesses were burned down. I didn't think that ever happened in these little towns, but I guess it could."

"Protection money. That's hard to believe. Hmm." Ray shifted in his chair, ran his fingers through his sparse hair. "You could be right, Mart. It sure sounds like something is going on."

Chapter Twenty-six

This business of bodyguarding was so boring Martin almost wished something would happen. No, on second thought, not to Mary and the boys. Not to Ray. Just be happy that nothing had happened, he told himself. But damn, this could have a feller chasing rabbits where there wasn't any.

"No, Josh," Martin said in answer to a question, "coyotes don't run in packs. Wolves do. But coyotes are usually loners. Except when they have a mate."

"But I seen 'em. I seen a bunch of 'em around a dead cow once."

"Sure, when one of them finds a meal, others will find it too. But when they get their bellies full they drift off in different directions."

"My thirty-two can kill a coyote."

When Luke came in at noon, mud on his rubber boots, he answered, "No, ain't seen nobody. Grass's about as high as it's gonna get. Gotta start cuttin' purty quick before it starts turnin' brown."

Ray, when he came home, agreed. "I've already started lining up some help. I've got the Williams boys ready to start work any time, but I need three or four more, and I've got Mrs. Woodly's promise to come over and help with the cooking and dish washing."

"Mrs. Woodly is a good worker," Mary said.

"Martin, would you mind moving into the bunkhouse? We need your room for the kitchen help."

"I didn't expect to stay this long," Martin said, "but sure, I'm right at home in a bunkhouse."

"Not just yet, but in a few days."

Ray washed his hands and face in the tin basin outside the kitchen door. "In the winter we use the room you're in for a washroom, but in the summer this suits me fine."

Martin was smoking his last cigarette before supper. "What did the sheriff say about my talk with Sis Able?"

"Seemed surprised. He won't believe anyone in Vega is paying protection money. Said he knows the town too well. But he said he'd question her."

"Well, I'll trot to town again after supper." Frowning, Martin added, "I know Mary thinks I'm a carouser and boozer, and maybe I am, but you know, every time I go to town I learn something."

"Mary . . ." Ray shrugged. "Mary is Mary. But as long as you don't come home drunk she'll keep quiet about it. And she's truly sorry about your headaches. She doesn't believe whiskey can help, but she admits she can't speak from experience."

The Ore Bucket was like a hundred other saloons Martin had seen: long narrow room, pine bar at one end, tables at the other end. Whiskey bottles lined a wooden shelf behind the bar, and cattle brands and initials were carved in the bar itself. There were a baize-covered dice table, a monte table, a blackjack table, and a half-dozen card tables. Two miners were playing blackjack—and losing.

The monte dealer stood alone behind his table, ruffling the cards and looking hungry.

Martin had plenty of elbow space between two men at the bar as he studied the room. His eyes settled on a professional gambler who wore a laboring man's rough denim and muslin clothes, but stood out like a sore nose. He just had the look of a gambler: long, slender, uncallused fingers, muslin shirt with big cuffs down to his wrists, fedora hat tilted to one side. And that oily smile. Gamblers nearly always smiled.

Martin gulped his first drink and felt its satisfying warmth and anesthesia. Sipping his second shot of whiskey, he pictured in his mind the way the gambler allowed a working stiff to win now and then just to entice others into his web. But, Martin mused, when he wanted to win he won. He was the kind Ray and some of the other town fathers wanted to get rid of or to earmark as professionals.

"Come to town to get a job puttin' up hay?" The overall-clad gent on Ray's left was looking at him with interest.

"Well, no," Martin said, idly turning his whiskey glass around on the bar. "Not exactly."

"Should of knowed." Squinty eyes in a wrinkled face looked Martin over. "You're prob'ly more at home in a saddle. Me, I'm more at home behind hosses than on top of 'em. Know anybody's that's hirin?"

"My brother, Ray Mossman. He'll be in his store, the Mossman Mercantile, tomorrow. Been in town long?"

"Naw. Just drifted in from Leadville. Plenty of work over there, but bein' down in one a them shafts gives me the willies."

"I tried it once. Once was enough. I reckon you don't know who owns this place, then?"

"Wal, I never met the gent, but a feller tol' me he's that

long, skinny jasper standin' over there watchin' them card players." He nodded toward a man who was at least six three and weighed no more than one-sixty. He was bareheaded and nearly bald. He wore a striped shirt with no collar, exposing a long neck. And he carried a walnut-handled six-gun in a holster on his right side.

Martin wanted to talk to him, feel him out, but he didn't know how to approach him. He stood with his back to the bar, sipping whiskey and trying to think of a way. The saloon owner's name, as Martin recalled, was John Gilberts, and he was no doubt opposed to the county board's proposals. As it turned out, Martin didn't have to approach the man.

Gilberts happened to look around and caught Martin staring at him. Shifting the gunbelt, he came to Martin. "If you're who I think you are, you must be lookin' for a fight."

"What makes you think so?" Martin asked, trying to maintain an amiable air.

" 'Cuz you been fightin' ever'body that's agin' the county board, and I'm an aginner."

"No, Mr. Gilberts, not all of them. I've got no quarrel with folks who don't agree with the board, as long as they're fair about it. Mind telling me why you're an aginner?"

"Hell, man, see for yourself. Drinkin' and gamblin' is what I make my livin' off of."

"If I understand the ordinances, they wouldn't stop the drinking and gambling. They'd make the gambling more honest, maybe, get rid of some of the sharps, but not stop it."

"We wouldn't get as much business, it'd cut into our profits, it'd . . ." The saloon owner's mouth suddenly clamped shut, and he looked like he'd swallowed something hard.

"You got a partner, Mr. Gilberts?"

Face red now, Gilberts snapped, "No. This's my place. Now see here, Mossman, if you start any fights in here, there's men that'll fill you so full of lead it'll take a team of mules to drag you out of here."

Trying a crooked grin, Martin said, "Why, I'm not going to start a fight. But I was wondering who your partner is?"

"Get out of here. I don't need your kind in here. Get out before you get carried out."

Coolly, Martin finished his whiskey, set the empty glass on the bar. "Well, it's your saloon. Adiós." He sauntered to the open door and went out.

Riding at a walk back to the Mossman Ranch, Martin pondered what the saloon owner had said—let slip, rather. And Martin was sure it was a slip of the tongue. Gilberts had a partner. The deed to the saloon was recorded in Gilberts's name, so the partner had to have invested in liquor and gaming tables. Or he held a mortgage on the saloon. But wasn't a mortgage supposed to show up on the deed? Martin wasn't sure. That was something Ray would know.

He offsaddled in a corral that had water piped from the creek, and fed his horse some hay. He was walking to the house, carrying the repeating rifle, when he heard hoofbeats—more than one horse. Four or five or six. Running, Martin got to a corner of the house in time to see them in the dim light of a quarter moon. They'd stopped on the road a hundred yards from the house. Stopped to talk in low voices. Martin jacked the Winchester's lever down, felt with his thumb for a round in the firing chamber. The gun was ready. He waited in the shadow of the house.

Martin muttered, "So you're gonna have your fun again, are you, yellowbellies. Come on and get some of your own medicine."

They came, suddenly spurring their horses into a dead run, holding their six-guns high.

Martin didn't wait for them to fire the first shots. He took aim at a big hat and squeezed the trigger. The rifle cracked, exploding the still of the night. The hat flew off. Martin continued firing as fast as he could work the lever, firing from dark shadows. The Winchester cracked over and over without one misfire.

Horses were yanked to a jaw-breaking, sliding stop. The riders milled a few seconds, then turned and rode at a gallop back down the road, firing a few random shots at the house as they left.

Yelling after them, Martin said, "Not so much fun when somebody shoots back, is it, cowards."

All was quiet for a long moment. Then Martin heard boots clomping down the stairs inside the house. He stepped back away from the shadows and yelled up at the shattered window, "Hey, up there, it's me, Martin. They're gone now. Is anybody hurt?"

It was Mary who answered in a shaky voice, "Martin? Are you sure they're gone?"

"Yeah, Mary, I saw them coming and going."

"Thank God."

What Martin was afraid of now was that Ray might come out of the house, pistol ready, and not recognize him in the dark. He started talking, "It's me out here, Ray. They're gone. It's Martin out here. They're gone, now."

"Martin? Is that you?" Ray came around the corner.

"It's me."

Then Luke hollered from near the bunkhouse. "Who's there? Who's over there?"

"It's all right, Luke," Ray hollered. "They're probably back in their saloons by now."

"I sure wish I could have got a look at them," Martin said.

"Any chance they'll come back?"

"I don't think so. They think we're watching for them."

"Well, come on in the kitchen, and we'll put the pot on."

While they were waiting for the coffee to perk, Mary came halfway down the stairs in a long, thin nightgown covered with a plaid wool robe. Her dark hair had been combed so it hung straight to her shoulders. She was a pretty young woman. "Are you sure they're gone?"

"Yes, Mary. Thanks to Martin."

As she went back up the stairs, the men heard her say, "It's all right, boys. Go back to bed."

"Well, anyway," Martin said, "I'm sure now two of the saloon owners have partners. Somebody's in business with them, and he wants to keep it a secret."

"I'll go back to the county clerk and see if there's a cloud on the title to the Ore Bucket Saloon. If somebody is holding a mortgage on the place it ought to be recorded."

"If we can find out who the secret partner is, we'll know who we're dealing with."

"Then the next problem is how to deal with him. Knowing who and proving it are different problems."

He wished he hadn't drunk the coffee. The headache was back, throbbing, keeping him awake. Swinging his legs off the bed, he sat up and reached for his makings, then changed his mind. He'd have to go outside to smoke. Lying awake, he knew Ray was right about trying to sic the law onto whoever had planned the two robbery attempts on Wilkerson Pass and who had hired the thugs to bully voters. The only way they could prove it was to get one of the hired thugs to point the man out in court.

There were ways of making a man spill his guts, but not before a judge. No, it couldn't be done. Legally.

In the morning Martin's face was pinched tight as he sat at the breakfast table. Ray was thinking about the day ahead, Luke was saying the time had come to cut hay, and the boys were arguing about what kind of dog they wanted. Only Mary noticed.

"Is it the headache, Martin?"

"Huh? Oh." He rubbed the side of his head. "Sometimes it's . . ." He shrugged.

Her eyes were warm and soft. "Isn't there anything that can be done? Anything at all?"

Trying to grin, Martin said, "This is one part of my carcass that can't be amputated."

"Doesn't laudanum help? Or anodyne?"

Everyone at the table was listening now. "Laudanum," Martin said, "is, well, it takes a lot of it, and it's . . . believe me, it's worse than whiskey."

"Can't they do anything at that hospital in Philadelphia? There must be something they can do."

Martin didn't want to talk about it, not at breakfast, and he answered simply, "No."

Ray said, "Even the best surgeon in the world is reluctant to open the skull. It could be fatal. I read that somewhere."

"Poor Martin."

Forcing a crooked smile, Martin said, "It'll pass. It hasn't killed me yet."

It didn't pass, not that day. With an eye on the surrounding countryside, Martin cleaned the corrals and shoveled manure into a wheelbarrow with a wooden wheel. He allowed Josh to try to push the wheelbarrow, but no matter how hard the boy strained, he couldn't move it more than a few feet at a time.

"Better let me do that, Josh. You're liable to bust a g—" It occurred to Martin that Mary might not like that expression. "You're liable to pull a muscle or something."

The headache got so bad that Martin had to sit on the ground and hold his head in his hands. Josh asked, "S'matter, Uncle Martin? You sick?"

Looking up with pain-filled eyes, Martin said, "To tell the truth, Josh, I don't feel so good. You'd better go to the house."

"Poor Uncle Martin."

When Ray came home he gave Martin something else to think about. It was a note from Sis Able, and it was in a sealed envelope. "A woman handed it to me in the store and asked me to deliver it to you." Martin opened the envelope and read:

"Martin Mossman. Please come to my house tonight. I have something to tell you. Please come to the back door and knock four times. Don't let anyone see you." It was signed Sis Able.

Martin folded the note and put it in a shirt pocket. "I think I'll walk to town tonight."

Chapter Twenty-seven

There were five horses tied to the hitchrails in front of the two-story whitewashed house. Staying in the dark shadows, Martin walked around the house and found his way between a stable and a woodshed, and then found the back door. No light lit up the door, and heavy lightproof shades covered the windows on each side of the door. Martin knocked four times, waited. Knocked again. A woman's voice came from the other side of the door, a weak voice:

"Who's there?"

"Martin."

Latches were undone from the inside and the door was opened a crack. It was dark inside. The voice asked, "Martin who?"

"Martin Mossman."

The door opened wider. Though he could see only a dim shape, Martin guessed from the height and width that he was looking at Sis Able. "Come in," she said. He stepped inside the dark room, and the door was shut behind him. "Don't strike a match yet."

Not liking the mysterious dark, Martin drew the Remington, stepped back until he was against the door.

Breathing shallowly, he waited for whatever was going to happen to happen.

"This is the kitchen," the woman said. "Come with me to my bedroom." Her hand touched Martin's left arm.

"No. Light a lamp."

"I know this room, and I'll lead you through it."

"No."

"Oh. You're afraid of what you can't see. All right, strike a match."

"You do it."

"All right."

A lamp was lighted, but it put out only a dim light. Martin's glance took in each corner of the room, the big kitchen range, the cabinets, tables, and chairs. Sis Able had her back to him, covered with yards of silk. "Come with me."

He followed her through a connecting door and kept the Remington in his hand, hammer back, until she lighted another lamp. Then she turned to face him.

Had it not been for her shape he wouldn't have recognized her. The round face was black and blue and swollen. Sticking plaster covered her nose, all but the nostrils. One eye was swollen shut, and the lips were puffed.

"Lordy," Martin said, "what did you run into?"

Through swollen lips, she said, "Two hoodlums were hired to do this to me." She backed up until her legs were against a bed with the quilt pulled down. She sat on the bed.

"Who hired them?"

Shaking her head, she said, "I don't know. I want to hire you to find out."

"Well." Martin holstered the Remington and stood with his thumbs hooked inside his gunbelt. "Didn't they say anything? They must have said something."

"They came in the kitchen door and sent the house-keeper to fetch me. Like a goddamn fool I came into the kitchen to see who it was. There were two of them. They grabbed me by the arms, and one clamped a hand over my mouth so I couldn't yell, and they dragged me in here and beat on me."

"They must have had a reason. What did they say?"

"First, they put a gun to my head and said if I made a sound they'd blow my brains out. Then they stuffed a rag in my mouth and tied it there, and then one of them held me by the arms while the other beat on me with his fists. I was a real live punching bag."

"Is that all they said? They'd blow your brains out?"

"No. One of them said 'This is for talking too much.' And just before I passed out, I heard one of them say, 'Don't kill her. He doesn't want her killed. Not yet.' Next thing I knew I was on my bed here and Doctor Hanley was bending over me, and the girls were standing around crying."

"They said he doesn't want you killed? Did they say who he is?"

"No. I'll pay you to find out."

Martin shifted his weight from one foot to the other. "They said they beat on you because you talked too much. What was it you talked about? Was it because you talked to me?"

"You're the only one I talked to about . . ." Sis Able shuddered, took a deep breath. "I'm paying someone to allow me to be in business here. He sends messages and doesn't show himself. He had one of my girls murdered to show he meant business. Her throat was cut from ear to ear. I'm paying him a hundred dollars a week."

"Who brings the messages?"

"First one and then another. He must have an army of hoodlums."

"Have you told the sheriff about this?"

"No. They'll kill me if I do."

"Huh." Martin lifted his hat and fingered the left side of his head. "I guess somebody saw you and me go in that little room, stay awhile, and come out. And heard me tell you I only wanted to talk."

"That's what happened, all right."

"Would you recognize these hoodlums if you saw them again?"

"I don't know. I didn't . . . they grabbed me so quick and started beating me . . . I didn't see much. Anyway, I'm not going to go looking for them."

"Well . . ." Martin reset his hat and looked down at his boots while he ran it through his mind.

"I'll pay you to find the man who hired them. I'll pay you five hundred dollars to find him. And kill him."

He didn't have much of a description to go on. Both men wore wide-brim slouchy hats. She thought one wore suspenders. They were average size, smooth-shaved. She didn't notice what they wore on their feet. Hell, Martin thought as he walked to First Street, that description fits half the men in the territory.

His first stop was the Silver Tip. Standing at the polished bar, he saw himself in the mirror behind the bar and quickly looked away. He didn't need to be reminded of how ugly he was. After gulping his first shot of whiskey, he turned to face the big room, and sipped the second shot. What was he looking for? Damned if I know, he told himself. Skinned knuckles? Sneaky glances his way? Two men with guilty looks on their pans? He counted twenty-nine men in the saloon, drinking, gambling, haw-hawing, or grumbling. A few sent curious looks at him, but that happened everywhere he went.

C. C. Vance was seated at a table, idly shuffling a deck of cards. He saw Martin, stood, and sauntered over, his two goons beside him. The husky, mean-looking one bumped shoulders with a customer and almost knocked him down. The customer opened his mouth to object, saw who had bumped him, and shut his mouth.

"Mr. Mossman." The dandy smiled and put out his right hand. Martin shook with him. "I trust you have no hard feelings about the outcome of the election."

"Well"—Martin forced a grin—"you've heard what happened. You can't expect my brother and the other board members to be happy about that."

The two goons stood beside Vance, the husky one looking like he'd eat alive any man who as much as insulted his boss, the skinny one looking like he wanted to shoot someone, anyone.

"You must admit, Mr. Mossman, that I tried to warn you."

"You did, Mr. Vance. What I'm wondering is how you knew?"

"Rumors. As I told Sheriff Little, all I know is what any saloonkeeper in town knew. I learned quite young in life that if you want to know what's going on in a town like Vega you ask a barman. Barmen hear everything."

"Yep, that's so. I don't suppose your barkeep remembers who he heard it from?"

"He doesn't. I asked him."

Martin finished his whiskey, but held the empty glass in his fingers. An idea popped into his head, and before he could think it over, he asked bluntly, "And I don't suppose your partner knows anymore about it than you do."

The smile slipped. The husky one's scowl darkened. The skinny one's hand moved to the butt of his six-shooter. Then the smile was back, although not quite as strong. "Partner? I have no partner."

"Oh," Martin said, wishing he hadn't mentioned it. "I guess I was mistaken. All this is yours alone?"

"The last time I saw the deed in the county clerk's office my name was the only one on it."

"I was mistaken, then."

"Whatever made you think I have a partner?" The smile was gone again, and the eyes had narrowed.

Martin shrugged and lied, "I don't know. I guess I thought this place was a lot for one man to own."

The dandy's eyes studied Martin's face for a long moment, trying to read his mind. Finally, the smile returned. "Well, a saloonkeeper has to circulate, see that everyone is happy. Enjoy yourself, Mr. Mossman." C. C. Vance left, his two watchdogs beside him.

The night was young, and with nothing else to do, Martin sauntered down the street to the Hardtack Saloon. Again he stood at the bar, sipped whiskey and looked over the men in the room. The owner, Newton Haley, sat at a table with four stacks of poker chips and a hand-painted sign on it that read Bank. He was banker for the three card games going on. Haley scowled at Martin, but kept his seat.

With eyes experienced from years of rambling, Martin spotted three professional card players. Three card games and three professionals. It was a profitable business for Haley. A percentage of the winnings from the professionals and probably a nickel on the dollar for selling and buying poker chips.

At least two-thirds of the men wore broad-brim hats, most slouchy. Five wore suspenders. No skinned knuckles that Martin could see. But then Sis Able's fat round face was so soft that beating on it wouldn't skin knuckles.

One shot of whiskey, and Martin went back out to the plankwalk. In the Ore Bucket, the mean-looking owner, John Gilberts, saw him come in and started toward him. Before he got there, a man in a bill cap spoke to him and nodded toward a card table where a loud argument was going on. The five men at the table were playing with cash, both silver and U.S. greenbacks, and one was red-faced and loud. Gilberts spoke to him, put his hand on his gun butt. The red-faced gent, a cowboy, pushed back his chair, gathered his handful of silver, stuffed it into a pocket, and stomped toward the door. On his way out, he grumbled, "Goddamned thieves. Goddamn 'em."

Yep, Martin thought as he stood at the bar, a man would have a hard time finding an honest game in Vega. After looking over the crowd, he knew his chances of finding the thugs who'd beat up Sis Able were next to nothing. If she would come to the saloons with him, she might pick them out. She wouldn't. She was afraid for her life. What else could he do to try to find them?

Another shot of whiskey dulled Martin's headache, and he felt like carousing, wishing he had a friend to drink with, to bat the breeze with, wishing the cowboy J.J. were in town.

But John Gilberts was coming toward him again, looking mean and determined. Not wanting a fight, Martin sat his empty whiskey glass on the bar, turned, and walked out the door.

If he went back to the Mossman Ranch now, he'd have too much time to kill. The effects of the whiskey would wear off and his headache would return. He walked, and when he stepped off the end of the planks, he turned toward the cribs one block over. No sidewalks here, only the dirt street. A few horses were tied at the hitchrails, but the men Martin saw were on foot, walking and staggering. Across the street was a lumber yard and weed-grown vacant lots.

A bearded gent in baggy miner's clothes staggered and sang loudly: "Oh, she jumped in bed and covered up her head and thought I couldn't find 'er. But she knew damn well she was wrong as hell when I jumped right in behind 'er."

Grinning, Martin knew the gent was feeling no pain. He walked the length of the dozen cribs. Most had the doors closed and the shades drawn, but lamplight showed behind the shades. Two women stood in open doors and yelled at him, "Lookin' for a fun time, cowboy?"—"Hey, you with the ugly mug, I'll give you what you want." Martin grinned at them, but went on by. One of the cribs was dark, and Martin guessed it had been occupied by the murdered whore, the one Sheriff Little had mentioned.

His footsteps took him out of town and onto the road to the Mossman Ranch. Now, he thought, was a good time to heed the advice he'd given his brother, and he left the road and walked parallel to it. The quarter moon put out enough light that walking on the prairie was easy. He walked along, his boots making only a little noise on the prairie soil. The whiskey had worn off and his headache was back. He paused long enough to take a sack of tobacco out of a shirt pocket, and by the dim light of the moon to roll a cigarette. He started to strike a match on the buckle of his gunbelt when another light caught his eye.

Standing stock still, Martin watched, straining his eyes to see better. The light was only a small red dot near the ground and near the road. The dot moved up a few feet, stopped, glowed brighter for a second, then moved down again.

A cigarette. Someone was smoking. Sitting on the ground and watching the road. Waiting for someone else to come along. Waiting for Martin.

Chapter Twenty-eight

Martin considered trying to sneak up behind the man, get the drop on him, see who he was. He wished he were wearing moccasins instead of riding boots. He took a few tentative steps as quietly as he could. Nope. No matter how he tried, he couldn't help making a small sound. And if he stumbled in the dark over a sagebush or stepped into a prickly pear, he'd be heard for sure. Then there would be a gunfight.

Damn, Martin said under his breath. He'd give a lot to see who that gent was, stick a gun in his face and make him tell who hired him. But he didn't want to have to kill the man and have to explain to the sheriff. Or to Mary.

For a long moment Martin stood still, trying to decide what to do. Finally, he gave it up, and turned his boots toward the ranch, again walking as quietly as he could. He wondered how long that bushwhacker would wait there. The man was no soldier. A soldier caught smoking on guard duty would spend a lot of time in an Army prison. Nope, this was some barroom thug, hired by . . . who?

Who knew he'd been in town that night? Hell, practically all the saloon customers. And C. C. Vance. Did

Vance want him killed? Come to think of it, Martin might have hit a nerve when he'd asked about Vance's partner. He'd sure ruffled his feathers some. And anybody who runs a saloon knows all the toughs in the territory. Vance knew who he could hire to ambush, rob, and kill and then get out of the territory.

For that matter so did the other saloon owners, Haley and Gilberts. Martin had mentioned possible partners to them too. Hell, all three of the saloon owners were against the proposed ordinances, and they'd all breathe easier if Martin was off their necks.

Did the three of them form a conspiracy? Or was everything that had happened the scheme of only one of them?

How to find out?

Before he went to bed, Martin chewed some of the peppermint candy he'd bought at the Mossman Mercantile and kept from the boys. Sleep was a long time coming, partly because he ran everything through his mind over and over, trying to figure out what to do next, and partly because of his headache.

At breakfast, he tried to smile and pretend everything was fine, but Mary read him like a book. "Poor Martin," she said. "I wish there were something we could do." For a second, Martin thought she was going to give him a sympathetic pat on the back, and he turned away from her, not wanting her to smell his breath.

He didn't mention the would-be bushwhacker, but he did advise his brother: "Better walk to town. It's probably safe enough to walk on the road this morning, but when you come home, stay off the road."

"If you say so, Mart."

He, or they, wanted one or both of the Mossman brothers dead. If they had to pick one or the other, they'd probably pick Martin. His murder would cause no outrage, no long investigation. Martin was a drifter, a fighter, and his kind wasn't expected to live long anyway. And his murder would be a warning to Ray, a powerful warning. Well, Martin thought, if one of us has to get killed it ought to be me. I haven't got a whole lot to look forward to, anyway. A face that almost makes some folks sick, and a headache that sooner or later is going to drive me out of my mind. To hell with it all.

He had to admit to himself, though, that one of the good things in his life was Josh. He liked talking to his nephew, even answering his many, many questions. People who asked questions learned.

"Well, I don't know much about dog breeds, Josh, but I do believe mutts, mongrels, make the best pets and watchdogs. I've never owned a dog, but I've known men who did and they all said they thought mutts were stronger and healthier."

"Papa said me and Bennie can have a dog. He said he's gonna keep his ears open and pretty soon he'll find somebody that's got some puppies to give away."

"Yeah, folks that have b—mother dogs are more than happy to find somebody who wants the puppies."

"Bennie's too little to play with a dog, but I'm big enough."

"Dogs can be fun, especially for kids, and the men I've known who had dogs wouldn't have parted with them for anything."

Ray came home in the dark, walking parallel with the road and approaching from behind the barn. Martin was watching for him, and was glad his brother had called to him before he came around the barn. Ray had news:

"Boy, I'll say one thing for Judge Whittman, he didn't waste any time. I got a letter from him today saying he'll be in Vega on tomorrow's stage from Fair Play and he wants to conduct a hearing within a few hours. As soon as I got the letter I sent word to the other commissioners, and I told everybody who came in the store to pass the word around. We'll need witnesses. You'll have to testify, Mart."

"Judges and courtrooms have never been good news to me, but maybe this time it will be different."

"We'll have the hearing in my upstairs storeroom where the polling place was. I don't think there will be any opposition."

Martin didn't go to town that night. A shot of whiskey would have been good medicine, but he could think of no other reason to go to town, and he could think of no more questions to ask of anyone. In his mind, he'd narrowed the suspects down to the three saloon owners, but he had no proof of anything. Maybe something would happen after the judge ruled.

Of course he could just shoot the three. Shoot them down, then hightail it out of the territory. That would end the problems for the Ray Mossman family. But then he'd be a fugitive, and with his face he wouldn't be hard to identify. Then there were his nephews. He didn't want them to remember him as a killer. Too, that Vance feller, he always had the two bodyguards with him. Why did he need bodyguards? Nobody else had bodyguards. He had to be afraid of somebody. Afraid of the killers he'd hired? Afraid they'd blackmail him into paying them more?

Afraid of the whores he'd taken protection money from?

Mr. C. C. Vance was looking more and more like the man behind the hired thugs.

How to be sure?

There were no lawyers at the hearing, and that disturbed the judge. But when Ray explained that there were no lawyers in Vega, the judge pursed his judicial lips and said, "Very well. Bring on your first witness." Judge Whittman, with his goatee and bushy eyebrows, sat at the table the two election judges had occupied, holding his gavel in his hand.

He seemed to be ready to conk someone over the head with that gavel, and he made it clear from the beginning that this was very serious business and everyone would behave in a dignified and respectful manner. Sheriff Little stood nearby, ready to slap handcuffs on anyone who angered the judge. A dozen or so townsmen had gathered in the makeshift courtroom out of curiosity.

It was a short hearing. First the election judges showed some figures that proved more ballots were cast than there were voters. Then two men told of being threatened by the three thugs, and one showed the judge a knot on his head where he'd been hit by one of the three. There was no opposition.

Bang, went the judge's gavel on the tabletop. "I hereby declare the election null and void, and I find that the county board of commissioners has authority to call another election." He marched with a straight back down the stairs and turned his steps toward the stage company's cubbyhole office next door to the hotel.

Before the room cleared the five county commissioners conducted a short meeting and agreed that another election would be called as soon as a clerk could be hired to register voters and ballots could be printed. Ray Mossman agreed to pay the clerk and to pay for printing the ballots.

Ted Wilson, hollow-cheeked rancher-commissioner said, "Know somethin', fellers? I didn't much care one way or the other how the election come out till I saw how the rowdies of Vega bullied ever'body. Now I'm for the ordinances."

"That makes it unanimous, then," Ray Mossman said.

The two brothers had their noon meal together, then Martin allowed he'd better get back to the ranch. Luke had been told to stay close to the house with a rifle in his hands while Martin was gone, but the brothers feared that Luke wouldn't be much protection. Martin went to get his horse tied behind the mercantile. But then he hesitated, thinking.

Whoever was scaring Sis Able into paying protection money was no doubt scaring the whores in the cribs too. When was collection day at the cribs? Every day? Once a week? Every day was more likely. The whores were footloose. They could pack what few possessions they had in a tin suitcase and catch the next stage out of town without paying protection money. Better to collect every day.

Let's see. Across the street from the cribs was a lumber yard and vacant, weed-grown lots. If Martin could keep out of sight and watch the cribs he might be lucky enough to see who did the collecting. As boring as it would be, he'd sure like to do that. Would Mary and the boys be safe the rest of the day?

As of an hour ago, only the county board and Martin knew for sure that a new election would be called. Word would get around before the day was over, but whoever was hiring killers would need a little time. A few hours. He—they—wouldn't send killers out to the ranch today.

Head down, standing at the hitchrail behind his

brother's store, Martin worried it over. He'd hate himself if anything happened to the family while he was gone. On the other hand, the family wouldn't be safe until the schemer—schemers—were found out and taken out. Martin couldn't learn anything while he was standing guard at the ranch.

Hiding in the weeds across the street from a row of whorehouses wasn't going to be any fun, and it might all be for nothing, but . . .

He left his horse behind the store and walked over to Second Street. It was too early in the day for the whores to be open for business, and the street was nearly deserted. No one in sight at the lumber yard either, just stacks and stacks of lumber. Instead of hiding in the weeds like a coyote watching a chicken yard, he'd hide among the stacks of lumber.

After searching for the right spot, Martin sat next to a pile of two-by-sixes, sat on the ground with his feet out in front of him, and watched.

Watched, smoked, waited, and waved away the flies. Not a sign of life across the street.

The sun was almost overhead, so there was no shade. Watched, waited, sweated. A drunken miner came staggering down the street, swigging whiskey out of a bottle and talking to himself. He stopped at a crib, knocked on the door. The door opened, a drawn, hollow-eyed woman looked out, saw who was standing there, and slammed the door. "Well, go diddle yourself, then," the miner yelled. He went to the next door and knocked, got the same reaction. "I cain't do it," he yelled at the closed door. "Thas im—burp—possible."

Well, at least the whores were answering a knock on the door. That could be a good sign. Two cigarettes later, the sun was far enough to the west that Martin at least had some shade from the stack of lumber. His butt was aching almost as badly as his head when he saw a familiar shape of a man turn the corner and start down the street. Martin stubbed out a cigarette in the dirt, scooted back a few inches, and watched.

Sure enough, the wide-shouldered, wide-hipped, block-headed bodyguard from the Silver Tip Gaming Palace knocked on the first door. Martin would have been sorely disappointed if he'd gone inside to satisfy an urge. But he didn't. The hollow-eyed woman gave him something, which he stuffed into his pants pocket. Then he went to the next crib.

While Martin watched, the biscuit-eared bodyguard went to every crib in the row except the vacant one.

Smiling inwardly, Martin believed the mystery was now cleared up. C. C. Vance was sending his personal thug to collect from the whores. And if C. C. Vance was collecting from the whores in the cribs, chances were he was collecting from Sis Able, and he was hiring killers and bullies to defeat an election—an election that would put a stop to his shakedowns.

Martin waited until pugface made his rounds and turned the corner, then stood and walked with rapid steps to the back of the Mossman Mercantile. He felt good about himself. Now he knew. But it occurred to him as he rode to the Mossman Ranch that the danger wasn't over.

So he knew who to point the finger at, so what? He had no proof. Pugface and the hired killers would lie. The whores wouldn't dare tell. And Sheriff Little would do nothing without proof. There'd been times in Martin's past when he'd appointed himself prosecutor, jury, and executioner, and this time he could be paid for being executioner. But he couldn't get by with that here, not unless he could claim self-defense.

Too, if anyone even looked hard at C. C. Vance, his skinny bodyguard would shoot him full of holes, and the other one would tear his arms and legs off one at a time.

There was no way. There had to be a way.

Chapter Twenty-nine

Luke was glad to see Martin. "This ain't the kind of work I hired out to do," he said. "If they didn't treat me so good I'd roll up my bed and move on."

"I don't think you'll have to do this anymore," Martin said. To Josh, he said, "Yeah, the judge nullified the election and said the board could hold another one. Your mother is probably wondering about it. Go tell her, will you?"

"You betcha, Uncle Mart." The boy took off for the house, running and skipping.

"Wish I could run that easy," Luke said.

"It's been a long time since I've felt like running," Martin said.

For the rest of the day Martin tried to think of a way to stop C. C. Vance, some way to prove he was extorting money from the whores. If only one of the whores would point out the bulldog as the collector, the sheriff could confront the saloon owner and arrest him. Once Vance was arrested, maybe somebody else would point out one or two of the hired killers.

And if Sheriff Little needed help in making the arrest, Martin would volunteer. That way he could kill Vance legally and be paid for it. More important than the money, though, was just getting rid of the man behind all the killing and bullying going on in Prairie County.

Of course, Martin could be killed.

Aw, well, he could have been killed before, more times than he'd kept track of. The big problem now was getting the whores to tell all. If only one of the whores would do it.

Maybe Sis Able would do it. After Vance had had her beat to pieces she ought to be willing to point out one of his hired goons. So she didn't recognize the two who had beaten on her. Maybe that's because she'd never seen pugface before. No, that couldn't be. Not if pugface was the collector.

Aw, hell.

That damned headache. It pounded on his brain so he couldn't think straight. Goddamn.

All right. Martin would have another talk with Sis Able. Could be she knew something she hadn't told him. Any little piece of information he could get from her might help.

At supper, Mary tried to talk Martin into seeing Dr. Hanley, but Martin reminded her he had already seen some of the best surgeons the Union Army could find.

"Morphia is a sure painkiller," Mary said. "I knew a woman who had terrible stomach pains, and morphia gave her some relief." After a short pause, Mary added, "She died. But at least the morphia kept her from suffering terribly."

Martin argued, "Morphia is a killer itself. Sure, it stops the pain, but a man can get trapped by it. It can trap a man as sure as a bear trap. Out in California I met a couple of men who lived in h—hades because of morphia. They were walking death."

"There just ought to be something a doctor can do."

* * *

As before, he walked to town, slipped past the stable and woodshed behind the two-story house, and knocked four times on the back door. The door opened almost immediately, but it wasn't Sis Able who opened it.

"Oh, pardon me, ma'am," Martin stammered, "but I was hoping to meet with Miss Able."

"Who are you?" The woman was fat and short but not as fat as the whorehouse madam. And she wore a plain blue cotton dress with no frills. "You'll have to go around to the front door like ever'body else."

"I'm here to see Miss Able, ma'am. That's all. Will you tell her that Martin Mossman would like to see her."

"Martin Mossman?" With her back to the lamplight, her features weren't clear, but Martin guessed her face was as plain as her clothes. She was hired help, a house-keeper or cook or both. "I heered about you." She peered closer. "Yep. You're the one. Somebody done cut your face up purty bad."

"What did you hear?" Not that it made any difference, but Martin was curious.

"You're the brother of Ray Mossman that wants to shut down this establishment."

"That's not so, ma'am. Nobody wants to shut down this establishment."

"That's what they're sayin'."

"Who's saying?"

"Some of the gentlemen that come here done said that to some of the ladies."

No use arguing with the hired help. "Will you tell Miss Able I'm here?"

"Yeah, but you wait right here." She slammed the door, and Martin heard a latch clicking shut.

Standing outside the door in the dark gave Martin a queasy feeling, and he stepped aside and turned so his back was against the outside wall. His eyes searched the darkest shadows, the stable, and the woodshed. Finally, he heard the latch being opened.

"Come in," Sis Able whispered. "Quick. Don't let anybody see you."

She had doused the lamp, and she took him by the hand and led him to her bedroom again. There she lit another lamp. Heavy makeup had hidden most of the marks on her face, all but the sticking plaster on her nose and the puffy lips.

"Did you learn something?"

"I think so, but I'm not sure."

She was impatient. "What, what?"

"Do you know C. C. Vance, the gent who owns the Silver Tip?"

"I've seen him. I don't know him."

"Have you seen his two bodyguards, the one with the big muscles, and the little gunfighter?"

"I've seen them, yes. They were pointed out to me once when I had the nerve to go into the Silver Tip for a drink."

"Oh," Martin said, disappointed. "Then they're not the ones who beat on you."

"No, they're not the ones. Why? Did you think they might be?"

"Well . . . Miss Able, do you know anything about Mr. Vance, anything at all?"

"No. He introduced himself to me when I went into his saloon. He seemed to be a gentleman."

"Does he ever come here? I mean, he's not married, and well . . .?"

"No. One of my customers—don't ask who—told me

Mr. Vance goes to Fair Play pretty often. He probably gets his satisfaction over there."

"I hadn't heard that. It could be."

"Most saloon owners have women working for them, but I'm told that none of the saloons in Vega keep women. The Silver Tip has a piano player and a dance floor, I noticed, but no one for the men to dance with."

"I've noticed that too. I've been told that Sheriff Little won't allow it."

"That's true. The sheriff told me that himself. The men have to go to the cribs or come here."

"You know the sheriff, then?"

"Sure. He comes here, in the back door. I send a girl in here so he won't be seen in the parlor. I shouldn't have told you that, but you must have guessed."

"I would have guessed if I'd thought about it. He's not married either."

"You won't . . . you won't let on that I told you?"

"No. That's his business."

"Do you want a girl? I can send one back here."

Lordy, but he was tempted. It had been too long. But he'd feel guilty, and Mary could read his face. "No, not tonight. I'm still trying to find out who beat you up. Mr. Vance, uh, I think he's gouging money from the women in the cribs. I've seen one of his bodyguards making the rounds of the cribs and taking money."

"Oh, he is?" Her eyes widened with surprise. She sat on the bed, frowning at the floor. Martin stayed on his feet. After frowning at the floor a moment, she looked up. "Why, that's . . . Could he be the one that's sending tough guys over here to pick up the money?"

"He could be and probably is. Didn't you ever get a clue at all as to who is behind all this?"

"Not a clue. He sends different men. The first I heard

of him he sent me a note demanding a hundred dollars a week and saying I'd be killed and my house burned down if I didn't pay up. Then two days later one of my girls was murdered, her throat was cut, then next day another note. I got the message."

Martin was silent a moment, thinking. She talked on, "The only man I recognized that tried to force me to do anything is the county clerk. He came in here once and tried to get me to sign over half my property, my house and lot."

"Sign it over? Sign it over to who?"

"That part of the paper was blank. He wouldn't tell me whose name was to go on it."

"Did you sign it?"

"I put if off for a while, but I got another note, and I was afraid that refusing to sign would just get another one of my girls murdered. I'd like very much to get out of this town, this territory, but I'm afraid for my life and the lives of my girls if I try to leave. That's why I'm willing to pay you five hundred dollars to find out who's responsible for this and get rid of him. Make that a thousand dollars. It would be worth every penny to me."

"I could get killed doing it, you know."

"I think you're the kind of man who will take a chance for a thousand dollars."

"A dead man can't spend money."

"Then I'll give it to whoever you name."

"The school?"

"That's a promise. I'm not a lady of virtue, but I keep my promises."

Martin pushed his hat back and rubbed the indentation on his head. "Everything points to C. C. Vance, but there's something . . . I just have a feeling that I don't know all about everything. I'm not altogether sure."

"It wouldn't help me at all if you killed the wrong man."

"You know, Miss Able, as much as I'd like to collect the thousand, the sheriff is your best bet. He has authority to ask questions and get answers. Does it matter to you whether the man who's badgering you is killed or arrested?

"Just so he's off my neck."

"Too bad you're afraid to tell the sheriff."

"I've been considering it. Maybe, now that I've got a strong suspicion, maybe he'll do some investigating without mentioning me. Since this started, Sheriff Little and I have become friends."

"Friends, huh?"

"I trust him and he trusts me. As a matter of fact, I've got a letter to the district attorney that he gave me to keep. He trusts me to keep it and mail it only if anything happens to him. Like if he gets killed or badly shot up."

"A letter to the district attorney? What does it say?"

Shaking her head, Sis Able said, "I didn't ask and I don't know. It's none of my business. He told me once, while he was drinking whiskey in here between girls, he left another letter with someone in Fair Play that was to be delivered to the district attorney if anything happened to him."

"Well, well . . . ?" Martin was rubbing his head again, puzzled.

"Listen, I've got to get back to business. Don't let anyone see you leave. And if you learn something else, come back. My housekeeper will fetch me."

He stopped in the Silver Tip for one drink of whiskey and to see what there was to see. A gent in a striped shirt and a derby hat was working hard at the ricky-tick piano, but no one was listening. C. C. Vance was playing cards with four other men, and didn't look up. His two goons were beside him, eyeballing everyone and everything. The big one looked like a giant snarling bulldog, and the skinny one kept his hand close to his gun butt, the look on his face challenging everyone.

The roulette wheel, the blackjack table, and the monte table were all busy. Only one card table was vacant. The Silver Tip was raking in the loot.

One quick shot of whiskey dulled his headache, and Martin walked back to the Mossman Ranch, staying off the road, keeping alert. At the same time new puzzles were running through his mind.

First, there was the county clerk. The deed he showed Ray had Sis Able the only owner of her house and lot. Now it turns out he has another paper showing somebody else owns half. He can show whichever paper he wants to. And if he's got two deeds to the whorehouse, he could have two deeds to the saloons too. Somebody either bought part interest in the saloons or scared the saloon owners into signing the deeds.

Then there's that letter to be delivered to the district attorney if Sheriff Little is killed. Two letters. There's only one way that makes any sense:

Sheriff Little's got the goods on somebody, and it's somebody he's afraid of. He's afraid he'll be killed to shut his mouth. The letters are his life insurance. If he's killed, somebody will be in a lot of trouble with the law. Knowing that is keeping the somebody from backshooting Sheriff Little.

Huh, Martin said to himself as he walked in the dark across the prairie. Is it all tied with what's happened to Ray and the election?

What the humped-up, holy, goddamn hell is going on here?

Chapter Thirty

Mary finally had her way. Martin would visit Dr. Hanley. The two brothers walked to town together, staying on the wagon road. There were only a few places a bushwhacker could hide on the prairie in the daylight, but both men carried six-shooters and kept their hands ready to draw and shoot. When they came close to a shallow gulch, where a man could stay out of sight by lying down, they watched it intently. And even after they'd passed it, Martin walked backward a ways so he could keep his eyes on it. They did the same when they passed a clump of sagebrush big enough for a man to hide behind.

As they walked down First Street, Martin asked, "Does she always get her way?" Then he quickly added, "Don't answer that. It's none of my business."

But Ray felt like talking about it. "She nags. Sometimes she gets on my nerves. But she's smart enough to know that I'll take just so much and then I'll blow up. She knows when to quit."

"Uh-huh," Ray grunted, thinking that was the end of that. But Ray talked on:

"Women can be a pain, but I'll tell you, Mart, there have been times when she was just what I needed. You

don't know, I guess, how good it is to have someone to
come home to, to always have someone on your side no
matter what. The whole world can be against you, can
hate you, but a good woman is always there to tell you
how wonderful you are. And my sons, I'd die and go to
hell for my sons."

Not knowing what to say, Martin only grunted, "Uh-
huh."

Dr. Hanley was slender in the shoulders and arms, but
so big in the middle he had to leave the top button of his
pants undone. He wheezed when he talked, and Martin
wondered if he shouldn't be taking some of his own medicine.

"Headaches, huh? I've got patients that would be more
than happy to trade their bodies for yours. Why, a little
old headache is nothing. Everybody gets a headache now
and then. A few drops of laudanum will take care of that.
Sit down over there."

Martin sat in a straight-backed chair in a small room
nearly filled with a six-foot-long examination table, a tall
chest of drawers, which, Martin guessed, held medical
instruments, and two chairs. The doctor's breath stank
when he bent over Martin to examine his head.

"Oh," the doctor said. "Oh my. I take it all back, what
I said about a little old headache. Why . . . why, you're
lucky to be alive. Good heavens. What hit you?"

Martin explained.

"Hmm. I see. Well, stranger things have happened. I
can also see why you have severe headaches. There has to
be some pressure there. My, my."

Stepping back, he said, "I wish I could help you. We
know so little about the human brain. Surgery could
relieve the pressure, or it could kill you or put you in an
insane asylum. Only in an extreme emergency would

even the most distinguished of surgeons tamper with the brain."

Martin said, "I might get desperate enough one of these days to take the gamble, but not yet. I've tried laudanum, anodyne, and even morphia. Morphia works best, but I'm afraid of it. I've seen what it can do."

"Yes, a person can easily become dependent on it and suffer terribly without it. You're wise not to become dependent on it."

Standing, Martin put his hat on. "What do I owe you?"

"Since I didn't do anything for you, nothing." Dr. Hanley repeated, "I wish I could help you."

Martin had known what the doctor would say. He knew too that the only thing that would help was whiskey. Whiskey or morphia. Which was worse, he wondered as he walked back to First Street, getting snagged by morphia or whiskey? Whiskey seemed to be more respectable. A boozer at least sobered up once in a while, but the dopeheads never sobered up. A dopehead was no good at all at any time.

He had a shot of whiskey at the Silver Tip, stopped at the Mossman Mercantile to buy more peppermint candy and to tell Ray what the doctor had said, then began the walk back to the ranch.

He was only a few hundred yards from the house when he saw a horseman coming toward him, coming at a hard gallop. The horseman was Luke. He pulled his mount to a stop, and yelled, "Got to get Mr. Mossman. Mizzus Mossman is goin' out of her mind. Joshua is gone."

"What?" Martin yelled. "What?" But Luke was whipping the horse with the end of the bridle reins, riding hard up the road.

For a second, Martin was dumbfounded. Joshua was gone. And then it sunk in, and he cried out in agony, "Oh,

Christ. Goddamn." And he broke into a run for the house.

Mary was running across the yard, dragging her youngest son by the arm. When she saw Martin, she stopped and looked at him with tears rolling down her cheeks. "Joshua's missing, Martin." Desperation had her face pinched, her eyes filled with pain. "He's just gone. I've looked everywhere."

Breathless from running, something he wasn't used to, Martin asked, "Where . . . where did . . . you see him last?"

"Right outside. I, I tried to keep watch, but I couldn't watch him all the time." Loud sobs had her shoulders shaking. "Something terrible's happened."

"Listen, Mary . . . Ray will be here soon. I'm . . . gonna look around here and if I don't find him . . . I'll saddle a horse and look everywhere."

Benjamin's sobs joined his mother's. Martin wished he could say something comforting, but he could think of nothing.

It didn't take long to search the barn, the sheds, and the corrals. Martin caught and saddled his brown horse and got mounted just as Ray rode into the yard at a gallop. He was riding the horse that Luke had ridden to town. Martin met him.

"I'm gonna look all around, Ray. He might have stumbled and wrenched his ankle or knee or something."

But Ray was holding his wife in his arms, close to tears himself. He only nodded at Martin.

With a sick fear in his guts, Martin began a slow, methodical search, looking down at the ground from his saddle and now and then scanning the terrain. The boy wasn't lost. He wouldn't wander so far that he couldn't see the ranch buildings, nor would he wander so far that he couldn't be heard if he was hurt.

Tracks were plentiful. Horse tracks. Man tracks. But there was no way of knowing whether they were Luke's or Ray's or Martin's tracks. And Mossman horses ambled around the place freely.

Fighting down gut-tearing panic, Martin reined up, sat still in the saddle a moment, rolled a cigarette, and tried to think. The most believable explanation was one he didn't want to think about. Had to think about.

The boy was snatched. Kidnapped.

Martin talked to himself, "All right now." He lighted the cigarette. "Supposing the worst happened. Either the kidnapper will kill him or hide him somewhere and demand money. Or something. If we don't find Josh's body, then he's alive. All right, old pony, let's do some searching. And hope to hell we don't find anything but tracks."

He rode in a wide half circle on the north side of the ranch buildings, hoping to cut the kidnappers' sign. The prairie was dry, but easy to track on. He crossed footprints and hoofmarks heading to and from Vega, but they were his own or Ray's. The snatchers wouldn't head for town anyway. While he was riding, he knew he could be on the wrong side of the ranch buildings. There was no way of knowing which way anyone went.

Martin reined up again and tried to figure it out. Straight south, there was nothing but a lot of prairie. Southeast was a range of high hills where prospectors had picked and scratched and searched for gold. North were mountains full of abandoned miners' camps. East was more mountains. The mountains to the east were closer than the mountains to the north. Mountains were easier to hide in than the prairie. Martin turned east. Still riding in a half circle, looking for sign, he reined up again when he heard a man yell.

Ray was riding toward him, riding hard. Martin waited.

"I told Luke to find Sheriff Little," Ray said, pulling his horse to a stop beside Martin. "Mary will tell him which way we went. Surely, he'll help us search."

"Sure."

"What do you think, Mart? How should we go about this?"

Shaking his head, Martin said, "Your guess is as good as mine. I'm thinking maybe they went east to tall timber."

"They?"

Still shaking his head sadly, Martin said, "Yeah, Ray. They."

Ray swallowed a hard lump in his throat and spoke with a strained voice. "That note. I'm afraid . . ." He couldn't finish.

"I hope to God I'm wrong." Then Martin straightened in his saddle. "This ain't getting anything done. I'll look for sign east. If I was you, I'd ride north, look for anything unusual. If you see anything, fire two shots in the air. I'll do the same."

Visibly, Ray gathered himself, his wits, his courage. "I'll do it." The brothers separated, searching.

Shortly before sundown, hope flared in Martin's mind. Hoofprints. Two sets. Going northeast toward the hills and woods. Martin had traversed the terrain, gradually widening his half circles. If he'd ridden a little more to the north he'd have picked up the tracks sooner.

"All right, old pony," he said to his brown horse, "we've got something to follow now. Let's lope."

The hoofprints were going in a straight line, and when

Martin lost sight of them, he continued on northeast until he picked them up again. While he was watching the ground he was also looking ahead, hoping that by some miracle he'd see the men in the distance. Two sets of horse tracks meant two men. One was carrying Joshua. The boy's arms had to have been tied, and he had to have been gagged.

Though Martin was riding at a lope, it occurred to him that he wasn't gaining. The two ahead were no doubt riding at a lope too, and they had a long head start. "Goddamn," Martin muttered, "there's too many places to hide up there. All right, old partner, we haven't got time to lope along easy. Pick 'em up and lay 'em down."

He spurred the brown gelding into a hard run, hoping to catch sight of the snatchers before they disappeared into the mountains. The horse ran its best, dodging sagebrush, jumping prickly pears, jumping narrow gulleys. "Sorry, feller, but I need all the speed you've got. Ray's boy needs you."

He lost sight of the tracks, found them again. "We're headed in the right direction, all right. Keep those legs pumping, partner." They were going uphill now, getting close to where the country sloped sharply up into the boulders, brush, and pines.

Then, looking ahead, Martin was struck a blow of disappointment. "Aw, goddammit. Shit. Goddamn." What he saw was the road coming down from Wilkerson Pass and going on to Vega.

When he reached the road, Martin reined up and sat his saddle. The horse's sides heaved and its nostrils flared. Martin cursed. "This just beats the hell out of everything."

The road was covered with hoofprints and wagon-wheel tracks, going in both directions. There was no way to separate tracks left by the kidnappers from the other tracks. Disappointment and frustration was like a hard punch in the stomach.

"Goddammit."

For a moment, Martin considered spurring the horse into a run again and trying to catch sight of the kidnappers before they quit the road and disappeared. The problem with that was they'd probably already left the road and Martin had no way of knowing which way they would have gone from there. He could ride parallel with the road and look for tracks that headed into the timber, but he couldn't ride both sides. Not only that, the sun was hanging on top of the western horizon now, and dark wasn't far away.

Martin needed help. Was Ray or the sheriff within hearing range of a gunshot?

He drew the Remington, then holstered it again and dismounted. "I've never fired a gun from your back, old partner, and this is no time for a bronc ride." Standing as far in front of the horse as he could and still hanging onto the bridle reins, he fired two shots in the air. The horse lunged back and reared, boogered by the sudden reports. But Martin kept his hold on the reins and talked calmly, "Whoa, feller. This takes some getting used to. Whoa, now."

Two answering shots came from the east. Martin fired twice more, then reloaded while he waited. Talking to himself again, he said, "I don't know if this is the smart thing to do. If Ray or the sheriff can hear my shots, the kidnappers can too. They'll know we're on their trail, and they'll try harder to be tricky." After he'd mulled it over, he added, "But maybe Josh will hear it, and maybe

. . . maybe it will give him some hope. Maybe he'll know we're not far away."

"Hang on, Josh," Martin muttered. "Hang on, boy. Your dad and me, we're gonna find you."

Chapter Thirty-one

When Ray rode up on a badly winded horse, Martin explained the problem. "I don't think they'll stay on the road any farther than they have to. There's too much of a chance they'll be seen by somebody. I'm guessing they'd got a spot picked out up there, some old miner's shack or a sheepherder's shack, or something like that. But the question is, which way from the road did they go?"

Ray understood. "So we'll have to ride on each side and watch for tracks."

"Correct." Glancing at the western horizon, Martin added, "We haven't got much time before dark. Let's get going."

They had to ride slower now and study the ground. Hoofprints weren't so easy to see in the rocks. Martin knew from experience there would be no clear prints, just a scuff mark here and there, a small indentation in the ground, an overturned rock. The brothers stayed within sight of each other, and at times stopped and dismounted for a closer look. Martin silently swore.

"Not even a goddamn Apache could track anything in this goddamn country. Given enough daylight we might get lucky, but pretty soon it's gonna be darker than a goddam stack of son-of-a-bitchin' black cats."

"See anything, Mart?" Ray hollered.

"Naw."

"It's getting too dark to see."

"Shit. Goddamn."

They had to give up and meet on the road. Martin said, "Somewhere in this territory they're camped for the night, and they might be dumb enough to have a fire going, coffee perking. We could keep riding and trying."

"Horses have good night vision and they won't run into a tree or fall off a steep hill, but there's an awful lot of territory up here. What chance have we got?"

"If they're smart they won't have a fire, and without a fire we could ride within a hundred feet of them without seeing them."

Ray looked at the sky. "No moon, no nothing."

"I guess," Martin said, "we ought to go back to the ranch, try to get some rest, and be back here at daylight tomorrow."

"I keep thinking about Josh, and . . ."

"Yeah," Martin said glumly. "It's hell."

"And Mary. She's probably going crazy, wondering and worrying."

"Yeah, we ought to go back."

"And there's a chance . . . I know I'm hoping for a miracle, but there's always a chance that something else happened, and Josh is at home now."

"Sure, Ray, strange things happen."

The brothers were quiet most of the way back to the ranch, then Ray said bitterly, "They saw us walk into town. They saw their opportunity and they took advantage of it. No telling how long they'd been gone with Joshua before Mary noticed he was missing. Then she looked all over the place before she sent Luke after me. They had a good head start."

Martin could only grunt in agreement.

"They had everything their way. We're all so . . . so vulnerable. No matter what we do, what precautions we take, we're vulnerable."

Martin was just as bitter, but he kept his thoughts to himself.

Mary heard them coming and ran to meet them, carrying a lantern. When she saw that Joshua wasn't with them, she stopped suddenly and burst into tears again. Ray dismounted and held her in his arms.

"I'll take care of the horses, Ray."

Luke came out of the bunkhouse, carrying another lantern. "Did you find 'im?"

"No, Luke," Martin said sadly. "We're going back up in the timber first thing in the morning and look some more."

"I'll go with you."

"Is the remuda nearby? I mean, the saddle horses? We'll need some fresh mounts before daylight."

"I kept up three of 'em in the water lot over there. You can turn these out if you want to."

"That's good thinking, Luke. That will help."

When Martin stepped inside the kitchen, Ray was sitting at the table, staring dumbly at another torn sheet of paper. Without speaking, he handed it to Martin. It was another note, written in a scrawly fashion with a lead pencil. It read:

Ray Mossman if you want to see your boy again resign from the county board. Do not call another election. Sell all your property and get out of the county. Do not tell the sheriff about this. Do not tell anybody. If you do not do as this note says your boy will be killed.

Martin put the paper on the table, and sat in one of the chairs. "Well, I expected this." After a moment of silence, he said, "Speaking of the sheriff, has he been here?"

"Yes," Mary said. "I told him you both went north, so he went south. He got back just a few minutes before you did. I . . . I showed him this. It was wrapped around a rock and thrown through the window, as before. Sheriff Little said he won't tell anyone, and said he'll return early in the morning."

More silence, then Ray said, "I'll do what they say. I'll resign in the morning and make it known our store and our ranch are for sale." He swallowed hard. "That means I'll have to go to town in the morning and leave it up to the rest of you to continue the search."

"You can't sell a ranch and a store in a day," Martin said.

"No, I'll just put it up for sale and take the first offer." Ray put his elbows on the table and his face in his hands. His voice was muffled, "I'll do anything to save my son."

Martin didn't say it, but he couldn't help thinking: No matter what Ray does, there's no guarantee they won't kill Joshua. He wanted to swear. He wanted a smoke. He wanted a drink of whiskey.

Mary said, "I had a stew simmering when all this . . . started. It's ready to eat now. You two have to be hungry. Benjamin has been fed, and he's upstairs in bed."

Mary ate nothing. Ray ate very little. Martin ate what he thought he needed to keep his strength. He volunteered to help with the dishes, but Mary said, "Thank you, but I have to keep busy."

Outside, rolling a smoke, Martin never felt sorrier for anyone than he did then for his brother and Mary. They were going through the worst kind of torture. And Martin silently vowed that if that boy was hurt, he'd do anything to find and kill the men who did it.

Anything.

He didn't wait for breakfast. He didn't wait for the sheriff. He pulled on his boots, buckled on his gunbelt, and went into the kitchen where he discovered that Ray hadn't even gone to bed. Sitting in the dim glow of a lamp, Ray told Martin he'd go to the store and start doing what the kidnappers had ordered him to do. "Yeah," Martin agreed. Martin and Luke were horseback before daylight. Luke was carrying a repeating rifle.

"I've never pointed a gun at anybody," he said, "but if I see them sons of goddamn bitches that took Josh I'll shoot 'em down 'thout blinkin' an eye."

Martin didn't feel much like talking, so he said only, "I believe you."

They rode along the road all the way over the pass and a half-mile on the other side, then they doubled back, riding slower, sometimes walking and leading their horses. About midmorning Martin picked up their trail. It was nothing more than an overturned rock. The top side of the small rock was darker than the bottom, and Martin guessed that the top had been the bottom, in the ground, and turned over by a horse's hoof. A few yards from there he found a small print on the hard ground where the toe of a horse's hoof had hit the ground.

At least, he said to himself, I know now they went north.

He yelled at Luke and motioned him over. "Horses have been here not long ago. Let's both see if we can find any more sign. Two hundred yards farther north they came to fresh horse manure. It was scattered northward instead of piled, and that told Martin something.

"Give a horse his choice and he'll stop to shit," he said to Luke, "but whoever was on this horse kept him moving. He was wasting no time."

Looking north, Luke allowed, "They could be plumb up to Buckskin by now."

"Then we'll go to Buckskin. Ever been there, Luke?"

" 'Bout a year ago. It was a purty busy little town once, but it was dyin' on its feet. Prob'ly ain't much left of 'er now."

"Might be enough left to make a shelter, but I don't think they're there. They're smart enough to know we'd look there."

"Yeah, you're prob'ly right."

"Well, let's keep going in this direction and see what we can see."

Neither man had had breakfast and their stomachs were growling, but they paid no attention to that. They went on, finding just enough marks on the ground to keep them going north. Then Luke reined up.

"Yonder." He pointed with his chin to more horse manure, but this was off to his left. Martin reined up too, and mused aloud, "Now why would they change direction and go west?"

The two searchers changed directions too and went west until they found more sign. This worried them.

"Why?" Luke asked. "Did they split up? Did one of 'em go back to Vega?" Martin was too deep in thought to answer. Luke said, "If they did, the one that kept going north is the one that's got Josh."

Martin got down and walked, leading his horse and studying the ground. He stopped, squatted and picked up a small granite rock. He could see a small indentation in the ground where the rock had sat for thousands of years before it was tipped over. Then off to his right he saw a clump of timothy grass that had been stepped on by a horse. Straightening, he said, "They both went this way."

"Then," Luke said, "they either went to Vega or they rode zigzag to fool us."

"Yep. They could have tried to fool us into thinking they doubled back to Vega. They could have us loping for town right now, while they'd changed directions again."

"They had to know this country to do that in the dark."

"Say, Luke, there's supposed to be a stage relay station down west somewhere. Ever been there?"

"Yep. I know where she's at. You think maybe they saw or heard something down there?"

"You know what scares the hell out of me, Luke? What scares me is if they went back to town . . . town is no place to hide the boy. If they went back to town, they . . ."

Luke finished the thought, "They left the boy up here sommers."

"Yeah."

Luke reached for a bandanna in his hip pocket and blew his nose. His eyes were moist. "He's just a little kid. They could hide his body where it'd never be found."

Bitterly, Martin said, "Yeah." He was silent for a long moment, deep in thought. He rolled a cigarette, lighted it, smoked. Then, speaking slowly, thoughtfully, he said, "You know, this is all a scheme to force Ray to give up on the two county laws he wants the voters to pass. Whoever is behind this scheme is down there in Vega right now." Martin took another drag on his cigarette. "Whoever he is, he knows where Josh is."

Stepping into his saddle, Martin said, "Luke, you can keep riding this country and looking or you can go back to the ranch, or do whatever you want to do. Me, I'm going to town." With that he touched spurs to his horse and rode west, downhill, at a fast trot.

Chapter Thirty-two

Martin didn't look back to see what Luke was doing. If Luke continued searching the hills or rode down to the relay station, he might do more good than what Martin had in mind to do. And that brought up a question that Martin had to ask himself:

What was he going to do?

How in hell could he force any information out of C. C. Vance? Even if he did somehow get past the two goons, he couldn't torture the saloon owner into spilling his guts. Get the sheriff to help? The situation was desperate enough that Sheriff Little might help—some way. But then there was something strange about Sheriff Little too.

When Martin rode into Vega he didn't go to the sheriff's office. He went to the whorehouse.

It was the housekeeper who opened the back door. This time she said simply, "Wait here," and slammed the door.

By the time the fat madam opened the door again, Martin was so nervous with impatience he was ready to kick the door in. "Did you learn something?" she asked.

"We've got to talk."

Stepping back, Sis Able said, "Come in." She again led

the way to her bedroom. "There's something on your mind, as anyone can plainly see."

"Yeah. I want a look at that letter, the one Sheriff Little left with you."

"Huh-uh. You know I can't let you see that. I promised, and a promise is a promise."

"Listen." Martin was talking through tight jaws. "Ray Mossman's son was kidnapped. This is no time to argue. Get me that letter."

"Well, I'm sorry about the boy, but . . ." Sis Able shut her mouth as she found herself looking up the barrel of Martin's six-gun.

"I want that letter. You can tell yourself later that you were forced at gunpoint to hand it to me. You can tell yourself anything you want, but I'm ready to start shooting and you're right in my way."

The fat, bruised face opened its mouth, shut it, opened it. "All right, all right. Point that pistol somewhere else, will you."

"Right now."

"All right, all right. Just be careful with that thing." Silk gown swirling around her feet, Sis Able turned to a dresser in a corner, a dresser that was covered on top with powder boxes and perfume bottles. She opened a bottom drawer, took out a tin box, and handed it to Martin. "I'll get the key," she said as she opened a top drawer.

"Hold it. Let me see." Martin moved over to the dresser, groped through the open drawer with his left hand, found nothing but silk underwear. "Where's the key?"

"I'll get it." Sis Able reached into a near corner of the drawer and took out a small key, which she inserted in a lock on the tin box. She opened the box and took out a long envelope. The envelope was addressed to the district attorney at the Park County Courthouse, Fair Play, Colorado.

"Sit on the bed and don't move," Martin ordered. He holstered the Remington and tore open the envelope. What he found inside wasn't a letter, it was a flyer, a wanted poster, the kind that was mailed to law officers all over the west. The picture on the poster wasn't much more than a dark, dotted outline of a face. The name was Charles Victor. He was described as a riverboat gambler, and he was wanted in St. Louis, Missouri, for a double murder and robbery. A five-hundred-dollar reward was offered for his arrest. At the bottom was a one-sentence handwritten note.

Speaking more to himself than to anyone else, Martin said, "Now we know." He folded the poster and stuck it in his shirt pocket. To Sis Able, he said, "Keep your mouth shut today. Tomorrow you can holler your head off if you want to. In fact, I hope you do."

"Are you gonna keep it?"

"Yep." Martin went through the kitchen and out the back door.

Outside, he untied his horse from a hitching post, then paused. How was he going to do this? He had no chance by himself. Even if he got lucky and put a gun up Vance's nose, he couldn't force him to tell where Josh was. And killing him wouldn't bring Josh back.

Wait a minute.

It came to Martin in a flash. The kidnappers did circle back to Vega. They were holding the boy here in town. Martin knew where. Sure. The last place anyone would look. It had to be the place.

But as he mounted and rode at a high trot to Second Street, he suddenly realized he wasn't so sure. It was just a guess, a hunch. Maybe it was because he'd just come out of a whorehouse, or maybe . . . something had suddenly glowed in his mind and just as suddenly gone out. But . . . well, by god, it was worth checking.

Let's see now, he said to himself, it was the third crib from the corner. Yep. He got down and wrapped the reins once around a hitchrail. He turned the cylinder of the Remington, made sure it was fully loaded. He glanced up and down the street. Not a soul was in sight. The window was dark, a heavy blind drawn on the inside. No sign of life at all. It had all the appearances of a deserted crib, once occupied by a whore who was later murdered. He knocked on the door. No answer. He tried to open the door. Couldn't.

Martin took four steps back, then ran at the door, ramming it with his left shoulder, at the same time drawing the Remington. A latch inside tore loose with a splintering of wood. In the semidarkness of the room, he saw a woman jump up from a bed, a cigarette between two fingers.

And then he heard an exclamation that was an answer to a prayer:

"Uncle Martin."

Josh was sitting on the floor in a corner behind the bed. Only his head showed above the bed. The woman dropped her cigarette and screeched, "Don't shoot, don't shoot."

"How are you, Josh?"

Excited, close to crying, the boy garbled, "They tied me up and they put a chain on me and they made me sit on the front of a saddle and I wanta go home. Are you gonna take me home, Uncle Martin?"

"You betcha."

"I didn't hurt 'im, I didn't hurt 'im." The woman was

middle-aged, with a pockmarked face and straggly brown hair. "They made me do it. I didn't hurt 'im."

"Are you hurt, Josh?"

"They got this chain on me, Uncle Martin, and I can't get away."

To the woman, Martin said, "Stand right there. Move one muscle and it'll be the last thing you ever do. And shut your mouth."

"I won't, mister, I won't move. Don't hurt me, I didn't do nothin'."

"Shut up."

She shut up.

"All right, Josh, let's see what they've got you tied to." He shoved the narrow bed aside and helped the boy to his feet. Josh's right wrist was held tight in a handcuff, the kind that law officers carried, and the other cuff, on a foot-long chain, was locked around the bedframe.

"Can you get this off of me, Uncle Martin?"

"Sure, Josh." To the woman he said, "Where's the key?"

"I ain't got it, I swear I ain't. They took it with 'em."

"Who are they?"

"I don't know. I seen 'em before, and I know they're killers, but I don't know nothin' else about 'em. They said they'd kill me like they done to Marie that used to stay here if I didn't keep this kid here."

Turning his back to her, Martin said, "Let me figure out the best way to do this, Josh." The best way was to get a chisel and hammer from the blacksmith shop and chisel it off, but he'd have to leave the boy and woman to do that.

"All right, here's what we're gonna do, I'm gonna try to bust that lock with a bullet. It might work and it might just jam the lock tighter. We'll try. Sit down and cover your face with your hands." Martin yanked a blanket off the bed and wrapped it around the boy from feet to the top of his head. "There might be some pieces flying around and I don't want you to get hurt. Here goes, now."

He put the muzzle of the gun two inches from the locked handcuff on the bedframe and squeezed the trigger.

The explosion rocked the room. The percussion knocked dirt clods from the ceiling. The handcuff jerked, but held fast. Martin didn't know whether it was still locked until he holstered the Remington and pried it open with his fingers.

"Whew. All right, Josh?" He unwrapped the boy and helped him to his feet.

"Gosh. Goshdamn."

"Don't use that word. Are you hurt?"

Swinging his arms, enjoying his freedom, the boy answered, "No. Boy oh boy."

Martin glanced at the woman to be sure she hadn't moved, then asked, "Know where you are, Josh?"

"Up in the Pumas. They tied my arms and made me set on the fork of a saddle, and last night they covered my eyes with a rag. I got awful tired of sittin' on a saddle that way."

"You're only three, maybe four town blocks from your dad's store. Come on outside and see for yourself."

With a busted handcuff dangling from a wrist, the boy stepped outside and blinked in the sunlight. "Gosh. Goshdarn."

"Know where you are now?"

"Well . . ."

"Come on, I'll show you." Martin led his horse with one hand and the boy with the other to the end of the block. "Look over there. Now do you know where you are?"

"Yeah. Yeah, I can see the store."

"Go on over there. Your folks are worried sick about you. Go show them what a brave boy you are."

"Are you coming with me, Uncle Martin?"

"I'll see you later at home, Josh. Right now I've got another job to do."

Silently, he reminded himself: It wasn't over. What had happened could happen again.

Chapter Thirty-three

Martin led his horse down the street and tied up in front of the Silver Tip Gaming Palace. He no more than stepped inside when he heard his name called, "Mart Mossman. C'mere, you rangy old son of a pup. Let me buy you one."

Martin took in the whole room before he answered, "Not now, J.J. Later, maybe."

A wide grin vanished from the young cowboy's face. He turned to get a closer look at Martin. "Something's chawin' on your innards, pardner. Can I help?"

"No. J.J. Stay back."

Vance was sitting at a table in a far corner, idly riffling a deck of cards. The pug-faced one was on his right and the skinny gunslinger was on his left. Martin walked directly up to them.

"Need to talk to you, Mr. Vance."

The saloon owner smiled, let it slip, got it back again. "What's the trouble, Mr. Mossman? Somebody shoot your dog or something?"

The two bodyguards read the danger in Martin's face and they were standing spraddle-legged ready. He considered just shooting the gambler without warning, but the skinny gunslinger would probably draw and shoot him before he could get off a round. There was just no way. No way at all. Unless he lied. He might try. He wished he were a good actor.

Forcing a crooked grin, Martin said, "I'm leaving this territory, Mr. Vance. Think I'll drift over to Idaho. I hear that's good country. I just wanted to let you know you win."

"I win?" The smile slipped, returned. "Win what?"

"You know." Still forcing a smile himself, Martin held out his right hand. "No hard feelings."

He had a plan. It had worked twice before. Which was no guarantee it would work again. But he could think of nothing else. He'd have to move fast.

The saloon owner stood, lost the smile, and studied Martin's face. "You're leaving?"

"Yeah, I'll be on my way within an hour, and Ray is resigning from the county board. Just thought you'd like to know." Still holding out his right hand, his gun hand, Martin stepped around a corner of the table. "I'll shake with you if you want."

"Well . . . if it will make you feel better." Vance carefully put out his right hand. The two men shook. Then Martin moved as fast as he'd ever moved in his life.

With all his strength, he jerked the saloon owner in front of him, wrapped his left arm around his neck, got him in front of the gunslinger, and started dragging him into the corner. In the same instant he dropped Vance's hand and drew the Remington.

Pugface was coming at him. The skinny one had a six-gun in his fist. Both stopped immediately when Martin shoved the muzzle of the Remington into the gambler's right ear. Then the skinny gunslinger tried to work his way around to where he could get a clear shot at Martin, but Martin had backed into the corner now.

"One more move," Martin said through clenched teeth, "and I'll kill him."

The saloon owner squawked, "Don't."

No one moved.

Still hissing through his teeth, Martin said, "No matter how fast you can shoot, you can't kill me fast enough to keep me from killing him." He raised his voice, "Tell them, Mr. Vance."

"Don't," Vance squawked. "Don't do anything."

"All right, tell them, Mr. Vance, tell everybody how you hired killers and bullies to try to get rid of my brother. Tell them how you hired thugs to beat up voters. Tell them how you and Sheriff Little are in cahoots, how the sheriff knows you're wanted for murder in St. Louis and how he's holding that over your head like an axe to get you to do his dirty work. Go ahead, tell them."

"You're choking me. I can't talk."

"You just did. The sheriff is shaking down the whores, ain't he? He's shaking you down. He's taking a rakeoff from you with one hand and holding that axe over your head with the other. He's forced you to sign over a part-interest in this place, and he's got an interest in the other saloons too. Tell them."

Martin's left arm had Vance choking now, gagging and strangling. His two bodyguards were ready, looking for a chance, death in their eyes. Then Vance choked out a few more words:

"Sheriff. Sheriff Little. Help me. Get this crazy man off me."

Martin hadn't seen the sheriff come up, but he was there, right in front of C. C. Vance. He barked, "What's going on here? Mossman, let him go." His voice was full of authority, but it had no effect.

"Not likely, Sheriff. Not until he tells all about the scheme the two of you cooked up."

"Kill him, Sheriff." Vance was barely able to talk now. His knees were sagging. Martin had to hold him up with his left arm. He couldn't hold him forever. This wasn't working.

Then, slowly, deliberately, the sheriff drew his six-gun. He aimed it at Martin's head, and Martin warned, "If you shoot me he's dead. This gun has a hair trigger."

The sheriff's trigger finger tightened.

Martin ducked his head and at the same time yanked the gambler up a few inches. The sheriff's gun boomed, and Vance went limp with a bullet in the face.

Another cartridge exploded, and Sheriff Little fell with a hole in the center of his heart. Martin half-turned and shot the skinny gunslinger in the left temple, dropping him instantly.

Then it was quiet. The biting smell of gunsmoke drifted over the room.

Three men were down. Two of them had died with guns in their hands. Martin looked around the room, at the startled faces. No one moved, not even pugface. Someone muttered, "Well, I'll be goddamned."

Finally, Martin spoke, trying to force calm into his voice, "You all heard what I said. It's true. I've got the proof in my pocket." He was silent again, then turned to pugface. "You. You've been collecting from the whores in the cribs. Somebody else has been collecting from Sis Able. You tell them." Pugface stood still, seemingly in shock, and said nothing. Martin continued, "Your boss is dead. You're out of a job."

More quiet.

Seeing nothing threatening, Martin holstered the Remington. He didn't know what to do or say now.

It was the young cowboy, J.J., who spoke next. "Whatta you wanta do with 'em, Mart?"

"I don't know. I'll see if I can find Harlan Longacre. He's on the county board, and he's got some authority. Maybe he'll know what to do. My brother is at his ranch."

Knees a little shaky from all that had happened, Martin walked weakly toward the door. He needed to get outside. He needed air. But he didn't get outside. A man stepped in front of him, blocking his way.

It was the red-bearded punk, the first man Martin had spoken to in Vega. He stood with his feet apart, his right hand near his gun butt. "You think you're tough," he growled. "Well, I'm tougher." He drew his six-gun and fired.

The slug hit Martin in the stomach like a ramrod. He staggered back, but stayed on his feet, suddenly numb.

A man cried out, "You goddamn son of a bitch," and another gun roared. The redhead bent at the waist, dropped his gun, then pitched forward onto the floor.

"I got 'im, Mart. I got the son of a bitch. Are you hit bad? I'll run and fetch the doctor."

"No, J.J." His vision swam, but Martin shook his head and his vision cleared again. "I've got to get to my brother's ranch. Got to get on my horse."

"I'll help you, Mart." J.J. got a shoulder under Martin's left armpit. "Can you walk?"

Martin held his hand over the wound in his stomach, tried to hold back the bleeding. But blood seeped between his fingers as he staggered outside to the hitchrail.

J.J. yelled, "Go get the doctor. Tell 'im to meet us at the Mossman Ranch. Run, goddammit." A lumberjack took off running.

* * *

Pain forced Martin's already twisted face into an ugly grimace and brought a groan from between clenched teeth. At times the pain cleared long enough that he realized he was horseback, hanging onto the saddle horn with both hands. The young cowboy J.J. was riding beside him.

In the ranch yard, J.J. hollered, and Ray and Mary ran outside and helped Martin to the room off the kitchen. "The doctor oughta be here any minute," J.J. said.

"What happened?" Ray asked.

"A lot of shootin' in the Silver Tip," J.J. answered. "The sheriff is dead, Mr. Vance is dead, and a couple others. Mart was shot by a worthless piece of crud that wouldn't make a pimple on a real man's, uh . . . I'll wait outside for the doctor."

A wave of pain went through Martin's stomach as he lay back on the bed, but then it cleared, and he asked, "How's Josh?"

Mary answered, "He's fine. He's telling his little brother all about it."

"Ray," Martin said, "it's over now. Sheriff Little and C. C. Vance were behind it all. Here in my shirt pocket is a paper that will explain it. I should have figured it out sooner. The sheriff was out of town on election day, and Sis Able was beat up the day after you told him she'd talked to . . ." A long groan came through Martin's teeth, but he managed to add, "The county clerk is a crook too."

"Don't talk, Mart. Save your strength. Here's the doctor."

Dr. Hanley cut Martin's shirt half off and used the width of his hand to measure the distance of the wound from the hip bone and from a lower rib. He motioned for Ray to follow him out of the room.

"He's bleeding inside. The bullet has punctured the liver. I could go in and extract the missile, but that would only increase the damage."

Solemnly, Ray asked, "Do you mean . . . ?"

Dr. Hanley shook his head sadly.

Silently, Ray and wife went back into the room. Mary knelt beside the bed and put her hand on Martin's forehead. "You know, Martin," she said softly, "there have been times in the history of the world when men like you were needed. Thank God you came along when you did. You'll always be a hero to us, Martin." She leaned down and kissed Martin on the forehead.

Grinning his crooked grin, Martin said, "Know something, Mary? My headache's gone."

"I'll leave you and Ray to talk."

Another spasm went through Martin's insides like a hot poker. Ray stood silently, jaws tight, blinking, trying to keep a straight face. Then the spasm passed for a moment.

"Ray, you've been after me to settle down, get some roots down." Martin fought off a wave of pain. "Well, I'm gonna do it." He managed another grin.

"Yep, I'm gonna stay in one place now."

Author's note:

The town of Fairplay, Colorado, was originally spelled with two words.
The town of Vega is fiction.
The original wagon road over Wilkerson Pass was somewhere south of where U.S. 24 now goes over the pass.